Super Moon Protocol

J.T. Fluhart

This is a work of fiction. Names, characters, places, and incidents either are the product of the author's imagination, (which is extensive) or are used fictitiously (which is likely). Any resemblance to actual persons, living or dead, events, or locales is entirely coincidental (unless it's obvious).

First paperback edition February 2021

ISBN 978-1-7364741-0-5 (paperback)
ISBN 978-1-7364741-1-2 (ebook)

For my Mom, my wife Alma,
and my closest friends for their encouragement.

It Started with Colonel Sanders....

Hello Everyone!

As an avid reader of suspense and thriller novels I have always aspired to write one myself. A few years back I decided to sit down and hammer out my first attempt at a short story. I used many elements of my real life on a small farm in North Texas. The finished effort was The Revenge of Colonel Sanders based on a crotchety rooster I had. The short story had all the elements of what I love to read... fast paced, heart pumping suspense, descriptive creativity and subtle humor. Writing that short story created an even bigger itch to write a novel where I could add depth and even more of those elements I love in a story.

I hope you enjoy reading Super Moon Protocol as much as I enjoyed writing it!

PS. You may be thinking, a rooster? Throw in the CIA, Mexican cartels, smarty art psychologists, Vietnam survivalists, redneck truckers, Nazi librarians, hi-tech weaponry, lots of horsepower, heart tugging moments and yeah well, you won't look at roosters the same again. I can promise you that!

- JT

Chapter One

Anna, Texas, 1970
The Event

Joe tried to put pressure on the slice in his calf muscle as he limped back toward the farmhouse. Banging the kitchen door open, he let out a yell, "Erma! Help! He's at it again!"

Erma stood from her crossword puzzle and went to the bathroom to fetch some gauze and peroxide. She didn't need to reply or even see Joe to know what had happened. He no doubt had another tangle with Colonel Sanders, the temperamental rooster of the family's chicken flock. He and Joe did not get along, so Erma proactively had plenty of first aid supplies on hand.

Earlier in the year the marketing company Joe was growing into a success financially collapsed. Their main account, the Chow company, mysteriously cancelled their contract with Joe. This left him home with their two kids, five year-old Annie and seven year-old Tommy. While he worked with the Chow company he learned he enjoyed animals, specifically chickens. Joe focused his newly found free time expanding the flock he had put together as live props for his marketing photography. He learned the eggs from the specific breed he had were in high demand for hatching all over the country. This helped Joe bring in a few more dollars to the family. Plus, they added to the feel of "farm life" which his family enjoyed, but also invited these combat interactions with the Colonel.

Joe propped his leg up on the kitchen table for Erma to inspect as she prepared to dress the wound.

"The sorry sap sucker got me when I was coming around the house with Max." Joe explained, wincing. Max was the family German shepherd that Joe acquired to help keep predators at bay.

"Well, it's not safe for the kids anymore," she replied. She half listened to Joe and half listened to the weather forecast on the kitchen TV.

"Yeah, but he's never attacked them. Seems his beef is just with me. Like I tossed Sara in the smoker. But I agree, I think the kids should steer clear until I figure out what to do with him," Joe contemplated. Sara was the Colonel's favorite hen. Two days earlier she disappeared. Most likely the victim of a predator attack.

"I hate to kill him. Kind've grown fond of the crotchety rascal." Joe listened wearily to the weatherman drone on about a unique supermoon coming in a couple nights.

The next day Joe needed to clean and wash several soiled water and feed bowls. He spied the Colonel and slowly moved in to deliver what he hoped would be a preemptive kick to keep the bird at bay for an hour or so. He learned if he struck first, then the Colonel was less likely to attack when Joe wasn't looking. When he saw his chance, Joe took several quick steps and kicked at the Colonel with such force he instantly felt he might regret it. He really didn't want to hurt the guy. He just needed to get the point across to back off for a few minutes. The Colonel locked in on Joe with his cocked-to-the-side stare. He quickly sidestepped the Red Wing boot that swept toward him like a sand wedge. The ground was wet with dew, and when Joe missed his mark, he lost his balance and landed hard on his back like he'd seen Charlie Brown do so many times when Lucy pulled back that football. However, unlike good ole Chucky Brown, it wasn't a pompous Lucy that barreled toward Joe's face. No, it was a pissed-off broiler named Colonel Sanders! His nemesis was now on his back and dazed. The Colonel ran flat out toward Joe's face. His wings flapped, and he screamed like a war eagle. He threw up his spurs and aimed for Joe's eyes. Joe turned his head at the very last second and saved his eyes, but earned a nasty slice across his scalp. His strike loosened a chunk of Joe's ear.

***

"Tell me again. How did a chicken do this to you?" asked the ER doctor with a bemused look on his face.

"It was a rooster, not just a chicken . . . big difference," Joe answered crossly.

"If you say so. Gonna leave a mark either way. But should heal up simply enough." The doctor applied four stitches. He stood to leave then turned and said, "By the way, gonna be a special kind of supermoon tonight. Happens every fifty or so years, and I hear the animals go crazy. Better keep an eye on that chick . . . I mean rooster you got there."

The door slammed closed and cut off a hard chuckle the doctor gave as he exited. All the way home, Joe contemplated how he would kill Colonel Sanders. His ear throbbed as the local anesthetic started to wear off. He was lost in his thoughts of how best to wring the rooster's neck when up ahead he saw the earliest sign of the supermoon. It loomed low in the sky and caught an ominous red glow from the setting sun.

At that same moment on his summer perch, Colonel Sanders settled in for another lonely, cold night. The rooster's instincts detected the temperature had fallen faster than previous nights, and that nearly sent him into his coop. But, even animals could be set in their ways. Out of habit he glanced over for Sara and still saw her missing. The hen's spot on their fence was still empty. In the distance Colonel Sanders noticed something bright, something huge on the horizon. He mechanically cocked his head to the side and stared intensely at the large red ball rising in the sky. He sat still as a stone

3

for the better part of an hour. The only sign he was alive was that his pupils grew and shrank ever so slightly.

Chapter Two

"Daddy's home!" screamed Tommy. He and Annie dropped their Tinkertoys and ran to the sound of Joe as he came through the kitchen door. Erma also heard the door close and went to see how the ER had taken care of Joe's ear.

"Yikes!" she said as she inspected the somewhat-put-together folds of skin.

"I know! Dr. Hatchet seemed too amused by the fact a rooster did this. Was chuckling the whole time. Surprised he was even able to sew at all." Joe winced as Erma further inspected his tender appendage.

"Well, come eat and relax," she said as she cracked open a cold beer and handed it to him.

After dinner, he took his plate to the sink and noticed out the window how light it still was outside. Even through the solar screens on the outside of the windows, he could still see details of things in the distance that weren't usually visible at that hour. He walked out his front door and was amazed at how bright and brilliant the moon was. Max heard him step out into the front yard and ran quickly around the house and nearly knocked Joe over.

"Hey! Easy, dang it. What the hell's wrong with you?" he asked his overly hyper dog. Max whined and yelped as he ran in circles.

Erma came out next with the kids and said, "Wow! That's bright."

The kids shielded their eyes, and Tommy started to howl playfully. A cartoonish imitation of werewolves he'd seen on *Scooby-Doo*. Max heard Tommy and chimed in with an authentic version. Instantly, Joe heard animals all around his property begin to howl—some that actually did howl and some he didn't think should have been.

"Okay, that's a bit freaky," Erma whispered as she continued to listen.

"Kids, let's go in and run baths," she finally said, and herded them into the house, obviously set on edge from the mangled symphony of noise. Joe stood there and listened as the howls slowly subsided and left their eerie echoes.

On the fence, Colonel Sanders lowered his head after he belted out a very crude and raw howl. It was nothing like the sing-song melody his crow usually took the form of. His head shifted mechanically, and he looked around as if he just woke up. He gazed up at the white brilliance the moon had become. He stood, shook his feathers, flapped his newly elongated wings . . . and took flight.

Back inside the house, Joe slipped his boots off and went into his bedroom closet. He pulled out his Benelli 12-gauge pump shotgun. He didn't know why, but something about the obscure howls outside made him want to get it out. He chambered four shells of three-inch Magnum 00 buckshot and set the safety on.

"That ought to drop any of the predators that feel like chicken tonight," he said to himself. He propped it up behind a tall plant in the foyer next to the front door then went into the living room to watch the news.

Kicked back in his well-worn recliner, he dozed off. Erma shrieked from the kitchen, "Oh my God, Joe! Oh my God!" Joe quickly jerked awake and thought Erma had revealed another mouse in the kitchen. The days had cooled in the evenings, which meant those little turd factories had started to burglarize their pantry. As he yawned and entered the kitchen, he realized Erma's eyes were wide with pure terror. She motioned for him to get the hell over there and pointed out the window into the backyard. It took Joe a minute to process what he saw.

Moments prior, as Joe dozed soundly, Colonel Sanders circled the backyard from above. His domain. His territory. That just a few nights earlier was invaded by a thief. A thief that stole his property. That stole Sara. Suddenly, Max trotted around the house. His long wet tongue lolled out of his mouth. The Colonel quickly eyed him with his newly enhanced vision and folded his wings into a deep, fast dive. Max sat on the deck and scratched at his collar. His winter coat had come in and caused it to tighten. It chafed his neck and irritated him. The sound of something moved toward him very fast from above. He heard this and it piqued his interest and caused him to sit up to listen.

Before Max determined the cause of the noise, something hit him hard in the head. He sprawled flat from the impact. Max growled deep. He tried to gain his feet, but the Colonel was already on his back. The rooster stabbed him in the side with long, needle-sharp spurs. Max yelped in surprise then attacked. He snapped his beartrap-like jaws at the rooster. Sanders easily dodged the sheer death of Max's bite and jumped on his head from behind. His spurs blurred. He stabbed them into Max's head dozens of times a second like a well-oiled Singer sewing machine that attacked a stitch. With succinct accuracy, the Colonel drove both spurs deep into Max's eye sockets. A torrent of fluid exploded. Max leaped around confused then rolled onto his back. He pawed at his face. The sound of his yelps caught Erma's attention as she went to the sink and got some dish soap for the kids to make bubbles in their bathwater. She looked out the window and saw a huge bird. It tore into Max's flesh. Its huge talons pulled the dog's skin back and exposed his bloody bones. She screamed for Joe. She waved frantically to put some urgency in his step as he casually strolled into the kitchen.

Joe peered out the window, stunned at the sight. The bird ripped a chunk out of Max's throat and caused a spray of blood across the wood deck.

"What the hell!" Joe screamed.

He ran out the back door to help his dog against this, this bird? As he approached, Max whimpered his last breath as his life's blood gurgled out the open gash in his throat. Joe looked at the bird as he stood victorious over his foe. Sanders now set his focus on Joe and cocked his head in that herky-jerky mechanical way. His stare penetrated his nemesis. The thief that stole his property and invaded his domain every single day.

Joe stopped abruptly. The moonlight illuminated the bloody scene like a black-and-white film remastered in high definition. He tried to understand what kind of bird brought down a full-grown German shepherd dog. Then he saw that mechanical movement of the bird's head. That intense focus a chicken makes when they eye something. Although the bird was covered in gore, Joe knew instantly where he had seen that mechanical cocked-to-the-side look . . . Colonel Sanders. But this version of the rooster was greatly different. Its eyes were larger with a subtle, golden glow as if it stared into a spotlight. Its beak was thicker and razor sharp with jagged edges. It resembled cutlery Joe had seen numerous times peddled on TV when insomnia carried him into the wee hours of the morning. The comb on his beak blazed red and rigid. It appeared to hold an edge that would make any butcher jealous. As terrifying as these recent evolutions seemed, it was the rooster's feet that made Joe take a step back. He was pretty sure Sanders was supposed to have just three toes per foot, but the abomination staring at him now sported six toes per foot! Each ended in a curved talon like a fish hook, and each still clung to bits of Max's flesh.

Colonel Sanders sucked in a huge breath, one that made his chest swell to the size of a large beach ball. He screamed an ear-piercing sound. It was sharp like ice picks and stabbed Joe's eardrums. His eyes rattled in their sockets. It gave him a headache like he'd only had when he became too eager with ice cream. Stunned by the audible blast, Joe didn't realize the rooster raced toward him with amazing speed. Before he could react, Colonel Sanders flipped his claws up and struck Joe in his thigh.

Through the years, Joe suffered sports injuries, even more serious injuries in a car wreck once, but never had anything sliced him completely to, and into, his bones. The pain blinded Joe as the Colonel literally tore a pound of flesh from his leg. Without thinking, which probably saved his life, Joe grabbed Sanders by his throat. He narrowly missed the rooster's razor-sharp comb. Joe slung the bird with all the strength he had. Colonel Sanders shrieked loudly as he spun round and round like a Frisbee. Joe rolled onto his feet. Pain seared through his leg, and blood now poured from the wound in his thigh. He braced himself for another attack he was sure was to come, but didn't. There, like a ninja's throwing star, the rooster's comb was buried deep in the trunk of the thirty-year-old oak tree that grew in the center of the deck. The bird thrashed violently. It viciously clawed at the tree to release itself. Splinters and bark flew everywhere. Joe realized this was his only chance to get away. He ran for the door that led back into the kitchen.

Inside, Erma screamed. She was completely beside herself as she watched the battle through the window.

"Go get the kids! Quick, now!" Joe yelled as he rushed in and bolted the door's lock. He heard a distinct clink from outside, like the sound of a knife blade that had broken in two. Erma rushed down the hall and got the kids out of their bath.

Suddenly, the outside-facing wall began to shudder from what sounded like a basketball being thrown against it. Harder and harder the impact was. BANG! BANG! BANG! The cabinets opened, and their contents spilled onto the countertop. Dinnerware and glasses shattered all over the kitchen. Shards of glass covered the floor. Tommy ran into the kitchen wide-eyed from all the commotion. He wore just his green Incredible Hulk underwear and ran through the jagged shards of dinnerware. The slices on his feet were so fine it took him a few seconds to realize the pain. "Mommy! Ahhh, Mommy!" he screamed at the top of his lungs and hopped from one foot to the other to find relief. This drove the glass deeper into each foot. Erma heard her oldest child cry out and raced into the kitchen. Fortunately, she wore house slippers. She grabbed Tommy and rescued him from the sea of glass then rushed him into the living room.

The force that slammed against the house stopped suddenly. Joe waited. In the silence, he headed to the living room to check on his son. Tommy lay on the couch. He screamed as Erma desperately tried to hold him still in order to remove the shards of glass from his feet. Strewn across the coffee table were bandages, gauze, and cotton balls. Blood poured from Tommy's soles. He was purple, unable to catch his breath as he screamed. Joe's thigh burned badly, but he pushed the pain aside. It then occurred to him Annie wasn't in the room.

"Where is Annie?" Joe asked in a panic.

"I don't know! Help me here, dammit!" Erma screamed as Tommy kicked her in the face and splattered it with blood.

Joe started to go to Tommy and comfort him. The force slammed into the house again. BANG! BANG! BANG! Pictures and decorations flew off the walls. The sheetrock cracked, and a large wall clock fell. It shattered its huge glass face on the floor with a deafening crash.

"Make it stop, Joe! Please, God, make it stop!" she cried out. She sobbed with Tommy wrapped in her arms, the glass removal effort abandoned.

Joe had no idea what to do. So far the Colonel hadn't punched through the walls. The force continued to move along the wall toward the brick chimney. Joe figured if the rooster punched into that, it would for sure break its neck. He shuffled along the wall toward the chimney and screamed at the force, "Come get me, you psycho son of a bitch! Over here!" He coaxed the bird to follow his voice so he would slam into the bricks.

He laughed like a crazy loon, but it seemed to work. The force from outside followed his voice and moved along the wall as Joe hoped it would. BANG! BANG! BANG!

"One more time, you bastard," he said to himself. He anticipated the next whack would be into the bricks. But it never came. All he could hear was Tommy and Erma as they sobbed, wrapped tightly together on the couch. Everyone froze and waited for what seemed like an eternity.

"Is it gone?" Erma finally whispered, afraid to speak.

"I don't know . . . Shhh!" Joe said. He strained to hear outside.

Suddenly the window on the other side of the chimney exploded in a spray of glass and startled them all. Joe screamed too and covered his head. Sanders had slammed into one of the windows and broken all the glass out. However, the thick solar screen sent him reeling back, like a vertical trampoline. Over and over, the screen extended into the room and denied the rooster, but it was no match for his talons, which were already ripping through. Joe ran and grabbed the poker from the fireplace tools and readied himself. In high school Joe led his team in home runs and RBIs. It'd been a while, but he felt like he could deliver a grand slam tonight.

Colonel Sanders finally tore through the screen and stuck his head in the hole he created. He cocked his head and trained his remaining, swollen eye on Joe and screamed that brain-piercing scream before he tore through the screen the rest of the way. Joe couldn't believe how battered the rooster's head was from being slammed into the sides of the house. The top part of his beak was broken, which left a jagged opening. One of his nasty little eyes was pierced. It oozed a greenish-pink mush. His feathers and skin were torn back from around his head, which gave a grotesque view of thick, sinewy jaw muscles. They were all pulpy and oozy. A huge shard of glass was stuck in the bird's large chest, but didn't seem to faze him.

"Run!" Joe screamed to his wife just as the rooster launched itself at Joe.

Joe was ready. Many years of practice and training took over as he stepped into his swing. He twisted at his hips, arms extended fully. He never took his eyes off that ball of beaked damnation as it hurled itself at him. In his baseball prime, Joe knew when his swing resulted in a home run just as the ball hit the bat. There was a solid connection. Not a single vibration of the bat in his hands, just that unmistakable crack! He would knowingly drop the bat and start his jog around the bases and watch his moon shot sail over the fence. Fans cheered his name, and his teammates all met him at home plate, where they traded high fives, fist bumps. Lastly, the inevitable slap on the ass from his coach.

That same satisfying, solid connection happened here as the poker connected with Sanders. It sent chills through Joe's arms. The room exploded with feathers, and he saw the rooster slam into the chimney bricks with a bloody WHUMP! The bird hit hard then bounced onto the floor. Joe gripped the poker with all his strength and cautiously approached the heap of feathers as it twitched and jerked. Colonel Sanders made wet sucking sounds that blew pink bubbles from his crushed beak. His knurled neck was twisted in a fashion that had to mean it was broken.

"Please, God, be broken." Joe silently prayed as he walked toward him, inch by inch.

As if the rooster sensed Joe's approach, he quickly cocked his head and looked up at Joe. This sudden movement by the bird caused Joe to shrink back then instinctively lung forward to smack the bird with the poker. He swung the poker down with all his strength. It hit something above his head.

With all his focus on the heap of feathers on the floor, Joe inched cautiously toward it. He wasn't aware his position was directly under the 74-inch ceiling fan above. "The Beast," Joe called it when he saw it on display at the local hardware box store. Erma had to have it. Their vaulted ceiling looked too open and bare with a regular 46-inch fan. The poker barely grazed the huge fan motor when he swung down, but it was enough to deflect his aim. Colonel Sanders was already in flight and flew at Joe with only one operational claw. The other dangled at an odd angle, clearly broken. However, the one that tracked his face was all the rooster needed to put Joe down. Joe instinctively dropped from his feet as one of the fish-hook-shaped talons grazed his head. It opened a nasty gash from his hairline down the side of his temple. The Colonel overshot his mark and slammed into the far wall. Joe took the opportunity and ran down the hall to where his family was.

"Erma!" Joe shouted as he searched for his family.

"We're in your office!" screamed back Erma. Joe rounded the corner and ducked into the office. He slammed the door shut and locked it.

"Oh my God, Joe! Your head is gushing!" panicked Erma as she ran to him.

"It's fine, it's fine. Where is Annie?" Joe asked, terrified.

"She's here, she's here. She was hiding in your credenza," Erma explained.

Joe had no time to register his relief, because suddenly there was a hard crash against the door of the office. Then another and another. Splinters flew into the room. Erma screamed and huddled with the kids in the corner. Joe had to think.

"We can go out a window and get to my truck. I have the keys in my pocket."

But before he could even get to a window a familiar BANG! BANG! BANG! slammed into the house. But it didn't sound like one basketball as before; it sounded like a whole basketball team! Dozens of forces slammed into the walls and ceiling. The windows exploded into the room. Erma screamed in unison with the terrified kids. Joe considered this was the end. He would let Sanders have him. He would surrender himself and allow the savage beast with his hideous lot of evolutionized cluckers to eat out his eyes and other soft tissues. Like buzzards do to fresh roadkill that litter the highways. Then he pictured Annie and Tommy picked to pieces as chickens fought over their young bodies.

"No . . . No . . . NOOO!" he screamed.

As more of the office door disintegrated, an idea popped into Joe's mind.

"Get the kids in the credenza! Hurry, shove them in! Now, dammit, move!" he shouted as he grabbed Annie and crammed her into one of the large bottom compartments. He shut its door tight. Erma finally gained some awareness and shoved Tommy into the other one. He was a bit too big, so Joe shoved hard on the door. That earned a loud, painful scream from Tommy. He turned to Erma and quickly told her to get behind the door. She positioned herself so that when the door to the office opened, she would be behind it.

Joe said, "On the count of three. One . . . two . . . three!" Joe opened the door as Colonel Sanders barreled into the room. The rooster scratched and clawed for him. Joe quickly sidestepped the bird into the hall. He limped as fast as he could to the foyer to grab his shotgun behind the plant. Blood from his previous entanglement with Colonel Sanders was smeared across the white tiles. This caused him to slip and land hard on the gash in his thigh. He screamed as a flash of hot pain shot up his body. Tears streamed down his face as he gasped for breath. From his office he heard Erma scream in torturous pain. Her anguish pierced his own.

"Erma!" he yelled back. She continued her screams of utter agony.

He knew then the solar screens on the office windows had finally failed. God knows what version of hell was streamed into his office and ripped his wife apart. Joe pushed himself up and grabbed his shotgun. He racked the slide, which loaded one of the buckshot shells into the breach. He struggled back to his office. When he turned the corner of the hall a demonized hen came at him. Its claws turned up toward him and drove deep into his gaped thigh. The pain was unbearable, and Joe thought he might pass out. Another scream erupted from his wife. This snapped him back from the darkness. He grabbed the feathered freak by the neck, ignored its serrated beak that dug into his wrist, and swung it around several times until its head popped off. Its bloody body splattered against the ceiling and fell to the floor. It flopped around like a fish out of water.

Joe turned into the office, gun raised. What he saw, he couldn't believe. It caused him to lower the weapon. Dozens of demon chickens poured in through the windows. Erma was on the floor motionless. Several chickens gouged chunks of meat from her back and legs. Triumphantly, balanced on one leg atop Erma's head, was Colonel Sanders.

He cocked his head to the side seemingly to tell Joe, "You took mine, and I now have taken yours."

With a piercing scream the rooster leaped into the air. Joe never had a chance to raise the shotgun. The pendulum of luck had made its way back in Joe's direction, however. From the hip he angled the barrel up and pulled the trigger. The sound was deafening in the small room. All the chickens jumped up and bounced off the ceiling in comical unison. As the feathers and chaos subsided, a pink mist still hung in the air. Against the far wall directly in front of Joe was a splatter of gore mixed with white and black feathers. He expected an onslaught of pissy hens, so he racked the slide of the Benelli to load another round. Instead, the chickens seemed suddenly normal. They clucked and ran into each other, confused in the chaos. The rooster's death must have broken whatever hoodoo they were under. Erma lay on the floor. She bled badly. Her clothes were shredded, and some fingers were ripped off her hands. The birds had taken chunks from all over her body. Even patches of her scalp.

Joe kneeled down and prayed, "Please be alive . . . please."

Erma stirred and looked up at Joe.

"The kids, Joe. Save the kids," she whispered before she fainted.

Joe quickly opened the two doors of the credenza. His kids spilled out onto the floor. He swept them up and shielded their eyes. He quickly took them to the next bedroom. Back in his office he grabbed the phone. He went to call 911, when he saw it: the rooster's severed head lay there on the floor.

With the rest of its body implanted into the wall, the severed head looked up at him. It cocked sideways in that robotic herky-jerky way. Colonel Sanders sized him up with his only little, beady eye. All of the evening's events raged inside of Joe. He lost his dog, his home was destroyed, his son lay in the next room with deep slices in his feet, and now his one-and-only love lay on the floor mangled, holding on to the last shreds of her life. Joe positioned the barrel of the shotgun so Colonel Sanders stared into its long cold barrel.

Then through gritted teeth, eyes narrowed and glowing like scorched embers that roared to life, he hissed, "Deep fry in hell."

Then pulled the trigger.

Chapter Three

Dallas, Texas, 2020
The Aftermath
Fifty Years Later

"Last call, buddy. Hey, fella? Last call." Rob looked up to see the bartender offering him a refill as the clock struck midnight. "No thanks," he replied, bringing his attention back to the warm, half-empty glass of beer that sat in front of him.

"If all my customers drank like you, my kids would be in the streets," the bartender muttered as he moved on to wipe the bar further down.

Rob was in his own world and didn't hear. His attention was on the last of the carbonated bubbles that freed themselves from the sides and bottom of his beer glass. One by one, they raced to the top as if fleeing the oppression of the heavy, amber liquid, then burst into the open air excited for their freedom and the happiness of their new life.

For the last two hours, these bubbles represented various friends and acquaintances Rob had grown up with and how eventually they all seemed to move on, starting careers and families. Their dreams fulfilled and being . . . happy. One solitary bubble clung to the bottom of the flat beer that remained. Unable to break free, it just sat there waiting to be consumed. Rob felt this last bubble was him here and now, with just one year left to finish his degree in journalism. On the bar next to him lay a letter that informed him he failed to finish his academic probation satisfactorily and the dean rescinded Rob's scholarship. Without a scholarship, there was no way he could afford to finish at this university or potentially any university.

Being put on academic probation wasn't due to Rob's inability to perform in his studies. In fact, he made the dean's list his first two years and earned a coveted spot as an editor for the university's newspaper, which was mostly reserved for upperclassmen. Writing was Rob's passion since he first learned to string a sentence together. It was his escape from the turmoil of his childhood. His father was committed to a mental hospital when Rob was ten years old, and shortly after, his mother dropped him and his younger sister, Mel, off with a neighbor. She was supposed to return in an hour after she ran errands. She never did. From that point on it was one foster family after another for him and Mel. Rob kept a journal at an early age and wrote creative stories as an escape from all the instability. Mel, just two years younger, was less fazed from all the drama and easily found friends, but not always the kind normal parents would approve of.

Foster parents would take them in with the promise of a loving family. Soon they would find Rob frustrating because he was not sociable and withdrew from attention, while Mel created attention wherever she could. This often left her in trouble with teachers and ultimately, the law. Once the newness of the brother-sister combo wore off, they would be cast away only to be dropped into another dysfunctional foster family that made the same fake promises. The degrees of dysfunctionality in these families were a crapshoot. Either the parents were neglectful or overbearing, or the siblings were awful to them or ignored them all together.

Making friends was virtually impossible. Rob had learned to read people very quickly to know if they could be trusted or not. He honed this skill to survive. Within mere seconds of being in the presence of a person, he would turn into a chameleon hoping to minimize attention to himself. Feeling he was part of the wallpaper, he would observe, watch and listen. He made mental notes he would later use to create characters in his stories.

One summer he met a neighbor kid, Josh, with whom Rob hoped a full-fledged friendship would flourish.

Josh was an only child that regularly used what Rob vaguely remembers his mother referring to as "questionable language." He seemed to have everything a kid could want. He had video games, nice new clothes, and a really cool bike—unlike Rob, who never had two pennies to rub together and rarely had anything new. Him having video games would be as ridiculous a concept as him having a Ferrari.

When Josh asked Rob what he liked to do for fun, Rob replied, "I like to write stories."

Josh looked puzzled and retorted, "What the hell is that? Sounds like boring crap girls do." After Rob explained how he could create wild adventures using characters created any way he wanted, Josh seemed intrigued as if using his brain for a source of entertainment was a newly discovered concept. "So like, all the chicks can have huge knockers, and I can be all famous and rich?" Josh asked excitedly as he came around to the idea more and more.

"Sure, I guess. That's what's so much fun about it. You can be anybody and be anywhere you want," replied Rob.

They began a creative writing project together in which one would write a few pages in a spiral notebook then hand it off to the other. This back-and-forth method allowed each writer to inject their own style and imagination into the story. When they started it seemed like a good idea, but soon they found themselves locked in arguments about why the other took the story in this direction or that. And frankly, Rob grew tired of all the huge knockers, as it seemed Josh's parts of the story centered around them.

In the story he and Josh had built a spaceship that took them far into space. They entered a new galaxy and found a planet on which, per the ship's computer, the atmosphere could support life. They landed and readied themselves with an arsenal of weapons and high-tech gadgetry. They exited the craft ready to destroy any foe. These were the parts Rob loved writing the most. The creative invention of weapons and gadgets, then going to battle. Instead, they were greeted by large-breasted green babes in revealing clothes that instead of walking, hopped everywhere.

When Rob asked Josh why they hopped instead of walked, he responded, "Really? Are you a dumbass? No, you must be a gay dumbass if I have to explain that to you."

Josh threw the notebook at Rob. This signaled his turn to take the story forward. He then put his fists under his shirt and imitated the green babes. How they hopped here and there.

That night Rob stayed up late and worked on his pages. The words flowed and the plot thickened. He was truly excited about the direction it was going. In the story, he had left Josh with the bouncing beauties and was going to answer a distress call that turned into a trap. A huge battle ensued as Rob and the crew fought hard. They took casualties as photon missiles slammed their spaceship. Fires and shrapnel exploded all around, but the crew held firmly together as they worked their posts and took orders. It was a fast-action, thrilling brawl to the death in which Rob and his crew barely escaped victorious. The next morning Rob couldn't wait to read to Josh what he had written. Once in Josh's room he began to read his latest edition, but before he could get to the battle scene, Josh interrupted, "So you left me behind?"

Rob replied, "Yes, I figured you would prefer to stay with the knockers."

"Well that sucks. What kind of stupid partner are you?"

"You always wanna be around the girls. It's all you think about, it seems," chided Rob. At this, Josh grabbed the notebook and began ripping out the pages and tearing them to pieces. Rob tried to grab it back, which led to

Josh throwing Rob to the ground. Rob wasn't a fighter, had never even been in a scuffle. This was a first, and he was outmatched.

Josh kicked him hard in the stomach, yelling, "Writing is stupid! Take your crap and run before I kick your dumb ass!"

Rob gasped for air, grabbed the notebook and the pages he could, and ran back home. From that point he was determined to never try to make friends with anyone and had pretty much held true to that.

Of his last fifty dollars, he peeled off a five and paid for his beer. He took one last look at the bubble. It still sat there pathetically at the bottom of the glass. Rob gulped it down.

Chapter Four

It was November, and the late-evening air in Dallas was nice and cool. The warm humidity had lessened. It was nice and brisk, so he walked back to his university dorm room in the fresh air. After all, sleep wasn't an option. For the last year a dream began to reoccur. Slowly at first, little bits and pieces wedged between forgettable dreams, but becoming clearer, more vivid, more unforgettable. It got to the point that Rob only caught snatches of sleep. Five minutes here, ten minutes there. But never more, which would risk sending him into rapid eye movement sleep, better known as REMS. REMS, Rob learned, is a unique phase of sleep in people, characterized by random rapid movement of the eyes and the propensity of the sleeper to dream vividly. It was the vividness that terrified Rob and had become the cause of him losing sleep and ultimately his university scholarship. Lately, this nightmare haunted his sleep every time he drifted off.

In the pocket of his jacket he felt a folded business card. He had folded and unfolded it so much lately it was close to being torn in the crease. He absently turned it over and over in his pocket as he strolled along the sidewalk. A few months ago he had left a writing class, when he saw flyers stuck on the windshields of several parked cars. He didn't have a car of his own, so he walked mostly. Money was too scarce to call an Uber or catch a cab. He had considered a bicycle, but figured the headache to keep up with it wasn't worth it. Curiously, he plucked a flyer off the closest windshield hoping for a coupon or some cost-saving service he could use. Instead, he discovered a locally renowned psychologist, Dr. Maria Sheltie, was going to be giving a lecture in the coming fall for the psychology students. However, all students of the university were invited. What caught Rob's attention was that *dream exploration* was listed as her area of expertise. A business card was stapled to the corner of the flyer. He tore it off, folded it, and stuck in his jacket pocket. He then placed the flyer back under the windshield wiper of the car from which he took it.

For the past month, Rob had referenced the card many times. The date of the seminar was tomorrow, and Rob had been torn about whether to attend or not. At first he was determined to overcome this on his own, but he had grown angry with himself for not being able to push this dream out of his thoughts.

"Am I so feebleminded I can't control this?" he asked himself repeatedly.

He felt this lack of sleep had pushed him into the same mental anguish that consumed his father so many years ago. Like father, like son. The inheritance of madness was bestowed upon him.

He arrived at his dorm building and swiped his access card. It turned green with a click and the lock released. He had no idea where he would live once the LED turned red. The smell of old carpet, mingled with ramen noodles filled the air. The food of choice for broke students in their academic struggle to succeed. A disparity of music and even some heavy, passionate breaths were heard as he passed the doors of other students. He swiped his access card again outside his room, and his luck held. The LED turned green. Inside, the room was not large and only had a bed that'd been hardly used lately and a threadbare chair. Next to the chair was a TV tray. There was a small studio kitchen Rob used to make strong drip coffee, which he was in need of right then as the late night pressed forward. He added two extra scoops of coffee and flipped the switch on to start the brewing cycle. As it began its gurgling process, he looked in the small fridge and grabbed the bologna. He gave it a sniff. Not sure if it smelled offensive or not, he peeled

23

off a slice and tasted it. Deeming okay for human consumption, he grabbed the mustard too.

As he made the sandwich his mind drifted back to when life was normal. He was six or so. Mel was just out of diapers and could keep up with Rob, so they could play together. He was happy with her in tow wherever he went. Truck and trailer, his dad would call them. Life was easy then. Fun as it should be for kids. His mother was in her prime, having friends over often, and there was always laughter.

It wasn't until just before his eighth birthday things started to get dark for his family. His father struggled to sleep and complained about everything. Rob's mother grew more and more detached from the family as she began attending social gatherings instead of hosting them. She often came home late, smelling of booze. His father's mood was becoming worse and harder for her to bear, and she seemed determined not to let it rub off on her. It was thereafter he recalled the biggest fight he'd ever seen them have, because they rarely fought at all. His father came home from work, for once, it seemed, in a cheerful mood.

"Nancy? Where are you?" he called as he searched room to room. Rob was with Mel in the backyard and raced in to see why his dad was so excited. They could hear him hollering for their mother even outside.

Rob's mom was lying on the couch half asleep. "I'm in here. What do you want?" she called back. He interrupted her thoughts of whether to go out tonight or stay in. This decision was becoming ever more difficult.

"You won't believe it. My childhood home is for sale!"

"That's good because . . . ?" His mother groaned as she sat up looking at his father, unable to see what was so exciting about that. When she married Tommy she knew very little of his tormented past, only enough to know there was a very traumatic event involving his father almost murdering Tommy's mother, so the papers reported. He and his sister were nearly killed themselves. The scars left on the soles of Tommy's feet from walking through shattered glass from the violence was enough for Nancy to know Tommy's father was a maniac. However, Tommy defended his father and claimed there was more to the story, but never would elaborate. Nancy knew there were demons in his past, but Tommy assured her that he had gotten therapy as a child and everything was well. He claimed he couldn't recall much of that night until recently when those dreams began plaguing him. She could see the loss of sleep and those repressed memories clawing their way back from the grave he had buried them in taking a toll on him, on his sanity. She figured even now he may be becoming delusional and she may need to go out tonight after all.

Handing his phone to her, he said, "Here, look at the realtor pics. It's been renovated, and the property is better than I've ever seen it. We should buy it!" Nancy flipped through them. She had never seen the house before, nor thought she ever would. It wasn't what she expected. For some reason she always figured it was a creepy old mansion, all run-down and dilapidated, complete with missing shingles and broken shudders. Somewhere a psycho would live. The pictures she was seeing showed a normal farmhouse. Actually, an attractive farmhouse serenely planted in Nowheresville, USA. It was a single story shaped in an L, very spacious inside. The whole property was ten acres, plenty of land for two youngsters that badly needed space to roam free without the fears of the city.

"You're serious? You want to buy it, and you want us to live there?" she asked dubiously.

"Yes! Very serious."

"After everything that happened to you there? This is absurd," Nancy said as she stood and walked into the kitchen.

Tommy followed her as he continued to explain his reasoning. "Look, lately I haven't slept well, and my moods have been up and down because of it. I'm thinking if I, if we live there, I can conquer whatever this is I am experiencing and things can get back to normal."

"As usual, it's all about you. Think of our kids. Think of me! Moving out into some godforsaken area without shopping and friends! Would you have the kids ride a bus to school too? My God, what are the schools even like? You can't just uproot a family like this. There are so many things to consider, Tommy!" She poured herself a large glass of wine and chugged half of it before walking to the bedroom. Tommy followed, trying his best to persuade her.

This argument elevated into the evening as more wine was consumed and insinuations bordering insults began rearing their ugly heads. Nancy claimed she had enough and was going to her friend's house to cool off. Rob couldn't recall if she returned that night, but ultimately she relented, and they drove out that weekend to take a look at the house with a real estate agent.

The coffee pot beeped, alerting him his strong brew was done and bringing his thoughts back to the present. He poured a cup and took his late-night snack to his chair and settled in. Once he was done with his sandwich, he hoped to start perusing job boards, so he readied his laptop on the TV tray next to him. As he ate, his mind went back to seeing the house for the first time. Rob shivered at the memory of his first being there. Compared to the house he was born in, it was sprawling. Five thousand square feet and one story. The hallway in the photos appeared endless and promised full-speed racing back and forth.

As they turned and drove up the long, winding driveway, Rob's and Mel's faces were glued to the car's windows. There was endless concrete for bicycle riding, roller blading, and Mel's favorite, sidewalk art. To say they both were excited was an understatement. The creek, woods, and huge lawn, all seemed surreal. Once the car stopped they bolted out their doors, eager to see it all at once. After they all had walked around the exterior of the house, his father called for them to come check out the inside as the agent raised the garage door and unlocked the side door to go in.

Chapter Five

Rob stood in the doorway. Ahead of him was a brick pillar that was one side of the stovetop island. There was a mirror that hung on the brick pillar. He saw himself standing there all of ten years old in his favorite SpongeBob SquarePants underwear. He looked down and saw a sea of shattered glass on the white tile floor. He wondered why the dishes were falling out of the cabinets endlessly—some shattering on the granite countertops and others crashing against the tile floor. He realized he was standing on several shards of glass. His feet were bleeding badly. The crimson color of his blood was in great contrast with the white tiles. However, he didn't feel any pain. Slowly, as if on cue, sound started to support what his eyes were seeing. Outside the kitchen wall he heard a BANG! BANG! BANG! as the walls shook violently, causing the dishes to shatter in deafening crashes. The noise and chaos were incredible. Without warning he began to walk slowly. He turned left to go around the stovetop island. He couldn't move otherwise. He slowly walked like he was a puppet. Or better yet, like he was an actor following a script that he mustn't deviate from. All good actors follow the script. Especially one so well written as this one. He wondered who wrote it. The visual effects were amazing. The sound effects were so authentic. He hoped he didn't screw up his part.

As Rob rounded the island, he saw his father there on the floor. He was covered in blood and squatting down with his arms wrapped around his knees. He was terrified, very afraid. He rocked back and forth on his heels mumbling something under his breath. Something incoherent. Drool dripped from his chin. Rob couldn't make out what he was saying through all the chaos. In front of his father lay a huge German shepherd dog. Rob didn't recognize the dog, but it had beautiful, thick fur. Its throat was torn open and laid back across its shoulder, exposing sinew and bones. Huge amounts of blood making gurgling, sloppy noises seemed to pour endlessly out of the gaping wound as the dog, though motionless,

28

seemed to still be gasping for air. His long, thick, pink tongue lolled out on the floor. Its eyes were dark marbles. Rob wondered what had happened. What could possibly do that kind of damage to such a huge dog? He wanted to ask his father what happened, but no sound came from his mouth. He felt he was on mute and just stared.

He heard cries and screams coming from the foyer leading into the living room. Rob's heart began pounding faster. The cries sounded like they might be coming from a kid and woman. A young boy screaming in utter agony and a woman trying to console him. Rob clearly heard the panic in her voice. Suddenly, a man hollered from the living room, "Come get me, you psycho son of a bitch! Over here!" His voice sounded unhinged and crazy. Rob started to walk again in that slow, numb way into the foyer toward the screaming. He didn't want to go in there and began wondering if this was a dream. He kept walking nonetheless and crunching broken glass underfoot.

As he passed through the threshold into the foyer, a sweet, floral perfume began to permeate the air. The smell was faint, but familiar. As Rob tried to remember how he knew it, the chaos and screaming behind him started to abate. In their place was the warm, soft humming of a woman. The tune she was humming was also familiar. But like the perfume, he couldn't quite place it. Behind him he still sensed the chaos and violence, but now in front of him was pleasant, calm, and bright. He continued into the foyer as the living room opened up to his left. Two large french doors leading outside to the front porch were on his right. Once centered to the doors, he slowly turned to his left, facing the living room. He felt his performance so far was right on cue. He was hitting his marks, and he wondered if the critics would love him for it.

The living room was spacious and lightly furnished with a large leather couch, coffee table, piano, and large flat-screen TV in the corner. The ceiling was vaulted with a massive ceiling fan turning slowly. Rob realized the room wasn't just clean, it was immaculate—from the fresh paint on the walls to a radiant bouquet of flowers on the piano. The foyer tiles on which he was standing were the same brilliant white as in the kitchen. Into the living room the floor turned to a rich, deep mahogany that shimmered slightly as if made of liquid. Directly opposite from him was a huge brick fireplace and a woman dusting its

29

mantle while humming that tune. She was only wearing underwear—a matching lace bra and a thong of pure white that seemed to glow against her smooth tan skin. Her silky hair was the color of honey and flowed down her back. Her legs were slender yet toned. She tiptoed to reach the entire surface she was dusting. Rob tried hard not to stare where her thong disappeared, but his eyes seemed to be drawn to that point. She didn't realize he was there, as she was completely focused on dusting every inch of the mantle. Finally, she exhaled and stepped back to inspect her work.

"All finished there!" she said in a light, breathy voice. She turned and began dusting the corner of the flat-screen TV. The feathers of her duster were a blur. The full profile of the woman made Rob gasp. He thought she was utterly gorgeous. His heart again began racing, but this time not from fear. Unable to speak, he continued to stare. All at once her duster froze and her head jerked toward him. "Rob, I wasn't expecting you," she said with what was clearly a forced smile. Rob slowly realized why the floral scent in the room and the pleasant tune being hummed was so familiar, yet the woman in front of him not so much. Then a thought burst into his head . . . Mom? He tried to speak, but the script didn't allow for it. He had no speaking lines in this scene. So he continued standing there, just staring. The woman held some resemblance to the mother in his memories. Enough to know the two must be related somehow, but in the way cousins tend to look similar. Her nose seemed different and her cheeks rose higher.

"What, you don't recognize me? How long has it been? Ten years at least?" she asked, then performed a perfect pirouette ending in a pose Rob recalled the models on The Price is Right *do to accentuate prizes to the contestants. She sauntered toward him, stopping just a few feet in front of him. Her perfume was intoxicating now. He wanted to breathe it in deeply, but to his dismay the script wasn't allowing for it. She then slid a finger up her tight thigh. She circled it around her navel, then further up between her large breasts, then pressed them together playfully. She leaned forward until she and Rob were eye to eye, resting her hands on her knees. He never really made note of his mother's breasts before, but surely they were never that full and . . . and . . . big.*

"Cat got your tongue?" she teased.

Her smile was dazzling. Lips full and plump. Teeth perfect and sparkling white. Why would the writers not give him any lines here? It was obvious she was needing a dialogue to play off of if she was to have any chance at making the podium for this performance.

"What's the matter, you don't like my mommy makeover?" She giggled as her eyes slowly looked down between the both of them. "Oh! But it appears you must."

Rob's eyes followed hers down. To his amazement SpongeBob's nose was extremely distended, giving Mr. SquarePants the illusion of being from the Far East. More giggles. She playfully flicked the tip of SpongeBob's nose with her perfectly manicured fingernail, tantalizing his naughtiness as she stood.

"What is Mommy gonna do with you?" she said flirtatiously as she mussed Rob's hair.

Rob moved his gaze up her voluptuous body to meet her dazzling green eyes and realized her smile was slowly fading. Her attention was directed toward the kitchen from he'd come. Her smile felt flat then continued down until her beautiful face twisted into a gruesome, exaggerated scowl. The corners of her lips pulled down so hard the skin of her high cheeks stretched like cellophane then tore in horizontal lines from her nose to her ears. Her eyes began losing their green luster, taking on a dull yellow glow as her perfect chest began heaving in anger, emitting the sounds of cracking twigs.

"What . . . have . . . you . . . done?" She said each word deliberately while clenching her teeth. Spit was flying from her lips. "You have tracked your nasty blood all over my clean floor! HE will be here any minute, and now look at this mess!" she screamed.

Her veins bulged garishly from her neck. Rob looked toward the kitchen and saw small, bloody footprints ending in a pool where he was now standing. His mother stomped into the kitchen and screamed at his father still huddling in the corner.

"Would you please shut up, you pathetic little man! I'm sick and tired of your sniveling and whining!" She then smacked him across his face with such force his head banged against the wall and he became still.

The chaos of the BANG! BANG! BANG! and the shattering of glassware in the kitchen began to grow louder again. Rob pictured a sound engineer wearing headphones in a booth somewhere, turning up the volume. He could hear his mother rooting around searching frantically for something. Glass crunched under her bare feet. She returned wearing a large rubber apron with matching rubber gloves, holding a pail. She dropped to her knees, making the bucket slosh its liquid, which was as crimson red as the bloody footprints. Out of the bucket she pulled a large rag soaked in blood and began scrubbing the footprints.

"This is why I left! This is why I dumped both of you brats and ran away," she explained while she scrubbed blood with blood. "Your father's incessant crying! His feeble fears! I am done with him . . . I am done with all of you! The best thing your miserable father ever did was introduce me to HIM!" She was scrubbing angrily now in a large pool of blood, splashing it high against the baseboards and onto herself. "HE is the only one who understands me! HE makes me truly happy. Not you all. You all make me sick!" she screamed at Rob with tears pouring down her wrinkling, now bleeding and torn cheeks.

His mother continued perpetuating the very mess she was trying to clean. Rob wondered who HE was that his mother kept referring to. As he got older, Rob figured his mother had run off with another man, but could never figure out who. The doorbell rang. His mother abruptly stopped her intense scrubbing and listened.

"HE is here! Look at this mess!" she exclaimed as she stood and threw off the soaked gloves and apron. "How do I look?" she asked while pretending to smooth down a dress, but in reality was just smearing blood down her bare stomach and thighs.

"Ah, what would you know anyway?" she spat as she shoved Rob aside and pushed him toward the hallway.

"You must go now. Mommy needs to be happy." She steadied herself and grabbed the doorknob and opened the door. As the door cracked open, a brilliant light blinded Rob. Just as he got a glimpse of the person's face, he heard crying from down the hallway. It was another kid. But a young girl this time. She was sobbing her heart out in such agony it hurt Rob to hear it. He began to turn toward the crying, but he wanted a better look at HIM.

He wanted to know who HE was. The script compeled him to turn into the hallway. His curiosity could wait apparently. The show must go on.

As Rob slowly walked down the hall, he saw it looked like a war zone. Holes in the sheetrock, a collapsing ceiling on ripped carpet. Gore and blood everywhere. The taste of copper was in the air, and it smelled of sweat and death. Feathers littered the entire space with what looked like various chicken parts scattered around. He saw a severed claw gripping a woman's finger. It looked to have polish on its nail and a simple gold wedding band around it. Approaching to his left was a doorway. The door itself had been shattered to pieces. Only chunks of wood were still attached to the hinges. From inside the office, the child's crying grew louder. He could hear her bubbling through snot and tears. Rob didn't want to look inside. He wanted this performance to stop. As if the script read his mind, he did stop, right in front of the door. However, he didn't turn to go into what appeared to be a home office. He kept looking straight ahead down the long hallway which ended in darkness. From the office, the sound of something large was breathing. He could hear the wheezing of its breath. He could sense the hatred in its gaze. Then the sound of something slightly moving its feet. Like adjusting its stance on a muddy surface, positioning to pounce. "Pleeeaase stop doing that to her, PLEEEASSE!" the young girl pleaded. As if the script cued Rob to turn his head to look into the room, he did so slowly. Dreadfully. Rob felt he might faint. He only got a glimpse of what was in there before he heard a whisper say, "La Casa Bailarinas." Then moving like lightning, with a scream so shrill Rob's eardrums ruptured, the most vile, hideous-looking winged abomination attacked his face, digging its razor-sharp talons deep into his mouth and eyes, crushing his skull.

Chapter Six

Rob gasped for air, screaming himself awake. He sat there breathing heavy, trying to calm himself, covered in sweat. He looked around and realized he was safe in his dorm room. He felt his face to make sure his head was uncrushed. His half-eaten bologna sandwich seemed to have taken the worst of things, as its contents were scattered from his chair into the kitchenette.

"Dammit . . . I fell asleep," he whispered.

He must have dozed before he had a chance to drink his coffee, all of which soaked his lap and chair. He checked his phone. It was 4:38 AM. That meant he was asleep for a little over three hours. It was the longest he'd slept in days, but this time his nightmare was much more terrifying, but potentially more telling. Rob tried to focus. A huge German shepherd dog. All the commotion in the other rooms he could hear but not see. What was it his mother had said? That the best thing his father had ever done for her was introducing her to HIM. "Who is HIM?" Rob wondered out loud and grabbed a pen and paper. He made notes. And the mommy makeover. If that even was his mom, or some Freudian creation of his subconscious. The details evaporated fast, like rain on hot summer pavement, so he wrote furiously. Then the final details that led to the end of the nightmare. He shivered thinking about them. The overall details may have be fading, but the beating of those strong wings that surrounded him at lightning speed along with that ear-piercing scream, wasn't. Especially the leathery feeling of its foot with needle-like talons on Rob's face, the lower inserting itself between his teeth, piercing his gums into the roof of his mouth, and the upper ones pressing through his

eyes. Ughh . . . he could still taste it. Rob shook his head and tried to free
himself from the skull-crushing sensation, but struggled.

There was something else. A detail he found most peculiar. A
whisper just before the attack from that monster. What did it say? La Casa
Bailarinas? Yeah, that was it, and he wrote it down. The House of Ballerinas.
Thankfully his Spanish was better than fair, due to the two years he took in
high school coupled with more during his freshman year of college. His
grandmother, or abuela, was Mexican. He only met her a handful of times
before he and Mel went on the foster freakshow tour of families. He recalled
she was always withdrawn and sad, but teaching him Spanish seemed to bring
her joy. She would sit in her chair, a colorful worn blanket across her lap, and
would ask him to repeat after her, uno, dos, tres, and so on. Never did he see
her do anything but just sit in that chair covered in that colorful blanket. Even
so young, he felt sorry for her and didn't know why. When Rob asked his dad
why she seemed so sad, he would simply say that she had been through a lot.
Then he would deftly change the subject.

Rob finished his notes from his dream and turned on the
coffeemaker's burner to reheat his earlier failed caffeination attempt. While he
poured a cup he determined he would attend the seminar of Dr. Sheltie at 9:00
AM later that morning. He took his coffee into the bathroom to get ready.
Later, he sacrificed another five precious dollars for breakfast on his way to
the lecture hall.

**

The Edith O'Donnell Arts and Technology Lecture Hall was the most
spacious room on campus with the capacity to seat 1,500 people. Its tall ceiling
painted black hid all of the support scaffolding, lighting, speakers and miles of
wiring and cabling that supported it all. Attached to the walls were sound
absorption panels creating vibrant yet soft acoustics no matter which seat a

person sat in. Rob had only been in this room one other time for his freshman orientation when he was eager and full of life, ready to take on the journalistic world. Now he was quite the opposite, rundown and full of exhaustion trying to hold on to the world he lived in now.

It was 9:00 AM, and students still filed in. Already the hall was mostly full, and from the looks of it, it was going to be a packed audience. Rob secured a seat on the far right in the back just in case he needed to duck out if he started to doze. Rob's answer when he began to nod off was to immediately get up and move around. These days Mr. Sandman was constantly tugging on his sleeve, which required Rob to stay vigilant to ensure the old Sandmeister didn't succeed.

At ten minutes past the hour, the dean made his way to the pulpit. He tapped the microphone and cleared his throat to introduce Dr. Sheltie. A warm applause greeted her as she walked out on stage. Dr. Sheltie was younger than Rob expected to have received such accolades. For some reason he pictured her as an older woman, studiously hunched over with a long nose and small round spectacles, complete with a pearl-beaded lanyard. An academic grandma. Instead she appeared in her early forties, tall and fit with long auburn hair. She mounted the podium with a practiced grace, obviously at home speaking to large audiences.

"Hello, everyone!" she greeted the students excitedly. For the next several minutes she made her introduction and described her various pedigrees and achievements, but did so in a way that was not stuffy and unbecoming. It came across as more of a pep talk. She encouraged the impressionable audience to follow their dreams. Anything they set their minds to could be achieved, so on and so forth. Normally Rob would have enjoyed her energy and eloquence, but today he wanted her—no, he needed her—to get to the meat of the issue on dream exploration. For the next hour Dr. Sheltie discussed challenges that the psychological community faced. New advances and breakthroughs, but sadly still more challenges to come. She discussed mental health in our criminal justice system and inequalities amongst the lower-income demographic. It was apparent Dr. Sheltie knew her stuff. Finally, she began to discuss dreams.

"Dreams are important. They have meaning in your life. They shouldn't be ignored," she said earnestly.

Yes! The segue into dream exploration Rob had waited for. Now she could tell him how to master them so he could finally rest and get on with his life. Maybe he could plead with the dean's office for an extension of his probation. With sleep, he knew he could bring his grades up and keep his scholarship. Rob literally was on the edge of his seat with anticipation, desperation. Then as if he was a balloon filling with hope, his knot let loose and he started to deflate as he realized she spoke of a different kind of dream. The Martin Luther King Jr. variety. The kind that guided a person. That filled them with purpose. Not the kind that tormented and destroyed the fiber of one's being and stole their sleep, crippling them mentally.

"And remember to dream big, which will allow you to achieve amazing things. Thank you so much. You've been a wonderful audience!" Dr. Sheltie said as she gave a final wave then disappeared behind the curtain.

Rob slid back in his chair and rubbed his face. "What now?" he thought in despair as he watched the crowd stand and start to exit the hall. Then it occurred to him what he must do. Rob quickly exited the hall with a small spark of hope, renewed.

The day was cool, crisp. Fall had won the battle with summer. Rob walked from the lecture hall to a corner coffee shop and sacrificed, rather invested in his alertness, another five dollars on some strong coffee. He sat outside and sipped his hot brew. He took out his phone. The flyer he found that pointed him to the lecture with Dr. Sheltie mentioned she was locally renowned. This meant she must have a practice somewhere there in the Dallas area. Rob typed in her name, and Google found her office phone number and address. He dialed the number. On the third ring a pleasant voice answered. It identified the office of Dr. Sheltie.

Surprised to be connected with a real person so quickly, he stumbled on his words. "He- hello, yes, I would like to schedule an appointment with Dr. Sheltie, please."

"Are you an existing patient of Dr. Sheltie?"

"No, ma'am."

"Unfortunately, Dr. Sheltie is not taking new patients at this time. You may try back in a couple months," explained the pleasant voice.

"I . . . I . . . wait, I," Rob stammered. He searched for something to compel her to change her mind, but nothing came before she said goodbye and the call went dead. Rob continued to hold the phone to his ear in disbelief.

"Not taking new patients?" he whispered. He felt his newfound hope and energy had drained away right there on the sidewalk.

Rob sat there staring at nothing in particular, his mind numb. The Sandmeister began to tug on him. He could feel him whisper sweet nothings into his ear. His eyelids grew heavy. He wondered what would happen if he just succumbed, let the dream have him, let the abomination consume him. Just as Rob drifted off with his head in his hands, someone bumped him from behind and startled him.

"Excuse me. I am so sorry," a woman apologized. She had pulled back the chair behind him for one of her three small children.

"No worries," replied Rob as the ruckus the kids caused began to resonate.

Rob let out a long breath. That was close: he almost fell asleep. He took another gulp of coffee then stood and left the coffee shop table. As he walked he tried to think of other ways to stay alert. A few months back when the dream initially started he went to a local clinic and discussed his situation

38

with the doctor. The doctor explained it was probably stress and Rob should exercise more between study sessions. He went on about how the stress of being a student was never fully appreciated by most people. When Rob asked if he could prescribe something to pep him up, the doctor looked at him skeptically and again fell back on his position exercise was the answer. Since that dreadful appointment, Rob had seen two more doctors with similar, unsatisfactory results. He could get pills all day long to help him sleep, but to stay awake, they looked at him like he was a junkie trying to score a high.

Rob walked on for another twenty minutes, lost in his thoughts. As long as he kept in motion, he wouldn't sleep, so he hoped. Even now he felt he could sleep and walk if he tried. He stood at an intersection and awaited the green indication he could cross. He realized that across the street there was a sign that declared the therapy practices of none other than Dr. Maria Sheltie. He blinked a few times to focus to ensure he wasn't hallucinating. Sure enough he had made his way to her front door. He crossed the street and brought his Google search up on his phone from earlier to verify the address. It was the same. Rob was flummoxed. He gave a brief laugh, but didn't know why. What was funny about this moment? This coincidence? Nothing of course, but when a person is so exhausted they find humor in everything. With no real plan he entered the lobby and approached the receptionist.

"Hello, may I help you?" came the pleasant voice Rob recalled from the earlier phone call.

Rob hesitated then answered, "Yes. I just attended a lecture by Dr. Sheltie at the university."

"Oh, are you a student?"

"Yes, ma'am. I was hoping to speak with her about some questions I thought of during her speech. I found her very inspiring and hoped to meet her."

"She will be happy you enjoyed it so much. I often hear her remarking how she thinks she puts the kids to sleep." With that Rob almost laughed again at the irony that he was a student that needed just that, her to help him sleep.

"Is she in? I would just need a few minutes."

"No, she hasn't returned yet. You must have come here straight away?"

"Well, yes, I must admit I had some time, so I walked over." Rob began to feel nervous. The pleasant tone in her voice turned inquisitive, protecting.

Her eyes narrowed just a touch as she asked, "Did I talk to you a few minutes ago about an appointment?"

"No, I don't think so. Like I said, I just attended her lecture and . . ."

"It *was* you! What are you up to? I told you she isn't taking new patients right now! I'm gonna have to ask you to leave," she said, cutting him off.

At that moment the door opened behind him and Dr. Sheltie walked in. She talked into her cell.

"Yes, Courtney, put us down for two seats, then lunch after. But don't sit us with the Murphys. You know how they are," Dr. Sheltie said into her phone.

Rob rushed over. "Dr. Sheltie!"

Dr. Sheltie stopped abruptly as the stranger approached her. Ms. Pleasant Voice struggled to make it around her horseshoe-shaped desk. For a split second she considered flinging herself over it. Dr. Sheltie was taken aback, not sure if she should acknowledge this man or act like she was busy and brush him off. Before anyone could react, Rob blocked her path.

"Please, Doctor, I haven't slept in days, and I am losing my scholarship. I just saw your lecture, and I need your help," Rob pleaded as Ms. Pleasant Voice, now a little out of breath, caught up to him.

"I'm so sorry, Dr. Sheltie. I asked him to leave. That you weren't taking new patients. Should I call the police?" she said in a less pleasant voice as she grabbed his arm and began to pull him away.

"No, Chelsea, that won't be necessary. Just give me a second." Dr. Sheltie turned and finished her conversation with Courtney. She disconnected her call and turned back. Politely flustered she asked Rob, "How may I help you, young man?"

Chapter Seven

Dr. Sheltie's office was half of the second floor of the building. It was large and open with her desk and workspace on one end and a conference/media center on the other. Although large, it still maintained a sense of coziness. To one side was a plush leather seating area with a couple large chairs and a sofa. "All therapists must require a sofa," Rob thought. He, though, stayed well away from anything that invited sleep, and opted for one of the chairs instead.

Dr. Sheltie sat across from him. She waited expectantly for an explanation for this impromptu invasion of her time. Rob explained as she continued to look at him intently.

"And you've seen a doctor about this?" she asked after a minute or two. It was evident she did not understand the urgency as Rob did. He told her of the doctor visits and how stress, per their professional opinion, was the root of his problem.

"I see. So briefly, and I apologize I only have a few minutes, tell me about the dream," she said as she checked her small, expensive-looking watch. After a few minutes she held up her hand to stop Rob.

"I must stop you there. Your situation is intriguing. However, I have a patient due in just a couple of minutes. Look, I will agree to see you again for a deeper dive into this, but you must go down and fill out the proper paperwork and set up an appointment with Chelsea. It's the best I can do right now," she explained, seeming genuine about his situation for the first time. She stood. Rob didn't. He stayed seated, bewildered. He knew if he didn't get help here and now he would go crazy. Rob just stared at her, his eyes pleading.

42

"I am afraid I am going to go crazy like my father," Rob said softly. "It's a curse going back to my grandfather. You don't understand."

"I am so sorry, but this is all I can offer. Come back later and we will go through all of that and I will help you, I promise," Dr. Sheltie said sympathetically. "This all came about so quickly, I didn't catch your name?" she said and held out her hand.

"It's Rob Florchett," he said, defeated as he stood and accepted her hand. Her hand froze in mid-shake.

"Did you say Florchett? As in Joseph and Thomas Florchett?" Dr. Sheltie asked. Her eyes grew wide.

***

Two hours later Rob once again sat in front of Dr. Sheltie, but this time not in her office. Instead he was in the small study of her home, and now he certainly had her undivided attention. That became apparent earlier in her office when she gave him her home address and asked him to meet her there in an hour. Rob inquired why, and she just motioned him out and said, "Not here. Not now." As he walked out of her office he heard her calling down to Chelsea to clear the doctor's schedule for the rest of the day. She would work from home.

Dr. Sheltie lived in a very expensive neighborhood west of downtown Dallas, mostly consisting of doctors, attorneys, and other high-earning professionals. Rob had to sacrifice another few bucks on an Uber. To traverse downtown Dallas to Colleyville on foot could be perilous for many reasons. Although the neighborhood was upscale, her house was a modest two-story on a couple of lush green acres. Since his arrival in her home, Dr. Sheltie said very little outside of offering him a cold drink. She was steadily focused on her laptop behind her small yet ornate desk. Rob sat and drank a soda. He hoped he didn't nod off before they could get started. He assumed she was busy and needed to catch up on things from the office before she could focus on him. The scent of light jasmine in the air pushed him to nod off when Dr. Sheltie came around her desk and sat down beside him. She placed a well-worn moleskin journal on the coffee table.

"How much do you know about your grandfather?" she asked. Rob hadn't expected this line of questioning. He hoped to just get on with his treatment.

"Uhm, well, he went nuts and tried to kill his family," Rob said. He couldn't see the relevance of the question.

"No, I mean, how much do you really know about that night?" Dr. Sheltie pressed.

"I guess not much," Rob returned. Now it seemed she was more interested in history than the present.

She let out a long breath as she summoned up courage. "I don't believe your grandfather went crazy and tried to murder his family. And I don't believe your father is crazy. My mentor didn't either."

"Your mentor?" Rob asked. Now totally lost.

"Yes, for my doctorate studies I had to find an internship, and my father had a close friend who was a retiring military psychologist, Dr. Klaskin. I worked for him the last year he practiced, for my internship. During that time he had a patient that came to him, or rather was sent to Dr. Klaskin by his mother. He was a teenager and had been in and out of therapy for some time and needed the special skills my mentor had in dealing with childhood trauma." Dr. Sheltie wasn't the confident doctor Rob had seen earlier today, but rather nervous. Skittish even. This raised his own anxiety level.

She continued, "As Dr. Klaskin began treatment, he confided in me that he felt there was more involved with this patient than he wanted to dig into. Certain things that certain people may be involved in. Something he felt could be dangerous if uncovered." Now Dr. Sheltie's hands began to shake. She realized this and folded them in her lap.

"I guess I am not understanding what this has to do with me?" Rob said.

"It has everything to do with you, Rob," she replied, now taking his hand into hers. She looked earnestly into his eyes. "The patient was Thomas Florchett. Your father."

Rob was stunned. "My father?"

"Yes. Dr. Klaskin believed there was much more involved in that night than a man going crazy. As a matter of fact, Dr. Klaskin didn't believe he was trying to kill his family. He believed your grandfather was defending it." Dr. Sheltie paused. She let that bit of new information sink in a minute before she continued. "But right now, we need to free you from this nightmare," she said as she picked up the ancient-looking journal and opened it to one of its many dog-eared pages.

***

For nearly forty-five minutes Rob explained his dream to Dr. Sheltie in great detail. He told her how he wasn't able to move or speak freely when in its grip, as if he was forced to follow a script. She took notes furiously as he spoke, like she was taking dictation. From time to time she would stop him and ask questions. Once she understood his answer completely she would slowly nod her head yes and prompt him to continue.

"Fascinating," Dr. Sheltie muttered as Rob finished his tour through freak land. Rob was sweating. He sensed her mind working a thousand miles an hour. He could tell there was much she wasn't telling him. Now she looked again like the doctor during the lecture. Confident. Eager. In her element.

"Okay. Let's have you lie back." She stood, giving him space and adjusting a throw pillow for his head.

"Are you going to hypnotize me?" Rob inquired nervously.

"Yes, in a fashion. Dr. Klaskin was a student of Dr. Milton Erickson, the pioneer of modern hypnosis. A truly brilliant man. He spent a great deal of time assisting Dr. Erickson in developing what now is known as Ericksonian therapy. Dr. Klaskin later enhanced Dr. Erickson's methods by combining them with elements of TLT, or time line therapy. However, there is one defining element he inserted into his hypnotic concoction." Dr. Sheltie paused, uncertainly.

"Should I ask what that was?"

"He found a way for the person administering the hypnosis to be inserted into the patient's point of view of their vision."

"You'll be with me in my dream?" Rob asked dubiously.

"No. Not in your dream per se. More like looking over your shoulder."

Rob must have looked skeptical.

"It's hard to articulate. Just relax." Dr. Sheltie prompted, then consulted the journal. She took his wrist in her hand. She positioned her thumb on the inside of it in a way that she could feel his pulse as well as the pressure of his grip. She perched herself on the edge of the coffee table.

"There are some instructions before we get started. There is a risk that if we both experience a certain level of duress together, I may become locked out, so to speak. Unable to reenter."

"What happens then?" asked Rob. He wondered if this was such a good idea after all.

Dr. Sheltie shifted on the table's edge.

"I have no idea," she admitted.

"You have no idea because it's never happened to you before? Or you have no idea because you've never done this before?" Rob inquired, becoming more concerned.

"It's never happened to me before," she said with an edge of defensiveness in her voice. "Now relax, close your eyes, and breathe deeply," she coaxed.

Rob did and could feel his eyes growing heavier by the second. He feared he would fall asleep and that would hinder Dr. Sheltie's efforts.

"Once we begin, if for any reason you feel scared or just want to stop, say the word 'crackers' and we will awaken together. Do you understand?"

"Yes," Rob answered sleepily.

"Good. Now describe to me somewhere you feel the most relaxed. Where you go to get away from your problems." Rob began describing to Dr. Sheltie his location of choice as she slowly closed her own eyes dreamily.

Chapter Eight

The place Rob described was a calm small lake. The weather was warm, but not hot. A steady, gentle breeze blew across a wet surface mirroring the clear blue above. Rob loved it there. It was outside of Prosper, Texas. Prosper was one of the first of Rob and Mel's many stops on the foster family express. They were placed with this Prosper-based family for what seemed a while. A total of nine months, he recalled, which was a lengthy stint comparatively speaking. This pair of foster parents were of the dramatic variety. Daddy worked as a healthcare executive for a local hospital group and seemed constantly under a great deal of stress resulting in binge drinking upon arriving home each evening. Mommy had socially noble intentions by fostering children, thus enhancing her stature with the stay-at-home-mommy club, as Daddy would call it. Rob could always tell when Daddy was in his cups and started looking for an argument with Mommy. Criticizing her from every angle. The way she dressed and how she acted around men was the most worn-out jibe. If that failed to arouse her, he would move on to her cooking, hairstyle, driving, housekeeping, or lack of higher education, searching for any way to get under her skin. All to get her engaged in a fight. However, once Mommy became fully engaged, she was a force to be reckoned with, erupting with all sorts of emotions. It seemed this was entertainment to him, pressing her buttons then egging her on. On one occasion Mommy began hurling dinnerware at Daddy, delivering a shattering performance. The chaos of her screaming and glass shattering triggered something in Rob, terrifying him to his core. He recalled bursting out the door running at top speed with no

48

destination in mind, running to get away as fast as he could from that shattering sound.

It was on this occasion he discovered the lake hidden inside a small wooded area. From that day forward while enduring Prosper, he spent almost every spare second there, resting on the bank daydreaming and writing stories. He had never felt calmer anywhere else.

Quietly, Dr. Sheltie said, "This is nice." She was heard, but not seen to Rob as he stared across the blue expanse.

"I used to do my best writing here."

"What are you writing now?" Dr. Sheltie asked, prompting Rob to look down and realize he was holding a pen and a Super Mario Brothers journal. Rob recognized Mario in his red overalls, jumping with one fist in the air. He recalled some of his best stories had been written in it.

"I'm not sure what I am writing about right now," Rob answered, trying to recall the last story he had written in this place.

"Maybe it's a script?" Dr. Sheltie suggested.

"It could be, I guess."

"Maybe it is, and maybe it is the script from your dream. The one that's been directing your performance."

"You think so?" Rob asked curiously as he opened the journal and began reading its words. "You are right, it is!" Rob said, thrilled, although he was not sure why.

He flipped through a few pages confirming it was in fact the script of his dream. He began to feel more in control, having this tangible instance of it in his hands.

"Tear it out," Dr. Sheltie instructed softly.

"Why? It will ruin my journal," Rob replied hesitantly.

"Do it," Dr. Sheltie said more forcefully. "Find the first page and last page then tear out that section."

Rob sat there staring at his journal a beat longer, then complied. He found the first page, marking it with his finger. Then he flipped until he found "The End" and began to tear out that section. It wasn't tearing at first, so he gripped the pages tighter and pulled harder until finally the glue in the spine started reluctantly releasing the papers.

Once he had the papers in one hand and the journal in the other, he asked Dr. Sheltie, "Now what?"

"Now tear it in half."

Rob did.

"Now again."

Again Rob complied.

"Keep doing it until you can't tear it anymore," she told him.

Rob did so, turning the sheets over and over, ripping them into smaller and smaller pieces. As the pieces shrunk in size, they grew in thickness, becoming more difficult for Rob to tear.

"Once more," Dr. Sheltie instructed when he paused.

"I can't. The pieces are too small."

"You must. Focus on your effort."

Rob closed his eyes and squeezed his fingertips against the small thick stack of papers as hard as he could until he felt them start to tear. His fingertips burned. He thought his fingernails might tear instead, but he pulled against the thickness of the paper even harder.

"You can do it, Rob. I can see it tearing!" Dr. Sheltie encouraged.

The paper gave way as Rob let out a huge breath, relieved to feel his hands pulling apart completely, resulting in each hand a large pile of tiny squares.

"Now what?" Rob asked, slightly exerted.

"Throw them into the wind!" Dr. Sheltie exclaimed triumphantly.

Rob did just that and tossed both handfuls of confetti into the breeze. They both watched as the pieces went from dozens to thousands blowing about, going this way and that way, climbing higher and higher. As they continued watching them swirl against the gorgeous blue sky, they noticed something transpiring in the pieces. The pieces began to take shape like a stereogram, slowly exposing images. Rob began recognizing the images, causing him to catch his breath. The German shepherd dog, his father, his mother, then something more ominous began to take shape. As the pieces swirled, the sky began to darken, and the wind now was whipping across Rob's body. The water in the lake went from shimmering to reverberating as it darkened and swirled.

"What's happening?" Rob whispered.

"I'm not sure. Just breathe and focus on my voice," Dr. Sheltie said with shaking confidence. She could feel Rob's pulse quickening under her thumb and his grip tightening. Her own eyes now were sealed shut, locked into his vision. Something about what was happening didn't feel right to her, but she dare not panic, fueling Rob's uneasiness.

"Stay calm. I fear we must endure this to cure you," Dr. Sheltie explained, mustering her courage as she watched helplessly. The pieces of paper began to swirl like a water spout over the lake, rising high into a now-stormy sky. It twisted back and forth in a serpentine fashion as if trying to free its head from the darkening clouds. Thunder boomed and lightning began streaking across the sky. Rob stood paralyzed, trying to be brave, but as the aberration of the water spout grew in size and strength, his bravery waned just the same.

"Stay strong. This is only your imagination bringing your fears to bear," Dr. Sheltie encouraged, her voice wavering a bit.

The water swirled black and frothy as the spout began sinking into the lake, creating a giant whirlpool. It turned slowly at first, and Rob could feel it pulling on him. As it gained more momentum, sticks, rocks, and other debris around him began scooting toward the water's edge. The tall grasses along the bank began bending toward the center of the liquid vortex. Faster and faster the water spun in a circular motion like water draining in a bathtub. Rob flinched at the thunderous cracking of treetops being pulled into the abyss, snapping like twigs. The suction now became unbearable, and the howling of the wind was so loud. Rob grabbed hold of a sturdy pine tree, trying to keep from being swept out into the void.

"This feels pretty real, Doc!" Rob shouted as a tree branch lashed him across his face.

"You're doing great! Hold on! I know you can win this battle! Your subconscious is a strong force, and you seem to be carrying a lot of baggage it's having to work through!" she yelled through the chaos, hoping to encourage him.

Now everything around them was flying or bending into the intense vacuum. Even the storm clouds and the sky itself began swirling into the vortex. Dr. Sheltie could feel the pull, too, so intense she began losing her grip. From behind them as Rob frantically held on to the tree, the lake began rising and turning toward them. The black vortex began to take on the shape of a huge throat. Its edges became jagged, serrated like so many rows of razor-sharp teeth.

"What the hell is that!" Rob screamed, looking back into the swirling darkness.

"I don't know, just focus on your grip!" Dr. Sheltie screamed back, her own grip of Rob's wrist tightened.

"What did you say?"

"I . . . know . . . cus on . . . grip!" Dr. Sheltie's words began breaking up like staticky reception on an old radio. She felt herself slipping out of the hypnosis, leaving Rob alone. Her focus to stay in the vision with him was so intense she didn't realize her fingernails digging into Rob's wrist.

Suddenly Dr. Sheltie gasped deeply and her eyes fluttered open. She realized she had slipped out of the vision and was back in her home office. Panicked now, knowing Rob was alone battling the evolving vortex, she grabbed his bleeding wrist and attempted to reenter the vision.

"Dammit!" she exclaimed, frustrated, seemingly locked out of it, unable to reenter. How did she let herself become so distressed? She was supposed to be the trained professional, the calm one to ensure this didn't happen. She knew better, and now she was locked out and Rob is alone potentially fighting for his life. No longer just his sanity. She grabbed the journal, smearing blood on the pages as they stuck to her tacky fingers. Reading furiously, she searched for a way back into the vision. Maybe a back door or something. Rob looked pale, sweating and growing more restless by the minute.

Back in his mind Rob's feet lifted from the ground in cartoonish fashion as the suction intensified. His grip slipped on the tree. He felt a shoe let go and looked back as it quickly disappeared into the blackness.

"What is that thing!" he screamed. No answer. He realized Dr. Sheltie wasn't there any longer. "Dr. Sheltie!" he screamed. "Dr. Sheltie, where are you? What do I do?! I can't hold on any longer!" But all he heard was the deafening noise of the world being inhaled around him.

Chapter Nine

Dr. Sheltie slammed the journal on the coffee table discouraged. Dr. Klaskin didn't document any contingencies other than saying the safe word, and why Rob wasn't screaming it now at the top of his lungs! She racked her brain, trying to recall watching how Dr. Klaskin performed this same therapy years ago. He was always so cool and calm as he moved in and out of the hypnosis so seamlessly. He would come out of the vision and scribble a note or do research in real time based on what he saw and experienced while inside the patient's vision. Then he would insert himself back in to continue his counseling with the patient. Then together the doctor and patient awoke, and the patient seemed renewed, refreshed. Cured.

In his last months, Dr. Klaskin coached her in this unique kind of hypnosis. He even allowed himself to play the role of the patient so Dr. Sheltie could enter his vision in the role of the doctor. From there, he would use his superior intellect to challenge her, in order to condition her to stay calm and rational no matter the situation. He emphatically said that was the most critical key when decoding dreams, keeping calm.

"If the doctor becomes distressed with the patient, that negative energy amplifies the patient's existing anxiety creating a very dangerous state of mind. If the patient's state of mind becomes too volatile or overloaded, it will defend itself, thus locking out the more aggressive energy or locking both sources of energy together indefinitely," he warned her.

Clearly, it was her emotions in Rob's vision that became the aggressor, and his subconscious now had her locked out because of it. She cursed herself for her stupidity. Dr. Klaskin was also well versed in linguistics, understanding the power of the spoken word. This led to the safe word, "cracker." Dr. Sheltie asked him the reasoning in choosing that specific word, and he explained it was because of its distinct double consonant emphasis. It was a unique word in its pronunciation. It required the person saying it to purposely exhale sharply, twice. The 'cr' and the 'ck' sounds. It's hard not to say the word crisply and sharply, which is of paramount importance when acting as the emergency brake to visions going awry. In other words, it was easy to say and easily understood. *Awry* was an understatement here as Rob thrashed around more and more, lying there on the couch. *Off the rails* seemed more fitting.

Rob's fingers were steadily slipping, and he knew he was done for. His life wasn't flashing before his eyes, as he had heard happens in these moments before death. Rather one person was standing there, undisturbed by the gale-force suction that was literally ripping the clothes off his back. It was his sister, Mel.

"You must find the truth, and you must restore your family," she said calmly, and turned and walked into the dense trees.

"Mel! Help me!" Rob pleaded, but she had already disappeared into the foliage. At that moment his grip failed and he felt himself hurling toward the dark vortex, but just as he knew he was done for, the suction stopped. Rob hit the ground, skidding backward to a stop across the dry and crusted lake bottom. He coughed as dust filled his gasping lungs. He lay there relieved, his arms, hands, and fingers burning from exertion.

He slowly gathered his knees under him and sat up, sucking air, catching his breath.

"I guess we did it, Dr. Sheltie." Rob laughed, out of breath as he looked around wondering why he wasn't back in Dr. Sheltie's home office. From behind him he could feel an intense heat, giving him the feeling of something large behind him. Reluctantly, he turned to look.

"What the—" Rob exhaled. His blood turned cold.

Rob realized the reason the suction has stopped, and it wasn't because he had beaten his fears. No, the reality was, his fear was now just becoming apparent. Rising up behind him in the middle of the dry lake was the most terrifying abomination: a rooster, if it could be called that, so tall he could barely see its hideous face. In that instant, Rob's bladder failed him and he began shaking uncontrollably. The massive creature's chest was swelling from the huge intake of air. Before Rob could make any sense of what he was seeing, the creature exhaled, making a hideously high-pitched scream with a lethal burst of wind. In a blink Rob was rolling across the crusty soil like a ragdoll. The searing heat of its breath reeking of the stench of death replaced the air around Rob as he was flung into the trees. He slammed into the trunk of a huge pine, snapping it in half and sending him spinning to the ground. With the wind completely knocked out of him, he tried to get up, but struggled getting his bearings.

Finally, the stars in his vision began to clear and the stench lessoned. He felt the earth shaking, and he looked back and saw the huge eighty-foot pine trees in the distance snapping over in bunches. They gave no resistance to the abomination smashing them with its claws. Rob did the only thing he could do, which was to run.

Chapter Ten

Dr. Sheltie knelt next to Rob and held a cool rag to his forehead, pleading with him to say the safe word, but to no avail. He couldn't hear her. She bandaged his wrist and monitored his pulse, which seemed to steady. Maybe he was coming out of it, she hoped. As soon as she thought he was out of the woods figuratively speaking, he was literally being thrown into them. A wet spot formed in his crotch. He began thrashing, hitting her in the face, sending her toppling backward. His body jolted this way then that way as he screamed silently. His eyelids opened and closed, revealing his rolling eyes. He started jerking his legs in a way that Dr. Sheltie thought he might be running. Yes, he definitely was running.

"Run, Rob!" she screamed, now more terrified than ever not knowing what he could be running from. "If you can hear me, run as fast as you can!"

And he was. The abomination was gaining ground. Up ahead Rob could see the edge of the woods opening up. He sprinted harder now with his mouth open, sucking wind. His legs high-stepped over branches and stumps. As he approached the tree line, he caught sight of Mel running too.

"Come on, Rob! This way!" she screamed over her shoulder.

Ahead in the center of the clearing was a white, swirling light. Mel reached it first and turned, motioning him to hurry. The ground thundered as the abomination gave chase, and continued its hideous shrieking. It stomped down the last few trees before the clearing, and they fell with a mighty whomp. The very top of one hit Rob in the back, sending him sprawling into a heap.

Rob found himself in a clear-cut where several pines had recently been harvested. He remembered as a kid playing in these open spaces during a foster stint with a rural family. This might be that actual one, he thought briefly. Clear-cuts were notoriously littered with branches, tangled treetops, stumps, and the huge ruts left behind from the harvesting machinery. Very difficult to walk in, let alone when running from a two hundred-foot abomination. He scrambled to stand and tripped on branches scattered around. The abomination stopped short of entering the clear-cut. It stood higher than the tall trees and was fighting viciously to break through an invisible wall dividing the forest from the clear-cut. Its chest was heaving and massive wings flapping, moving the air around Rob like several helicopters landing on him. The air turned putrid and hard to breathe as the monster screamed, making Rob's eyeballs vibrate in their sockets as he gagged from the smell. Violently it attacked the invisible force using its massive talons. Its twenty-foot spurs rattled against it like machine-gun fire. Rob could sense the amazing strength as it struck the wall. Sparks of electricity shot in all directions with each blow. It didn't seem the wall would hold it back forever. Rob turned to see Mel leaping into the swirling light. Afraid the light would disappear, he ran toward it, diving in headfirst.

Rob's eyes fluttered open as his nose registered a hint of familiar jasmine being churned in the air by the blades of the slow-turning ceiling fan above him. He swallowed hard as he realized he was back in Dr. Sheltie's home office. Dr. Sheltie applied a cool rag gently to his forehead.

"You made it," she said, relieved, brimming with emotion.

"Yeah, I guess I did." Rob exhaled. "What happened to your face?"

"Well, you punched me." Dr. Sheltie winced as she touched her swollen lip.

"I'm so sorry."

"Oh, don't worry about that. You were thrashing about pretty good there for a minute. I tried to get you to say the safe word, but I guess you couldn't hear me," she replied, helping him sit up. She took up her notebook and pen then sat in the chair across from him.

"Honestly, I totally forgot about it," Rob said, feeling dumb now knowing he might have avoided the whole experience.

"I can only imagine you had more pressing things to worry about. Besides, you may not have been cured if you had used it. Tell me what happened?" Dr. Sheltie asked, concerned, her pen poised to take detailed notes.

"I realized you were gone, and then all hell broke loose," Rob said, staring at the fruit basket centerpiece on the coffee table, dazed.

"That was my fault. I failed to control my fear, and your subconscious locked me out. It was stupid of me. I knew better," she said, ashamed.

"Don't sweat it. I can certainly understand why. I know I was freaking out," Rob answered, hoping to ease her guilt.

Rob continued explaining the series of events thereafter, about his sister and what she told him.

"You must find the truth and you must restore your family," Rob repeated what Mel had said before walking into the trees.

"When was the last time you saw Mel?" Dr. Sheltie asked.

"Seven years ago, I think. She ran away from the foster family we were with. That daddy had a thing for young girls, and Mel nearly killed him, and took off," Rob said, remembering that day.

Rob recalled that this particular flavor of foster family lived outside of Mesquite, Texas. They never should have been allowed children. Of course, he felt most foster parents shouldn't. Even now Rob felt guilt for what had happened. He, as usual, would find quiet places to get away and write his stories. That was his coping mechanism. This usually left Mel alone to either find trouble or for trouble to find her. She was fourteen and in her rebellious prime. Daddy had all the earmarks of a pervert and was keen to be more friend when she needed a father. She would come into Rob's room at night and crawl in his bed freaked out.

"He's watching me. I can feel it," she would tell him as she slid in.

"Everyone is asleep. What are you talking about?" Rob asked sleepily.

"I don't know. It's how he looks at me. Like he knows something. Like he has a secret with me, but only he knows what it is. He gives me the creeps."

"We've only been here a month. Everyone is still adjusting. Get some rest," Rob urged, and turned over.

Three days later Rob walked up the street toward their foster family's house. It was early evening on a Saturday. He had been behind a warehouse for most of the afternoon writing in his journal. He had found an old industrial desk and chair next to a dumpster in the back. He settled in to do some writing. Seeing the sun begin to set, he felt his stomach rumble. He realized he hadn't eaten anything all day and decided to go home.

He stopped when he saw all the emergency vehicles. Several police cars, a firetruck, and an ambulance. Paramedics rushed a gurney out the front door into the ambulance, causing Rob to take off running toward the scene.

Rob yelled, "What happened? Where is Mel?" But a police officer grabbed him and kept him from going into the house, questioning who he was. And who was Mel?

Rob later learned from Mel that she was getting ready in the bathroom to go out with friends. They were going to see a movie she was excited to see. Mel loved movies like Rob loved reading. They constantly debated which was better entertainment. She had her makeup out, and a curling iron sat heated on the sink's counter. Daddy snuck into the bathroom and undressed. It seemed he had plans to join Mel for a little shower-time fun. A struggle ensued, tearing down the shower curtain and rod. In the struggle Mel broke free. She grabbed a steel fingernail file and stabbed Daddy in the throat, nearly severing his jugular. Bleeding profusely, Daddy scurried away on all fours showing her his ample ass and meager manhood. Her fierce temper took control. She grabbed the scorching-hot curling iron and proceeded to shove it, as Rob recalled her saying, "Where the sun don't shine." The police officers had a good laugh about the whole thing.

"Geez, she was a feisty one!" an officer said at the scene as he laughed about the situation.

"A woman scorned and a man scorched!" joked another as they finished processing the scene then left Rob there alone.

Early the next morning child services from the state of Texas joined in the foray with a check of the home and discovered there were two cameras hidden in Mel's room.

"And I feel horrible I didn't believe her," said Rob regretfully. His exhaustion now pulled at him more than ever.

"I think I would like Mel very much. What happened to her?" Dr. Sheltie asked, looking astonished with her hand to her chest.

"I don't know. She ran away from the scene and only called me once to explain what happened and tell me she was alright. She said she would make her way on her own and she never wanted to go back to another foster family as long as she lived. She said she loved me and hung up. I never saw her again, and I have no way to reach her," Rob whispered quietly, picking at his fingernails. "She could be anywhere. I honestly don't know if she is even alive." Rob looked up, utterly exhausted, with tears in his eyes.

"What you need now is rest. You can stay in my guest room. From the looks of you I doubt you could even make it back to your dorm. You can't even keep your eyes open sitting there. Besides, I would like to keep an eye on you. I assume you are cured from that nightmare's grip, but just to be safe," she said worriedly.

Dr. Sheltie took Rob into a spare bedroom and went into the adjoining bathroom and set out toiletries and a fresh towel.

"You can take a shower if you like," she hollered from the bathroom. When Rob didn't answer she looked in the room and found him snoring, already fast asleep. She pulled off his shoes and tucked him in.

"Mel is alive. We will find her," Dr. Sheltie whispered as she switched the light off and gently closed the bedroom door.

For the next day and a half, Rob slept like the dead and Dr. Sheltie researched, feeling more alive than ever.

Chapter Eleven

"Dallas County Sheriff's Office, how may I help you?" the dispatcher inquired robotically.

"This is Dr. Maria Sheltie. I am a local psychologist and . . ."

"*The* Dr. Sheltie? Yes! I know who you are!" the dispatcher interjected, to Dr. Sheltie's surprise.

"My daughter attends UT and told me about an inspirational speech you gave a few days ago. She won't believe I am talking whichoo. Gonna text her right now."

Dr. Sheltie heard the woman go on speakerphone and her long nails tap dancing against her phone's screen.

"She be lovin' her some Dr. Shel-tie. Girl, she ran down to the bookstore and bought your first two books already. Oh, honey, she says you so beautiful and so full of yo-self. I mean that in a good way, you know what I'm sayin'? It's all she talks about, becoming a psychologist and helping people like you do. She so smart. She is HUGE into the girl power thang. I mean, I am too, don't get me wrong. It's such a man's world still. I mean imagine working here behind the blue curtain! Testosterone overload, let me tell you, honey!" She laughed hysterically without taking a breath. "Sharmane is going into her second year. I been concerned she hadn't declared no major yet, but now she wants to go into psychology! You believe that? My baby girl a psychologist!" she rattled on to Dr. Sheltie, who was amazed she still hadn't taken a breath. "My baby daddy took off years ago, that douchebag, just like a man. They just play and don't stay. You feel me? So it's been just us . . ."

"Ex-excuse me?" Dr. Sheltie asked, trying to shoehorn herself into the conversation.

"Oh, yes, so what can I do for you, honey?" the dispatcher offered, sounding somewhat put out Dr. Sheltie interrupted her diatribe.

"Firstly, thank you very much for your kind words, and, yes, I do enjoy blazing a trail through the machismo." She hated that she felt a stab of annoyance toward this friendly lady, but she was in a hurry. "Uhm, I have a patient that has been missing her appointments lately, and I was hoping to check in on her, but the address she put on her paperwork seems fictitious. I am concerned and am hoping you might give me what address you may have on file so I can check in on her? Her name is Melanie Florchett. She is nineteen and sometimes goes by Mel," Dr. Sheltie explained, and hoped her ruse would hold.

She hated to be deceptive, but her efforts so far to try to find a lead on Mel had turned into dead ends. The tapping cadence of the dispatcher started again, but more distant on a computer keyboard.

"Give me another minute, suga," the dispatcher cooed, breathing into the phone as the tapping intensified.

"No worries, thank you so much for this," Dr. Sheltie replied.

The tapping stopped abruptly.

"Honey, I tell you right now why she ain't been showin' up for no appointments."

"Oh good, why is that?"

"'Cause if it be the same Melanie Flochett I see here, it's 'cause she a guest of ours right now."

"I'm sorry. A guest of yours?" Dr. Sheltie asked, not understanding.

"She locked up, girlfriend."

"Locked up!"

"Yep, says she got picked on a skin hustle."

"A skin hustle?" Dr. Sheltie asked, struggling to keep up.

"Prostitution, honey." A couple more taps on the keyboard. "Good luck fo you, though, she on the last day of her thirty-day sentence. Should be let out tomorrow. Be back in yo office before ya know it," the dispatcher said happily.

"She doesn't have any family around. I'd like to meet her when she gets out. Where would that be?" Dr. Sheltie asked, now encouraged.

The dispatcher explained the release process and where it would happen.

"Thank you so very much. You've been amazing! And . . . and give your daughter my kindest regards."

"Oh, I will, she textin' me right now all excited and stuff. I can't read all her emojiness. You know how these kids are and technology. I tell you everything is an emoji now. Kids can't talk no mo . . . Hello? Dr. Sheltie? Hello? She gone." And with that the dispatcher picked up another call ringing in. "Dallas County Sheriff's Office, how may I help you?" the dispatcher inquired robotically.

Chapter Twelve

Dr. Sheltie was returning home after she ran out to a Nature's Way grocery store nearby. Nature's Way was a store that was part organic food and part holistic wellness. A place one could grab grass-fed Kobe steaks and heart-healthy krill oil capsules just two aisles apart from each other. Dr. Sheltie was partial to their organic rotisserie chickens, and they made an addictive skim milk latte she was fond of too. Her Porsche 718 Spyder smelled of succulent chicken as she sipped on her steaming beverage while zipping through traffic. On the radio the weatherman forecasted clear skies all week and a fifty-year supermoon on Friday night.

"We see supermoons often enough, Brian. However, this one will bring the moon the closest it's been to Earth in fifty years," the weatherman said to his counterpart.

"Sounds spooky, Chuck, and to make things even more spooky, this Friday is the 13th! Moo ha ha ha!" Brian exclaimed in his scariest Halloween-style laugh.

"Sounds like a true apocalypse in the making, Brian!" With that comment from Chuck, Bobby Pickett began singing:

I was working in the lab, late one night

When my eyes beheld an eerie sight

For my monster from his slab, began to rise

And suddenly to my surprise.

He did the mash, he did the monster mash

The monster mash, it was a graveyard smash

Dr. Sheltie cranked up the volume of the Porsche's premium 1,000-watt Bose stereo. She was always a Bob Pickett fan, even though he only succeeded in becoming a one-hit wonder. His homage to Boris Karloff in the "Monster Mash" struck an endearing chord, as she was a huge classic horror movie buff. Hearing Pickett's croon now bolstered her spirits further after finding Rob's sister. She couldn't wait for him to wake up so she could tell him the news.

"The zombies were having fun, the party had just begun!" Dr. Sheltie sang out, tapping the soft leather steering wheel as she eased into her driveway. As she exited her car with the groceries, she noticed her office light on and the shadow of someone through the silk shade. She figured Rob was awake as she fumbled with her keys and stepped onto the porch. Suddenly a hand cupped her mouth.

She struggled, but the person pulled her tight against his body then whispered into her ear, "Shhh, don't make a sound." His breath was hot on her ear. "Seriously, I'll take my hand off, but don't make a sound. Do you understand?"

In her purse, Dr. Sheltie carried a concealed Sig Sauer P365 nine millimeter with a custom-fitted hot-pink grip, fitted with Trijicon night sights and a green laser. It was a gift from her youngest daughter who was afraid one day a disgruntled patient might confront her. She had gotten very proficient with it at the local range, grouping together her shots within the size of a silver dollar at thirty feet. Quite good for such a small pistol. Fortunately for the man holding her, with a bag of groceries in one hand and her keyring in the other, she couldn't make a move for it.

She nodded yes, she understood, readying herself to turn and give him a hard knee to his balls. The man removed his hand. Just as she was about to turn and swing up her knee, Rob put his finger to his lips indicating to be quiet.

"Rob! What the hell!" she whispered, surprised.

"Shhh! Follow me," Rob whispered emphatically as they went around the corner of the house in the shadows.

"Who is that in the house?" she whispered, her wits returning.

"I don't know. I got up to pee and heard glass break and peeked into the kitchen when the door started to open, so I snuck out the front door and have been waiting here."

"Waiting on what?"

"Either that person to leave or you to get home."

"Well, I'm here now and he is still in there."

"What do we do?" Rob wondered aloud, but Dr. Sheltie had headed back to the porch already with her Sig in hand. Rob thought she was stone crazy, but found himself following her. There was definitely a mystery surrounding this lady that intrigued Rob.

She eased open the front door and slowly moved into the foyer. Silently, she crept down the hallway to her office door. She could hear the person rummaging through papers then the digital camera sound a smartphone makes when snapping photos. With her pistol at the ready she swung around, fixing her emerald laser on the intruder.

"Don't move!" she yelled, a green dot locked onto his center mass. "I mean it, or I'll carve my initials in your back with nine-millimeter bullets. Put your hands up! Now! Higher asshole!"

The intruder dropped the papers he was holding back on her desk and complied slowly. The man was tall and lean. He had a mop of graying salt-and-pepper hair.

"Good evening, Dr. Sheltie," he said in a smooth voice without turning around. She approached him from behind and pressed her gun against his spine then checked under his black suit jacket finding a very large pistol.

She pulled it out and tossed it to Rob, who fumbled it like a hot potato, nearly dropping it.

She took a step back and said, "Turn around slowly."

As he did he looked at Rob and smiled. "And good evening to you, Master Rob," he said in his velvety voice. "How's your mother these days?" he asked, smiling a rugged smile with perfect, gleaming-white teeth. However, his smile did not hide the weariness around his eyes.

"Do I know you?" Rob asked, wondering how this guy knew who he was, better yet, knew his mother?

"I don't know, do you?" the man looked at Rob quizzically.

"Enough of the trivia. Who are you, and why did you break into my house?" Dr. Sheltie demanded, and leveled her gun, setting the laser between his eyes.

"Wait! I do know you! You're from my dream. You're the guy at the door! You're HIM!" Rob said loudly, completely taken off guard. He recognized that rugged smile. He quickly raised the pistol Dr. Sheltie had tossed him. Rob had never shot a gun before, and it was heavier than he imagined as he struggled to keep it steady.

"Whoa, whoa there. Easy, cowboy. Let's not get all worked up causing someone to accidentally get shot," the man cautioned in a playful manner.

"If it's from my gun it won't be an accident, I assure you," Dr. Sheltie said, sensing the man's nonchalant demeanor. It irked her. "Where is your ID?"

"In my jacket pocket."

"You take it out slowly, and I mean slow-ly," Dr. Sheltie warned, not wanting to get within reach of his long arms.

He did so, and Rob took it as Dr. Sheltie told the man to sit on the couch.

"Benjamin Masters, CIA. Retired," read Rob, surprised.

"CIA? What's this all about?" asked Dr. Sheltie.

The man didn't answer as he glanced at the folders and documents covering her desk. While Rob was sleeping, she searched through several filing cabinets full of Dr. Klaskin's patient files and private journals she had stored in her basement. Finding the specific ones she was looking for, she had been reading through them at her desk and had them organized in neat stacks.

"Dr. Klaskin was right. There was something to that night being covered up. He warned me before he disappeared," she said as her anger grew.

"Disappeared? You never told me that." Rob said, shocked.

"Don't worry, Robbie. He turned back up," Masters said with a smirk.

"Yeah, floating in Lake Lavon!" she retorted, her hands starting to shake.

"Yes, his boating accident was unfortunate. However, I assure you we had nothing to do with it," he said, still wearing that playful smirk.

"You murdered him. You murdered a brilliant, sweet man!"

"He was helping us. Why would we kill him?"

"I don't believe he was. You killed him because through his treatment of Tommy Florchett, he discovered what really happened that night in 1970, and the proof is there in those journals." Dr. Sheltie indicated with a couple quick jerks of her gun barrel toward the desk.

"You weren't aware that Dr. Klaskin enhanced Dr. Erickson's methods of hypnosis to enter inside the patient's hypnotic vision through immersion. You figured he was just another run-of-the-mill psychologist like the ones that failed treating Tommy before him. You foolishly assumed your cover-up techniques would fool him, too, but they didn't. Dr. Klaskin was able to maneuver around them and reconstruct much of that night through his immersion technique, but not all of it. But he figured out enough the CIA feared he was a threat to their secret, so they staged a boating accident and killed him," she explained.

"I'm confused. He maneuvered around what exactly?" Rob asked Dr. Sheltie.

"I caution you, Doctor, to stop right there. That information is classified. Don't put master Rob here in a position of hearing something he is not cleared for," the man said as his eyes narrowed, becoming menacing. It seemed Dr. Sheltie was hitting too close to the CIA's home, and Masters wasn't taking too kindly to it.

"I don't have any level of security clearance, and now I know. The only way to protect ourselves, Rob, is to expose the cover-up. Shed a bright light on what we know. Once it's out, the CIA will shrink back into the shadows like the cockroaches they are," Dr. Sheltie said as she picked up a red folder from her desk and held it up in the man's face for emphasis. "So tell me, what will happen if Rob knows the truth?" she asked defiantly, still holding the folder.

"Consequences," he said, then slapped it into her face and grabbed her wrist in which she held her gun. It fired errantly into the wall, just missing Rob. Masters then punched Dr. Sheltie in the face, and she spun around and hit a bookshelf that contained a large scented candle. It rolled under the heavy drapes, catching them on fire. Dr. Sheltie lay on the ground knocked out cold. He then lunged for Rob. Rob tried to move, but the man was fast and grabbed Rob's hand holding the gun. Rob fired the pistol, and the bullet struck the man in the stomach just under his sternum. His inertia carried him into Rob, and they continued to struggle for the gun, but the man's life seemed to drain out of him, leaving him limp and Rob pinned to the floor as fire and smoke engulfed the office.

Chapter Thirteen

"Wake up, princess. Your Prince Charming is here," said the sheriff's deputy dryly as he unlocked the cell door.

"What do you mean? I am supposed to be released tomorrow," replied Mel as she sat up on her cot. For the last twenty-nine days she had been enjoying her confinement. The escape from the stress of the manipulation and violence of her life was much welcomed and she was determined to stay every last second she could.

"Your bail has been posted. I just do what I'm told," the deputy said as he swung the heavy door open, "Let's go."

Under any other circumstances, being bailed out the day before a person's scheduled release would seem strange, a waste of money to some people. But Mel knew this was standard operating procedure for this person. Most of his girls carried a debt to him that they were constantly required to work off. This debt further accumulated when they messed up or got out of line, like getting arrested. Five thousand dollars here and ten thousand dollars there to a billionaire drug and human trafficking enterprise was no greater a value than a dull penny lying on the ground. But its binding effect on the girls to the organization was absolute. However, Mel had been fortunate enough not to have a debt assigned to her until now. She feared the worst if she didn't find a way to escape.

"Get a move on, princess." The deputy began motioning with his hand. "Not all of us are paid by the hour." Mel slowly got to her feet and shuffled out of the cell into the long corridor leading to another locked door.

The guard swiped a badge that released a lock. Holding her by the arm he led her to a counter where she collected her personal items, which consisted of a tight-fitting teal sequined bodycon dress, matching stilettos, a rhinestone-studded clutch, its matching small wallet, a hair brush, a makeup compact, breath mints, wet wipes, and condoms. The usual items of the trade.

In a small change room she swapped the county's orange jumpsuit for her own dress. From there she was led to a more open area and sat on a wooden bench in line with the other women being processed for release. Some she recognized, some she didn't. This business was a revolving door for young women such as her. As she sat there she recalled when she was seduced into it. She had just run away from her foster family after she made a searing rump roast out of her foster father's rectum. Even now she still smiled at the satisfaction of hearing that pig scream. The only thing she regretted from doing that to him was not using both hands to drive it even deeper into his bowels.

She and her brother Rob had only been with this foster family for about a month. Mel was never with a foster family long enough to develop any meaningful friendships, but easily made acquaintances. Rob seemed content being alone, withdrawing into his imagination and writing. Mel needed social stimulation. She hated being alone. She met some girls at the local mall just a few days after arriving at the Mesquite family's door. Now on the run, she didn't know where else to go. She thought it was so cool they were her age and lived alone. No school, no responsibilities, and seemingly always had money. In no way did she fully understand they were actually captives, with little to no freedom, being emotionally hollowed out little by little.

On the second day she was with them they went to a club. Being sixteen was no obstacle to getting into eighteen-and-older clubs, as any one of the three girls had standing agreements with the bouncers for later favors, allowing them to walk right in to any club in the area. Those favors, Mel eventually learned, were the social currency to enjoy nonstop partying. Initially she felt the return on them was worth it for the lifestyle. It wasn't until meeting Jimmy that she started questioning whether what she had been sucked into was worth it after all. But by then, unbeknownst to her, it was too late.

Once in the club, they met up with other girls, and those girls were with some older guys. The ringleader was Jimmy. He was Mexican, lean, well muscled, and dressed very sharp. Mel began to feel his eyes on her more and more until he came over and introduced himself. Mel wasn't shy by nature, but she found herself that way around Jimmy initially, which seemed to play well with him, as he bought her numerous drinks and frequently requested to dance. Later, a hit of ecstasy soon removed any inhibitions for her. Much after was a blur, but she recalled very well the feeling of the amazingly plush leather seats of his Range Rover against her bare backside.

Eventually, she moved in with another girl named Meeka who worked closely with Jimmy. She claimed she was like an assistant to him. Bringing him coffee, making reservations, running errands, that sort of thing. Jimmy invited Mel to dinner with his boss who was in town just for the evening, something usually reserved for Meeka. Mel was afraid Meeka might take this as a slight, but Meeka acted as if she didn't care one way or another. Jimmy had provided Mel with a pretty expensive and elaborate wardrobe. He requested she wear a certain black cocktail dress and fix her hair up and explained his boss was keen on meeting her, so he wanted her to look stunning, to show off her long neck and lean athletic build. He even gave her a solitary four-karat diamond pendant necklace, which took her breath away and accentuated her lean features. She had never owned any jewelry that wasn't a cheap imitation. She remembered standing there in the full-length mirror amazed how her fortune had changed after she had run away. She looked like a celebrity and was beginning to think her life was going to be full of opulence and happiness.

As they drove to the location for dinner, Jimmy held her hand and stroked her thumb with his as he complimented her beauty. She was flush with gratitude and excited to see what this amazing night held for them. She began to realize they were going further from the city center and wondered why. As if Jimmy sensed her growing anxiety, he laughed and explained his boss was mobile and soon she would see what he meant. And boy did she.

Twilight had set in as Jimmy turned into a random parking lot of a sprawling industrial park. They weaved in and out of several warehouses before turning a corner around a very large empty one. Looming in the distance was a large jet-black bus, gleaming in sodium lights, black rims and all. As they drove closer it grew from large to huge. Mel had never seen anything so sleek, powerful, and even ominous. Jimmy explained how the nearly sixty-foot-long custom Volvo FH Globetrotter had four massive slides, nearly tripling its width. Underneath, the storage bay doors were up, revealing two Tesla Model X electric cars tucked away neatly. Mel noticed Jimmy getting a thrill explaining its various details, especially the powertrain, which was two twin-turbo Volvo D16C diesel engines producing a combined 1,220 horsepower with an astonishing 5,600 foot pounds of torque. He let out a long whistle then explained its near invincibility with bullet proofing, run-flat tires, underbody armor, and even infrared missile-deflecting decoy flares. Of course none of this moved Mel's needle, as Jimmy might as well have been speaking an alien language.

So she simply asked, "How much?"

"No one knows all its capabilities, so no one knows for sure the price tag, but I've heard north of three hundred million," Jimmy said, glancing at Mel to see her reaction.

That figure had every needle in Mel's body pegging out as the Range Rover coasted to a stop.

"What does your boss do?" she asked, astonished, not taking her eyes off the sleek black body of the massive coach. She realized she had never asked much about Jimmy's work, but it never really interested her until now.

"Import–export. Come on, he doesn't like to be kept waiting," Jimmy answered as he pushed his door open and exited quickly. Mel could tell he totally dodged that question. Two armed men seemingly materialized out of nowhere as Jimmy opened her door. Both carried fully automatic Heckler and Koch .45-caliber USC rifles and dressed in full tactical gear. They flanked each side of the door leading into the bus. Upon approach they frisked both Jimmy and Mel. Mel gasped from the brazenness of it. If they enjoyed copping a feel of her, they didn't show it. They were very professional, which added to her uneasiness.

"Who is this guy in the bus?" she kept thinking.

The doors hissed open and escalator stairs extended out. Mel stepped up first and was slowly carried inside followed by Jimmy. The ambience was perfect, and the smell of roasted meats wafted around her. Absolutely no expense was spared on the interior. There was nothing mobile about what she saw. It by far was the most luxurious space she had ever been in. Straight ahead was a den, complete with a large rug made of some exotic animal on a creamy marble floor. Two large leather recliners and a plush wraparound sofa maximized the space around a faux fireplace that looked so real it commanded the same respect as its real counterpart. A ceiling fan slowly turned above, and light classical jazz filled the air. Mel could hear chop, chop, chop to the left where there was a fully featured kitchen. A chef steadily worked chopping herbs and vegetables and paid no attention to the arriving guests.

"Please come with me," said a slightly accented voice from behind them. Mel turned and saw a maître d'-looking individual as he gestured toward a short hall leading into another room of the bus. In this area the lights were dimmed further, and in the center of the room was an elaborately furnished rectangle dining table. In the center were two large crystal candlesticks. Each burned two tall candles, creating a very intimate atmosphere.

"Please," the maître d'-looking man said as he pulled a chair back for her and indicated to sit.

Mel slowly sat. She noticed the gorgeous dinnerware was laid out perfectly with everything in its place. She ran her fingers around the elaborate designs on the edge of her plate.

"Flora Danica, madam," the maître d' explained as if reading her mind. She looked around slowly, taking it all in. The golden spoons, forks, and knives were set on silk table linens. The maître d'-looking man opened her napkin to place it on her lap and said, "Gianni Versace," as if expecting her to ask.

"It's beautiful," Mel replied, wondering if she could even bring herself to wipe her mouth on it.

He then poured each of them a glass of wine and announced their host would be joining them soon. He then quietly departed and left Mel and Jimmy listening to the soft jazz.

Chapter Fourteen

"Mi amigo, Jimmy! ¿Cómo estás esta tarde?" the dinner host proclaimed as he entered the room. Jimmy stood to shake his hand. He was what Mel considered a typical Hispanic of medium height and build. Somewhat handsome, but nothing about him stood out except his eyes. They were a deep gold color, feral even. Everything from his perfectly cut Brooks Brothers suit to his impeccable handmade John Lobb shoes dripped opulence. He looked at Mel all over with an intensity that she felt conveyed an absolute alpha male. Her body immediately responded under her thin tight dress. She stood slowly as he took her hand and gave it a light kiss.

"Ah, veo que trajiste una flor fresca," the host said to Jimmy, his eyes locked on Mel.

Then in perfect English, "I am Manuel Dominguez. You may call me Jefe Manuel. It is a pleasure to meet you," he said, nodding his head slightly, allowing his eyes now to track slowly down her body. "May I say, you look ravishing this evening."

"Thank you. You look very handsome yourself," Mel said before she even realized it. Where did that come from?

"Creo que me va a gustar este, Jimmy. Ella me está mostrando un gran potencial!" Jefe Manuel said to Jimmy with a loud chuckle.

Mel had no idea what he said, but Jimmy grinned big and replied, "Sí, Jefe Manuel. Sí. Éste tiene un gran potencial. Even more so than Rosa." Both sets of eyes settled on her. Mel wondered who Rosa was. As if Jefe Manuel sensed her uneasiness from their stare, he snapped his fingers and asked the maître d'-looking man to serve dinner.

The food was served in multiple courses, and each one seemed to top the one before in taste and appearance until a small roasted pig on a large ornate serving platter was rested in the center of the dining table. Although Mel's stomach was full of various appetizers consisting of lobster and cheeses, light brothy soups, salads, and other complementary morsels of food, her belly grumbled as she eyed the suckling pig in front of her. Never before had she been served such an amazing meal.

"Ah! Marcel has outdone himself on this!" Jefe Manuel gushed with open arms, loud enough for the cook to hear. He entered the room and took a bow.

"Merci beaucoup, Jefe Manuel. It is an honor my food delights you and your guests," Marcel replied in a thick French accent.

"Marcel is a sixth-generation French chef who has worked for several Mexican presidents over the years. I have him on loan to me for a couple weeks from Presidente Obrero as a birthday present. His culinary skills are most amazing!" Jefe Manuel doted. "Please, you must taste for yourselves."

The maître d'-looking man finished serving everyone a portion of the meat and then offered a pour of gravy. The meal was as amazing as it looked. After dinner they moved into the den for drinks. The men smoked long Cuban cigars while Mel just sat and enjoyed the expensive port and the plushness of the couch as she listened. Jefe Manuel offered Mel a position as one of his private assistants. He explained these assistants lived in various houses, called waypoints, Jefe Manuel had across Mexico and the United States. These houses were not his private residences; they were lavish holding facilities for various aspects of his business. His only private residence was this bus. Her job was to maintain appearances and ensure nothing became a hindrance to the daily business as people and product moved through her waypoint.

"Something like an office manager," Jimmy explained.

"There is one condition, you see," Jefe Manuel cautioned gently. His eyes became like ice as he leaned forward to her. "Once you are in my service, only I can release you. Parts of my business are very secretive and must be kept that way at all costs. If you do a good job for me, then one day I will release you from your duty and reward you generously to live a full, happy, and wealthy life."

Mel thought this over and determined it wasn't a bad gig at all for an orphan on the run and penniless. This luxury was definitely something she could get used to.

"Do you understand?" Jimmy asked.

"Yes," she said.

"Do you accept?" Jefe Manuel asked, his icy eyes still locked with Mel's.

"Absolutely."

Chapter Fifteen

"Melanie Florchett!" called the sheriff's clerk from behind a glass window, yanking Mel from her memory.

Mel stood and walked over while she searched the busy room for a specific face. She didn't see it, but knew he was watching from somewhere.

"You are hereby released. Please sign here . . . here . . . and here," the clerk indicated with a long red fingernail.

"Here are your copies." She handed an envelope to Mel. "Have a nice day," she said dryly, without looking up.

Mel went to the front doors of the station and walked out. The sunlight was bright and the air smelled of exhaust. She stood there letting her eyes adjust when she heard a familiar voice.

"Over here," Jimmy called, sitting on top of a picnic table to her right. She turned and walked over.

"Let's get this over with. Jefe Manuel just arrived an hour ago and hopes to be back on the road as soon as possible," Jimmy said, his features cold and distant. Mel said nothing and got into the Land Rover. Jimmy pulled out of the parking area and accelerated into the street.

Several minutes passed, and then he said, "I tried to defend your situation to him, but I'm not sure if it did any good. You know it will mostly depend on his mood, and I hear he is in a foul one today."

"Thank you, but I don't need defending," she said curtly.

"You might. You know what he is capable of." Jimmy sighed. Most of the girls that came into Jimmy's orbit were just objects. Some proved themselves useful, but they mostly just existed as a means to an end. Mel was an exception, and Jimmy had always held a special place for her. Jefe Manuel did, too, although he would never admit it. Overall she had been trusted and performed well, sometimes with a coldness Jimmy admired. To manage girls in this business, one had to be heavy-handed at times. Mel could handle business when it mattered.

Mel didn't need Jimmy to remind her of what Jefe Manuel was capable of. She knew exactly and had the scars to prove it, some physical and some not. What she had witnessed over the last few years had hardened her in many ways. But some of the atrocities as of late, she struggled to deal with. She wasn't a killer, but she knew very well Jefe Manuel was.

Too quickly the huge black mobile fortress came into view. She had only been in the thing once before when Jimmy had brought her to that amazing dinner to meet Jefe Manuel initially. They parked, and Jimmy got out and opened her door. The two same men, armed and deadly serious, materialized as before. Their thorough frisk failed to shock Mel this time. Her innocence had long since vanished. Instead it had been replaced with something that could easily have found pleasure in such rough handling. Jimmy stepped toward the door they had entered before and abruptly was told to halt.

"La puerta de atrás," he was told—the back door.

This was definitely not what Mel had hoped to hear. The back door of the bus had the reputation of once a person entered it, they never came out of it. It led to a cold office where Jefe Manuel meted out his justice. An office with stainless steel flooring, walls, and ceiling. A room made for executions, torture, and easy cleanup. It was rumored there was a trap door leading to a holding tank full of formaldehyde to pickle fresh corpses until they could be dumped somewhere in the desert wilderness. Even Jimmy hesitated.

"Move it, amigo. Jefe Manuel needs to be on the road in twenty minutes." The guard motioned with his rifle toward the back of the bus. As they walked, Mel could see their reflection in the black glossy side of the bus. She wondered if this was to be the last time she saw herself. With the exception of her messy hair, she thought she looked pretty. A tear rolled down her cheek as she considered all in life she had hoped to do but now wouldn't. Rob slipped into her mind briefly for the first time in what seemed like forever. He was the only person she had in life that mattered and instantly regretted she never reached back out to him since that night in Mesquite.

They rounded the back of the bus, and the door hissed open. There were no automatic stairs, just plain steel ones that seemed to climb endlessly. She stepped up, and on weakened knees she took one, then another, then another until she emerged in a cold rectangle room . . . of stainless steel. "So the rumors are true," she thought as another tear left a moist trail down her cheek. She felt weak, as if she was going to be sick. Jimmy stepped up beside her, silent. His face was hard to read, but she sensed he had been here before. What other girls had he brought here, and to what end?

In front of them was a steel desk, and nothing else in the room. Behind it was a steel door with a keypad. Next to it was a mirror she assumed was a one-way window. At least she was wrong about one thing: she would get another glimpse of herself. And she still looked pretty. Now a third tear rolled down her cheek. Suddenly the steel door opened and Jefe Manuel walked in. On his hip was a platinum-plated Les Baer .45-caliber pistol with pearl grips.

"I am saddened to be here today," he began as he leaned forward on the desk with his hands. "I am a forgiving person. You both have been loyal to me in our years together. I am also saddened to learn senorita Mel's run-in with the law may have been part of a conspiracy to expose my operations to law enforcement." Mel closed her eyes tight. Guilt washed over her, and she then knew she wasn't going to walk out of this room alive.

"I am not senor Perry Mason. I do not seek the truth, I haven't the time. Therefore, I do not care to hear arguments and appeals. This is not a courtroom. However, I do believe in second chances." With that said, his gaze locked onto Jimmy. "But not third ones."

"Jefe Manuel, please," started Jimmy as he realized between him and Mel, it was only he that had been in this room before. With Rosa.

With the speed of a cobra, Jefe Manuel drew his pistol and shot Jimmy through his left eye. The soft-tip .45-caliber bullet exploded in his head and sprayed his brains across the wall behind them. Jimmy collapsed onto the floor, and blood began to pool quickly around him. The sound of the gun in the confined room was deafening. Mel startled and covered her mouth lest she began screaming hysterically. Instead she just whimpered, terrified.

Jefe Manuel stood there looking at Jimmy lying on the floor. He then looked up to Mel and said, "Follow me, por favor." He turned and punched a code into the steel door and disappeared through it. Mel followed, numb yet eager to leave the death chamber. Once the steel door was closed behind her, she heard an electric hum and felt vibrations through the floor. Then a splash. Then the sound of high-pressure spraying like a touchless car wash. Another rumor confirmed.

Chapter Sixteen

Dr. Sheltie woke up. She was confused about where she was. It was becoming apparent she was lying in a strange bed, but only one of her eyes worked, making it hard to focus. She tried to sit up, but her head immediately felt like it was splitting in half and caused her to fall back onto her pillow. She felt her face, and her right eye was swollen shut.

"Ouch! Dammit." She winced as she explored it gingerly.

"Hey there," Rob said as he gently placed a cold rag of ice against her face.

She let the cold ice soak into her swollen face until it began to numb.

"That's a heck of a shiner you got there."

"I'm beginning to feel like a punching bag," she said, and laughed weakly. "Ouch, ouch! Hurts to laugh." Then, as if she was stung by a bee, she jerked up. "My house! Rob, what happened to my house? Where is this? How did I get here? What happened to that man?" she said, now panicked as her memory returned.

"Everything happened so fast," Rob tried to explain. "That CIA guy punched you. Then he was on me before I could react. I must have shot him in the stomach somewhere 'cause he was dead on top of me. By the time I got him off of me and was able to stand, the room was ablaze. Somehow something caught on fire and everything was burning, so I grabbed you and dragged you out of the house. Thankfully you still had your purse looped around you, so I grabbed your keys and got us out of there. I didn't know where else to go, so I brought you to my dorm room."

"Your dorm room!" she exclaimed. "We can't be here. They will find us! Grab some clothes. We have to leave."

And with that she eased up off the bed. Rob held her steady until her balance returned. He then grabbed a backpack and emptied its contents onto the floor and began shoving the few first aid supplies he had into it. Then he grabbed some fresh clothes and toiletries as Dr. Sheltie made her way to the door and pressed her ear to it after she looped her purse across her body.

Rob eased the door open and peeked out, looking for anyone in the hallway. It was clear, so they stepped out and quickly walked toward the parking lot entrance where Rob had left Dr. Sheltie's car. Slowly, he opened the door to the parking area and stuck his head out. Gathered around Dr. Sheltie's Porsche Spyder was a small group of students, mostly guys gawking at the high-end sports car. He could hear whistles and catcalls as two more guys walked up.

"Your car is drawing quite a crowd," Rob whispered back to her.

"Yes, it tends to do that," Dr. Sheltie said.

Then a campus police cruiser pulled up causing several in the group to move on, leaving a few of the students to chit-chat with the officers.

"Campus cops," Rob sighed, speaking over his shoulder.

"If they run my tags it will cause a commotion, I am sure. Especially if they find out about the fire. Even if they don't put the two things together, why would I be parked here in a dorm parking lot?" Dr. Sheltie said, perplexed.

"Ever heard of a cougar?" Rob smirked.

Dr. Sheltie punched him in the back. "Real funny. Now what are we gonna do?"

"The cops don't look that interested. Let's wait a sec to see if they move on." They waited another couple of minutes, and finally the cruiser slowly drove on. It weaved back and forth through the parking area then exited the lot and drove away from them. The rest of the student gawkers moved on too.

"Now's our chance," Rob said, then exited the building. Dr. Sheltie followed close behind.

"You'll have to drive. My head is still spinning," Dr. Sheltie said as she held the ice to her swollen cheek.

When they both were in the car behind the dark tint, Dr. Sheltie let out a long sigh of relief.

"What now, Doc?" Rob asked, looking at her.

"Doc? You sound like Bugs Bunny," she quipped, giving him a droll stare. "Call me Maria. I think our relationship has moved to that level. Now take me home. I want to see the damage from the fire."

Rob pushed the ignition button, and the high-performance engine roared to life. He zipped out of the parking lot with little effort. The Spyder handled like a Formula One racing car. With very little pressure on the gas pedal, the engine wound up and propelled them into triple digits on the speedometer in mere seconds.

"Easy there, Mario Andretti. Let's not get pulled over right now," Dr. Sheltie cautioned, still holding the ice on her face, resting her head against the headrest.

"This car is amazing!" Rob squealed with excitement as he carved up the thick traffic.

They arrived at her Colleyville neighborhood and made the turn onto her street. Slowly they rolled up to her house. The whole front of her house was blackened with soot, and the roof had a gaping hole in it. Smoke could still be seen wisping here and there. Yellow caution tape was everywhere.

"Oh my God," she whispered.

"Should we stop?" Rob asked.

"No. Circle the block and pull over," she replied, then asked, "Do you have a cell phone?"

"Yes," Rob said, and fished it out of his pocket. He typed his unlock code and handed it to her. She Googled the fire department number and pushed to call it.

"Tarrant County Fire. How may I help you?" asked the voice.

"Yes, this is Maria Sheltie. I am out of town, and a neighbor informed me my house was on fire last night. I was hoping to speak with someone who can help me understand what happened and what I need to do," Dr. Sheltie explained to the lady, again feeling guilty about being dishonest with the second dispatcher in as many days.

"Please hold while I transfer you," the voice said.

"Captain Williams," a gruff voice came on the line a moment later.

Dr. Sheltie identified herself and explained her situation again.

"Yes, let me pull the preliminary report. The final report to provide your insurance company won't be ready for another couple of days." He paused as she heard shuffled papers. "Here it is. Says the fire started in a front room that appeared to be an office. Says the accelerant was a candle that fell and lit the curtains on fire. The neighbor called when he saw the flames, but we weren't able to save much, unfortunately."

"That's it?" she asked.

"That's it."

"No one was in the home?"

"Nope. Was there supposed to be?" the captain asked warily.

"No, no. I just wanted to be sure my housekeeper or someone wasn't there. You know, must have been a dangerous situation and all," she said. Then she listened as he explained the process going forward. Dr. Sheltie barely heard anything he was saying. Her mind was running a mile a second.

"Thank you so much for your help. Goodbye." She clicked off the phone and stared out the windshield for a moment then turned to Rob. "Are you sure Agent Masters was dead?" she asked Rob.

"I assume he was. I shot him. I know that. He was unconscious because I barely could get him off of me," Rob recalled as he answered her.

"Did you move him or anything?" she inquired further, pulling down her sun visor to inspect her swollen eye again in its mirror.

"It crossed my mind, but the fire was raging everywhere. I just wanted to get you out, and I barely did. Stuff started collapsing," Rob said as he stared out the windshield. "I wanted to grab the files, too, but they either were on fire or scattered everywhere. I feel like we ask this so much, but what are we gonna do now?"

"I wish I knew. But one thing I am certain of is we are being followed," Dr. Sheltie said as she looked behind them in the sun visor's mirror.

Rob turned and looked as a black sedan rounded the corner two blocks behind them. It stopped for a moment then accelerated fast toward them. Rob heard its big V-8 inhaling hard.

"Get us out of here!" Dr. Sheltie yelled. Rob shifted into drive and dropped the hammer down, which caused their even more powerful V-8 engine to roar. The Spyder listed to the left as the fourteen-inch-wide Pirelli P Zero tires struggled with the sudden burst of torque and laid down thick black rubber and smoke. Like a shot they were flying down the residential road. Houses and trees blurred as they flew by.

"Turn there!" Dr. Sheltie instructed.

Rob jammed the brakes and cut the steering wheel hard, and the car slid sideways. He slammed the gas down again, and the nimble Spyder flew down the street like a rocket. Dr. Sheltie led Rob out of the neighborhood and onto a service road heading north. The black sedan was still following but not handling the sharp curves as well as the Spyder as it fishtailed back and forth. He weaved around cars like they were standing still, until he was able to merge onto the onramp to the freeway. His heart pounded adrenaline through his veins as the Porsche passed 130 mph with ease. It seemed to enjoy the workout.

"I don't see the black car!" Dr. Sheltie reported as she looked behind them. "Keep right and take the turnpike. We need to get somewhere and hide for a while."

Rob did as instructed and exited onto the six northbound lanes of the George Bush Turnpike. From out of nowhere a brilliant yellow-colored Z51 Corvette came up fast from behind. In his rearview mirror Rob saw its owner's huge grin as if he accepted a perceived racing challenge. Rob had attracted a speed enthusiast who now hoped to prove his American Chevrolet superiority over Dr. Sheltie's German Porsche. Rob stabbed the gas to the floor, and the Spyder responded instantly as he and Dr. Sheltie were thrown deep into their seats. Within seconds the yellow Corvette was just a twinkle in his rearview.

Chapter Seventeen

Mel sat in the passenger seat of a Cadillac Escalade driven by a huge mountain of a Mexican man called Bronco. The vehicle reeked with marijuana and cheap men's cologne. Bronco had arms thicker than Mel's waist and covered in tribal patterned tattoos. Jefe Manuel assigned him to her as her driver and protection to work off her $6,000 debt to him for bailing her out of jail the day before. Bronco was taking her to her fourth appointment of the morning. At $200 per hour for her companionship, she had twenty-one such rendezvous left to have her debt paid back in full. A small price to pay compared to the alternative. Mel didn't dare complain.

After being led out of the bus's death chamber, she was allowed to shower and clean up. Jefe Manuel explained how she was to pay him back. She wasn't a hooker per se, but by now knew the ropes. As the Dallas waypoint lieutenant that looked after hundreds of working girls over the last few years, she was versed enough. Her latest stint in the clink was a case of wrong place at the wrong time with some legitimate call-girls in her charge. Or as one of her foster mom's once said as they waited in the school principal's office, birds of a feather flock together. Jefe Manuel's punishment required her to take up the skin trade until her debt was paid. Jefe Manuel set the hourly rate to $200. She knew this rate could vary. Based on what she had heard through the grapevine from other girls, $200 per pop was generous. He told her to report back in three days. If her debt was cleared he would consider allowing her to go back and manage the waypoint house in Dallas. Otherwise, another visit through the back door of the bus may be in order, and she knew how that would end. He explained his fondness of her and how this second chance was

91

a kindness he rarely expressed to anyone—and even more rarely to his "bitches," as he put it.

Bronco slowed and pulled into a Hilton hotel in Richardson, Texas. He received her appointments on his cell via text. Requests for female companionship came in from a web portal that resided on the dark web. They were vetted for security, and from there approved requests were broadcast via text to "handlers" like Bronco. They entered the lobby, and he turned toward the bar. She turned toward the elevators to find room 612. She knew the drill and had her burner cell phone programmed to Bronco's in the event the john became too rough with her. They rarely did, but on those occasions Bronco quickly showed them the error of their ways. He was not to be trifled with. She lightly knocked on the door. It was opened by a man in a robe trying to look casual, but Mel could sense his nervousness. A first timer. Good. She should be in and out in fifteen minutes with minimal effort. Then four down, seventeen more such meetings to go.

Chapter Eighteen

They parked her Porsche on the top level of a public parking garage two blocks over from the Hilton hotel in Richardson, Texas. She donned a pair of huge sunglasses she had in her glovebox to hide some of her swollen face. Rob received a couple of reproachful looks from people who assumed it was his handiwork on display. After they checked into a room, they decided to order room service for lunch to spare Rob the further embarrassment of a wife beater. Dr. Sheltie lay on the bed and explained how she had found out Mel was in jail and due out today. Rob quickly called the Dallas County Jail to learn she had already been released the day before. The deputy would not give him any further details over the phone.

"Probably if you go in person they can be persuaded you are her family," Dr. Sheltie suggested. "Maybe then they'll tell you who bailed her out, and you could look that person up."

"It's better than nothing, I guess," Rob concluded as their lunch was served. "I'll go after we eat."

They ate club sandwiches and plotted other possible ways to find Mel if going to the jail proved fruitless. They also discussed more about the CIA's involvement in this whole thing. Dr. Sheltie explained what Dr. Klaskin had notated in his journal that burned in the fire.

"Dr. Klaskin believed it was a CIA cover-up?" Rob asked, trying to piece the connection together. "My grandfather was a marketing executive, not a spy."

"How can you be so sure? You don't know much about him."

"No, I don't. But a spy? I'm just having trouble buying that idea."

"Well, that Masters guy wasn't a made-up character and my house really did burn down. So your grandfather did cross paths with the CIA somehow back then, and they are keen on getting their hands on you now," she said as she took a bite of her sandwich, wincing as she did so.

These facts Rob couldn't deny. It just seemed too cloak-and-dagger for him to believe.

"What was that you said to Masters about how Dr. Klaskin succeeded in maneuvering around something in my dad's head to find the truth?" asked Rob. He thought hard to remember their conversation through all the chaos.

"Your father's little sister was too young at the time of the incident for any long-term trauma to take hold. Your dad, on the other hand, wasn't able to shake it off as easily. He continued struggling with the emotional and physical trauma. They tried a couple of different therapists, but nothing seemed to help. The journal didn't say specifically, but it indicated your father was given some sort of genetically modified serum to scramble his memories of that night. Through his immersion technique, Dr. Klaskin described it as a brick wall in which he was able to circumvent and reveal hidden memories. These memories included a visit to a certain clinic that administered the shots to him, shots that his mother was very distressed over."

Dr. Sheltie finished her sandwich and wiped her hands on a napkin before she continued, "Dr. Klaskin speculated the CIA was concerned your father was going to say something that revealed their secret, so they gave him this experimental cocktail hoping that would seal the truth in his head."

Dr. Sheltie leaned back on her pillow and held the cool rag to her forehead. Her ice had melted.

"Rob, you need to find Mel. Then I think you need to find your father. Ask him what he remembers. I can locate what mental health facility he is in and let you know."

"I haven't seen him since I was ten," Rob said quietly as he contemplated it all.

"I've done all I can for you now. I need to deal with my house, and I have patients I need to see. And, oh yeah, this needs to heal," Dr. Sheltie said, motioning to her swollen face. "Call my office if you need me. Better yet, here is Chelsea's cell number. She will know how to find me. I'll get a new cell as soon as I can."

"I can't thank you enough, Dr. Sheltie. You saved my life," Rob expressed.

"Well, we are even. I would be a crispy critter right now if you hadn't pulled me from that fire," she added.

They hugged each other tightly. "Good luck, Rob," Dr. Sheltie said.

"Same to you, Maria," Rob said shyly.

"Here, wait a sec." She grabbed her purse and handed Rob a wad of twenties. "It's not much, but it's all the cash I have. Also, input my credit card number into your Uber app so you have all the transportation you need."

"Thanks. I will pay you back," Rob promised as he keyed in the digits of her Mastercard.

"Go find your sister. Go restore your family," she said, teary-eyed.

With that said, Rob said goodbye and left the room determined to find Mel and solve this mystery.

Rob left Dr. Sheltie's room and headed down to the lobby. While he rode the elevator, he brought up his Uber app and requested an economy car to take him to the Dallas County Sheriff's Office. Several cars were in the area. To Rob they resembled fleas as they moved in the app on Rob's screen. He chose the closest one. At the same time, Mel left room 612 with two hundred more dollars in her purse. Like she hoped, the guy finished fast and she was out in seventeen minutes. Both elevators opened on the ground floor at the same time. Rob was focused on his Uber mobile app, and Mel looked for Bronco. They passed within mere feet. Neither noticed the other.

Chapter Nineteen

The cityscape whizzed by as Rob sat in the back of a late-model Ford Focus lost in thought. Prostitution isn't an occupation normally chosen for fun or even by choice. He was concerned Mel needed help. Also, if the CIA was hunting him, was she also being hunted? She could be used as leverage to find him. So finding Mel quickly would be best for them both. Plus, he just really missed his little sis.

"I'm usually picking folks up from here, not dropping them off," the Uber driver quipped. Rob realized they had stopped in front of the Dallas County Jail. "Good luck to ya," the driver said as he looked back at Rob through his mirror.

Rob exited the car and made his way inside the lobby. There were two smudged plexiglass windows. One was empty with a sign that read, "Please Use Other Window." In the other window was a woman clerk. She talked on the phone as her fingernails tap, tap, tapped on her keyboard. She paid no attention to Rob as he approached. A long wooden bench ran the length of the wall. Two men and a woman sat on it with their heads down. They looked like they had been there a while. Each looked at the floor in despair. Rob stood there for several minutes and listened to the droning of a police scanner somewhere behind the plexiglass. The deputy hung up the phone and kept tapping away on her keyboard.

"Excuse me," Rob said.

Without looking up she held up one finger with a three-inch curved fingernail painted bright red. On the other fingernails were tiny, encrusted handcuffs. Rob hoped she meant one more minute with that gesture since it was her pointer finger, but the expression on her face could have gone either way.

This was ridiculous, Rob thought. After a few more minutes frustration set in and he rang the shiny bell on the counter. It was much louder than he thought it would be.

"I know you just didn't ring that bell"—she pointed her long red claw toward the bell—"in my ear? 'Cause I know you see me sittin' right here," the clerk said. Each word was emphasized as her eyes got large and her head moved back and forth on her neck.

Rob swallowed, now embarrassed. "That thing is pretty loud. I apologize."

"What? I can't hear you from the ringing in my ear!" she said sarcastically. "What can I do fo you?" she finally asked in a huff.

"I need to speak with someone about my sister. She was released yesterday, and I am trying to locate her," Rob said, relieved the conversation had moved forward.

"Name?" demanded the clerk.

"Melanie Florchett," Rob said quickly.

"She one popular girl. People calling all morning about her. I wish that many people cared about me," the clerk said as her fingernails tap, tap, tapped.

The clerk paused. "She yo sista, you say? Can I see some ID?" she asked as she finally looked at Rob with interest. Rob handed her his driver's license, and she compared something on it to her computer screen. Something wasn't feeling right. He had learned over many years in the foster system, where trust was scantily found, to trust his gut first and foremost. And right now his gut twisted in that old familiar way.

"Hold on a sec, suga. I just wanna check somethin," the clerk said. She slid his ID back to him and then scurried from her desk and down a

98

hallway a little too quickly for a woman of her build. Rob stood there. He shifted from one foot to the other, nervous. His anxiety mounted by the second.

Moments later the police scanner crackled with her voice, "Positive BOLO for Benjamin Florchett. I need a 10-18 on a 10-33."

Then, "Copy that. ETA three minutes. Proceed 10-61 until I arrive," replied another static-laced voice.

From the hallway, the clerk and two deputies rushed into the lobby, their guns drawn, as the front door clicked shut. That left the two men and a woman on a long wooden bench with their heads down. They looked like they had been there a while. Each continued to look at the floor in despair.

Chapter Twenty

Rob bolted through the front doors and cut across a picnic area. He ran until he was a couple of blocks from the jail, found an alleyway, and stopped to catch his breath. A sheriff's car sped past, then another. He realized that now that law enforcement was looking for him, things had just gotten a bit tougher. He continued walking until he came to a strip mall. He ducked into a sports apparel shop and bought a Dallas Cowboys cap and some cheap wraparound sunglasses. He hoped this might help any casual glances at him not to turn into easy recognition.

His biggest immediate issue was the usual recurring question, "What next?" He couldn't return to his dorm. Dr. Sheltie was unreachable, and he already felt he had imposed on her enough. He had no idea who bailed out Mel, nor where she went. He had a few clues, but ultimately he was back at square one. Except now he could sleep, which was good, but with Uncle LEO and the CIA hunting for him, he doubted that was going to be any easier. He exited the sports store and continued to walk. An idea took shape in his head. He headed for the library. He needed a place to hide that had online access and a place to charge his phone.

The library wasn't busy, which was a good thing. He found the computer lab area and sat down at a computer on the corner so he could see the door. He didn't know exactly what he was going to search for, but figured he needed to research that night in 1970 and better understand what exactly had been reported. He did several Google searches using "*Dallas Morning News*" as a prefix. There were a few articles, but just bland information. He read his grandfather had gone crazy and was arrested after attempting to murder his family. He was sentenced to thirty-five years in prison. Rob found another article later announcing his grandfather had died in his cell after a short bout with cancer. That was pretty much it.

Then it occurred to Rob this event occurred in a very small town on the outskirts of McKinney, Texas. The *Dallas Morning News* probably didn't think a country bumpkin losing his mind was all that newsworthy. They pretty much focused on Dallas politics the best Rob could recall from what people said. He himself hadn't read a newspaper in . . . ever? So he deleted "*Dallas Morning News*" from his search criteria and hit Search again. Bingo. Several news articles appeared in the results, and the one common denominator of them all was a reporter named Waylon Gentry. Waylon was obsessed with the story, it seemed. He knew Rob's grandfather and staunchly defended that Rob's grandfather didn't go crazy. Gentry went even further to say he believed he was railroaded by law enforcement.

Rob then searched for "Waylon Gentry" and was shocked to see Waylon had recently written an article on the urban expansion into rural Collin County and its horrible effects on just about everything.

"He's still alive and he still writes!" Rob whispered to himself and smiled.

Rob noticed the article was published by the *Collin County Community Sun*. He Googled that and found an address and a phone number. He quickly dialed the number.

"*Community Sun*," answered a nasally woman who didn't seem very motivated.

"Hello. I am looking for Waylon Gentry. I just read his article on urban intrusion on rural Collin County citizens and may have something interesting to share," Rob said. He hoped he didn't sound too excited about what, in reality, was probably a very dull topic.

"Waylon is a contributor. He just sends in his articles. He doesn't come into the office," she droned.

"May I have his number so I can call him?" Rob asked, hopeful.

"Sorry. Mr. Gentry has asked us to take a message and he will get back to you at some point. Or never, so I hear." She exhaled into the phone.

"I really would like to speak with him. Could you make an exception?"

"Sorry, I just can't. What's your message?"

"Can you at least give it to him right now? Please?" pleaded Rob.

"Wow, you must be seriously encroached upon by the urban folks of this county," she said sarcastically. "Yes, I'll give it to him straight away, sir."

Rob thought for a minute. "Yes. Please tell him my curiosity stems back to 1970."

"That's all?"

"Yes."

"Your name?" she asked.

"Rob Florchett. That's F-L-O-R-C-H-E-T-T," he answered.

"Gotcha. I'll get it right to him," she said. Then abruptly, the call ended.

Rob sat there wondering if his message would get through to Mr. Gentry at all. The lady on the phone sounded like she had no urgency to do anything outside of her normal routines. Just as he thought he might lay his head there and take a quick nap, the shrill ring of his phone broke the oppressive library silence. This earned Rob a stern, spittle-filled SHHHHH from the librarian who looked quite ancient. Her crooked finger pointed at a sign that commanded all cell phones be put on silent mode.

Rob ignored her and answered the phone quietly, "Hello?"

Rob heard a raspy breath, then, "Is this a prank?"

"I'm not sure what you mean," Rob replied, confused.

"Who is this?" the voice asked.

"Rob Florchett."

"I don't know any Rob Florchett, goodbye."

"Wait, please!" Rob said quickly and a little too loudly, which again attracted the attention of the Nazi librarian. She stomped from around her counter and made a beeline straight for Rob.

"You don't know me, but you knew Joe Florchett," Rob said as he kept one eye on the old librarian as she approached.

There was a long pause of raspy breath in the phone.

"You need to leave, sir," the Nazi librarian told him with her arms crossed across her withered chest. Rob looked at her and waved okay, whatever. He needed to focus on the next ten seconds, and this crusty old bat was not going to have it.

"The library demands quietness. Show your respect!" she commanded as she lunged at him. She grabbed his arm and then tried to grab the phone away from his ear.

"What are you doing, lady?" Rob said, now shocked at her forwardness. He dodged her grab for his phone, but instead, she grabbed his wrist. The old bat had some strength and yanked his arm hard, which sent his phone flying down an aisle.

"What the hell is wrong with you?" Rob shouted. She might have been stronger, but Rob was faster. He sidestepped her as they both went for the phone at the same time. She tripped on his feet and nearly toppled over a bookshelf as she caught her balance. Rob grabbed the phone up from the floor. "Hello? Mr. Gentry? You still there?"

Silence, no raspy breath. The line was dead.

Chapter Twenty-One

Rob's ear was tender and cherry red. The old librarian had come up from behind him and grabbed it and given it a hard twist that bent Rob into submission. With a grip like a vice, she marched him toward the exit. She mumbled something about kids these days, no respect, and a few other disparaging grunts and groans as she yanked him down the hall. He was sure she had torn it off as the library door slammed shut behind him.

He rubbed his ear as he walked over to the bus stop awning on the sidewalk beside the library. He sat on the bench under the awning and brought up his call history. He found the number Waylon Gentry had called from and dialed it. It went straight to a voicemail box that had not been set up.

"Dammit! That stupid woman," he said, angry that she ruined his chance to speak with Waylon. He sat back and watched the traffic. Cars and trucks drove back and forth as he tried to think of his next move. He figured he could go to the *Community Sun* and beg the unmotivated lady to send another message. With no better ideas, he got up and started to walk in that general direction. No sooner had he made it a dozen feet than an old tan club-cab Ford Super Duty 4x4 screeched to a halt beside him. The driver slammed the truck into park and rolled down the window. Behind the wheel was an old man wearing an oxygen mask. He pulled the mask away from his mouth.

"You Rob?" the driver asked in a raspy voice. The high-mileage diesel engine clattered loudly. Fuel and exhaust fumes from the old truck were overpowering. Rob wasn't sure how to answer, unsure who he could trust anymore.

"Son, if you are Rob, I'd suggest tossing your cell phone into that water"—the old man made a motion toward the small duck pond that sat in the middle of some park benches behind him—"and getting in this truck immediately."

Rob stood there unsure what to do.

"But suit yourself," the old man said, and put the truck in gear to leave.

"Wait! Okay, okay," Rob said, and jogged over to the edge of the water. He wondered how Dr. Sheltie would contact him about where to find his father if he got rid of his phone. Rob looked back at the old man, and he had replaced his oxygen mask on his face and motioned for Rob to hurry. No time to think, so Rob made his choice. He tossed it in the pond and ran back to the truck. The old man motioned to get in behind him, and Rob did. Even before the door slammed shut the turbo diesel whined and the truck lurched forward. The truck smelled of soured animal feed and wet dog.

"Damn, boy, I may be too late," the old man said as he rounded a corner that led to the main highway. Ahead was a sheriff's car askew in the road. Its blue lights flashed, and a deputy stood beside it. He held up his hand for the old truck to halt. Rob's heart froze.

"Duck down and cover with that blanket," the old man instructed. They coasted to a stop, and the deputy walked over to the driver's window. The old man waited until Rob was hidden in the floorboard. Rob tried not to gag as he covered himself. The filthy blanket was definitely the primary source of the stink.

Rob heard the electric window as it rolled down, which allowed the outside noise to flood the cab of the truck. Rob could hear the deputy's boots on the pavement and highway traffic ahead.

"Turn the truck off!" the deputy shouted over the clattering of the old diesel engine. The old man complied. The outside noises seemed even louder now, not having to compete with the engine clatter. Inside the truck he could now hear the old man's oxygen as it hissed.

"Where are you headed?" asked the deputy. He rested his right hand on his service weapon.

"I have an appointment with my heart doctor. Dr. Baker, you've probably heard of him. Best around when it comes to the old ticker," the old man said then patted his chest.

"Can I see some ID, please?"

"What's this about?" the old man wheezed, and handed his ID to the deputy.

"These are press credentials," the deputy said as he studied them. "Are you a reporter?"

"Yes, sir. Have been since 1969 when I was discharged from the service," the old man said proudly. "So what's going on with the roadblock? Sounds like a juicy story in the making. Lemme find my notebook," the old man said excitedly and dug in a pile of things on the passenger seat.

"Ah, here it is!" he said triumphantly. "Aww, blast, where did I put my pen?" he said, defeated, and started to rummage through the junk again for a pen. The deputy tried to see into the back of the cab, but the grime and bubbled window tint made it difficult to make anything out.

"This will have to do. So let's start with your name and designation," the old man said as he scribbled the date and time on a fresh page in the notebook with a small pencil. He then turned to the deputy and scrunched his face as he struggled to read the name tag on his chest.

"Deputy Chris Horn," Waylon dictated as he scribbled. "Is your daddy Max Horn, the oncologist? I hope I don't have to see him anytime soon, but I hear he is pretty good."

"No, sir," he replied, frustrated with the dirty windows, and wondered what the deal was with old people and their incessant conversation about doctors. He brought his attention back to Waylon.

"Okay, so what's with the roadblock again? We got a fugitive situation or something? Oh, and we are on the record here, but we can go off if you prefer. I'm not into tarnishing reputations, just getting the scoop," Waylon said with a friendly chuckle.

The deputy became flustered and had no intention to divulge anything about the situation to anyone, let alone an old codger in a ratty truck—not with who was behind his orders to be there. He had never dealt with a federal government agency before, and they scared the hell out of him. He had two small kids and he needed this job. His lips were sealed.

"Have a nice day," the deputy expressed. He handed back the old man's press credentials then turned on his heel and walked to the next car in line.

"Will do! Thank you, son," the old man said cheerfully then cranked up the old diesel and pulled away. He had just readjusted his oxygen mask when he saw the black sedan screech to a halt in front of them on the shoulder.

"Keep down a few minutes longer," the old man advised Rob through his mask. Even with the mask over his mouth, Rob could hear the concern in his voice.

The driver opened the door quickly and got out. He was tall. His features were rugged with thick salt-and-pepper hair, and he wore a black suit that hid a radio with a curly cord fitted to an earpiece in his ear. The wind blew open his jacket and revealed a huge pistol holstered on the man's side. He looked at the old truck through dark black sunglasses. He held his gaze on the old man, who gave a friendly wave.

"Commie pinko bastard," Waylon mumbled to himself as he feigned a charmed grandpa's smile.

The man in the black suit just stared at him as the truck slowly passed. Then he walked toward the deputy with a brisk step.

They turned onto the highway, and the diesel belched a huge cloud of black exhaust as it accelerated. The old man pressed his oxygen mask firmly to his face and inhaled deeply as he realized he had held his breath since he saw the black suit and earpiece. From under the blanket Rob asked if the coast was clear so he could get up. The old man said it was, and Rob lifted himself up onto the backseat. The blanket's stench was so bad, Rob could taste it. The old man swiped the passenger seat contents onto the floorboard so Rob could join him up front. Rob squeezed over the center console and sat in the passenger seat.

The old man held out his hand. "Waylon Gentry."

Rob shook Waylon's hand and said, "Rob Florchett."

Although the man was easily eighty years old, his grip crushed Rob's hand.

"It's a pleasure. Now let's get you somewhere safe 'cause I think you are in a world of danger, young man," Waylon said as he mashed the accelerator to the floor. The old diesel exhaled a huge cloud of exhaust and sped into the twilight.

Chapter Twenty-Two

The sun had set and caused Waylon to flip on his headlights. The glow from the dashboard gauges illuminated his face eerily. With the oxygen mask, he looked like a mix of crypt keeper and fighter pilot. He was very thin, but not frail. He had wispy white hair and bushy eyebrows. He hunched slightly forward with a turkey neck. Rob guessed it was from so many years at the typewriter.

They drove in silence for some time until Rob asked, "How did you know where to find me back there?"

Waylon took a couple more breaths from the mask then pulled it off and laid it in his lap.

"On our call I heard you arguing with someone, and when they said library, I recognized the voice. Hilda Green. She's been the county librarian as long as I have been a journalist. We go way back to when research was done in the library, not on a computer. She means well, but it sounded like you really crossed her," Waylon said with a chuckle.

"Yeah, I did. She nearly ripped my ear off," Rob said as he reached up to touch it and realized it was still very sore.

"You won't believe it, but fifty years ago she had a body that had every journalist's loins on fire. She was a firecracker," Waylon grinned as he reminisced.

Rob could tell that Waylon was fond of Hilda Green and enjoyed the churned-up memories of her.

"Even back then she was no-nonsense. I asked her out once, and she proceeded to tell me what a bush-league writer I was and that she would never be seen with such a daft reporter. Or any reporter that I can recall. She had a PhD, she would remind us. Much too educated to be dumbed down by community rag reporters like me. Damn, I loved her," he went on as a smile played on his lips.

"I haven't seen her in years. I'm sure she looks as run down as I do these days." With that he laughed, which turned into a cough. He pulled his mask up for a couple of hits of oxygen.

Rob seized the break in the conversation. "I read in one of your articles. You knew my grandfather."

Waylon lowered his mask, and his smile went flat. "Not now. We'll discuss that soon enough," he answered. His eyes darted from mirror to mirror. Rob wondered if Waylon thought the truck was bugged or something, but he did as requested and fell silent the rest of the way.

Waylon slowed and exited the highway onto a blacktop county road. They bumped down it for a few miles then it turned onto a smaller gravel one. Rob bounced around in the seat as he held the handle above the passenger door. The road was in need of more gravel and several repairs. Parts of it were washed out completely and caused Waylon to engage the truck's four-wheel drive. The diesel engine whined, and they continued to move slowly forward as mud slung up from the big tires and thudded down on the hood and roof of the truck. He slowed again and turned onto what Rob thought was more trail than road. Branches screeched down the sides of the old truck like fingernails on a chalkboard. Rob's skin crawled at the sound. Finally the trail opened up into a small clearing. Lit up by the headlights of the old truck was a cabin nestled in its center.

"Stay out here with the headlights on so I can see to unlock the door," Waylon said as he slid off the driver's seat and slammed the heavy door.

He pulled his portable oxygen tank behind him up the porch steps. He fumbled with the lock for a few seconds, and then the door swung into the cabin. He turned and waved at Rob to turn the truck lights off and come inside. Rob flipped the lights off, and everything went pitch black. He slid out of the truck enveloped in total darkness. A cool breeze was blowing, and he could hear insects making their evening serenades all around him. There was no moon in the sky. He wondered why Waylon hadn't turned any lights on in the cabin. His foot tripped against the porch stairs. He took them gingerly because there was no handrail. He walked across the porch and found the cabin door still open. He heard a beep, beep, beep which caused him to stop at the door's threshold.

"Waylon?" Rob whispered into the dark cabin. Silence, except for something that beeped as it moved around in the back of the cabin. A green light suddenly appeared and floated for a few feet then disappeared.

"Waylon?" Rob called a little louder. He waited another minute as the green light appeared again then vanished.

"All clear," Waylon declared. A match was struck, and a lamp began to glow. The light brightened and pressed the darkness into the corners. Waylon put a device into a black leather case and noticed Rob watched with curiosity.

"I always sweep for bugs. You know, listening devices," he said naturally, like it was the floor he just swept.

"Of course. As one does," Rob said mostly to himself with a touch of sarcasm as his eyes moved around the room. "You have that problem way out here? People snooping on you?" Rob asked as he took a step into the room for a better look. The room was tidy. A wood stove stood on one side, a couch and easy chair across from it. In the corner was a desk with a closed laptop on it. Several technical devices with all sorts of cables were nested in its various cubby holes.

"Not yet, but I wanna be prepared for the day when they might come calling on me."

"They being who?" Rob wondered aloud as he studied the various dials and microphone of an elaborate ham radio sitting on a table next to the desk.

"Come in and make yourself at home. We have much to discuss," Waylon said as he took the lantern into the kitchen.

"You have a lot of electronics for no electricity," Rob observed. Now in the kitchen he saw a coffee maker and a stand mixer sitting silently in the shadows. Waylon laughed, but said nothing as he searched in a drawer for something.

"Here it is," he said as he stuck whatever it was in his pocket. "Get comfy. I'll be right back."

Waylon carried the lantern back into the living room and motioned for Rob to sit. Rob did, and Waylon took the lamp outside and shut the door, which caused the room to pitch back into complete darkness.

"What the hell is going on?" Rob said to himself. He hoped he hadn't been led out into the wilderness by a truly crazy man. He sat there tense and listened to the night sounds outside. In the distance he heard a grunt, then another. It sounded like Waylon being punched in the gut.

Chapter Twenty-Three

Rob jumped up to run outside and check on Waylon when the cabin lit up bright as day. LEDs mounted flush in the ceiling caused him to squint.

Waylon came in the door. "Ah, there we go. Is that good enough for ya, city slicker?"

"Wow!" Rob said, now able to see everything. The cabin wasn't as rustic as he initially thought. It was quite high tech. Rob walked over to a huge 90-inch LCD display built into the wall. The picture was divided into eight squares. Each contained high-definition surveillance videos.

"Push that button there," Waylon said as he pointed to a red button just under the screen.

Rob pressed it, and a keyboard slid out from the wall. Rob stood aside and let Waylon expertly manipulate the screens. He flipped from infrared night vision, black and white to full color, then to thermal signatures. He zoomed in on an armadillo rooting around somewhere on the property. Its little body was a rainbow of colors with crimson red in the center where its heart was.

"That's so cool," Rob complimented as he took it all in.

"Yep. Under this floor is a thousand-gallon-capacity rainwater filtration system. Its collectors are the rain gutters around the roof. Hidden around the property in secret caches I have enough dry goods and vacuum-sealed food to last five people an entire year, along with a small arsenal of guns and ammo, of course," Waylon beamed proudly. "And we are sitting on enough natural gas to power this cabin for a million years, give or take a few centuries," Waylon said with a wink. "The natural gas generator is buried about forty yards that way"—he pointed—"and the solar battery I use to start it is on the fritz, so I had to hand crank it," Waylon explained while he stretched his back.

That explained the grunts Rob heard when Waylon was outside. They were his strained efforts to pull start the generator, not gut punches from federal agents. Rob continued to listen to Waylon as he explained something about the windows and bulletproof glass, but his attention was drawn to several framed photographs. He walked over and studied one of them. He had seen it before as a child.

Waylon noticed Rob walk over and stare at the picture and paused his verbal tour of the cabin. "Handsome devils, weren't we?" he said as he walked over and stood next to Rob.

"So you really did know him," Rob said in almost a whisper. The photograph was of two young soldiers as they posed next to a 1960 M-920 tanker truck. It was olive drab-colored like all army trucks were back then. Rob remembered his grandfather had this same photo in his den back when Rob was a kid. Next to his grandfather's picture, Rob recalled another framed picture of a colorful ribbon bar and a silver star. Waylon had a similar frame next to the photo Rob was looking at now, and it, too, contained a ribbon bar, but a different medal than his grandfather had. Waylon's had a Purple Heart.

"Did I know him? Hell, we were like brothers for two years in that hell," Waylon said, now too transfixed on the photograph. "He saved my life. It was 1961, and the Southern Vietnamese were getting their asses handed to them by the Viet Cong. The US involvement was still hush-hush. Your grandfather's job was to drive into enemy territory to refuel trucks and deliver certain supplies to the front lines. I was part of the army internal press corps, you could call it. The mainstream news wasn't on the scene yet, so the army created their own news mechanism. They called us the Deadpan Dummies. We were no Remington Raiders, no sir. We were shoulder to shoulder in the trenches getting blown apart like any other soldier," Waylon said defensively.

"I was assigned to ride with him. Since he was constantly moving from one embattlement to another, it was ideal for me to see firsthand how our progress was bolstering the ARVN, or Marvin the Arvin as we called them. Useless is what they were. When left to their own devices, we would half joke their mission was to search and avoid.

"Messages from a tense skirmish came back to HQ that they needed more soldiers, fuel, and ammunition badly. It sounded like a slaughter, but without hesitation your grandfather loaded up what we called a deuce and a half with all the above items. This attempt to get supplies to them would be a third of its kind. Two prior attempts failed with all involved captured or killed." Waylon paused to take a hit of oxygen from his mask. His eyes still fixed on the photo.

"Did you go with him?" Rob asked.

"That's a stupid question. Hell yes, I went with him. We were a team," Waylon said with conviction.

"Were you scared?"

"Shitless. But back then there was something called duty and honor. None of this patsy touchy-feely, everyone-gets-a-trophy bullshit. It was what it was and you just did it." Waylon turned and walked over to the couch and sat down with a grunt then continued.

"I just knew I was to die on that mission. Clearly it was suicide, but I jumped into the deuce without hesitation and we were off. Everything was fine for a few minutes. The captain of the crippled platoon radioed their new rendezvous coordinates and told us to meet them there. Your grandfather hoped the new coordinates would take us further east of where the two previous failed attempts passed through." Waylon clicked his teeth. "Boy was he wrong.

"The idiot captain botched the rendezvous calculation and sent us right into Charlie's loving embrace. Immediately we took a ton of fire. Bullets ripped through the deuce like it was made of paper. We were sitting ducks. Your grandfather yelled at me to bail out and find cover. The eight troops in the back were mowed down through the burlap canopy with no chance. Just as I opened my door and began running, the lights went out. A mortar struck the truck, and with all the firecrackers we were haulin', he told me the blast was insane."

"Were you okay?" Rob asked, riveted.

Waylon pulled up his shirt to reveal the nastiest scar Rob had ever seen. It looked like Waylon had been literally ripped apart, then hastily put back together by Dr. Frankenstein.

Rob gasped, "What happened?"

"Your grandfather found me forty or so yards from the blast with the side mirror of the passenger door buried in my side. He later joked all I needed was a turn signal to be street legal." Waylon cracked a smile and sucked in some more precious oxygen.

Rob walked over and sat on the couch beside Waylon as he continued.

"Of course I don't remember a thing. Your grandfather told me he had to pack my guts back inside me then carry my useless hide about a click further east to a small river. He put me on a log, and we floated back south until he could make it to base and get me some help. But I wasn't home free just yet. I caught a nasty bacterial infection from that toxic river water. That's what nearly killed me," Waylon said, and turned to Rob.

"A month later I was back stateside, and your grandfather's tour was over later in the year. I got hired on as a beat reporter at the local rag, and he followed in his father's footsteps in marketing. We kept in touch here and there. He landed a huge account the next year with a local emerging animal feed outfit called the Chow company. I remember I visited him and Erma, and they were so excited about what that meant to his new marketing company," Waylon said and started to stand.

"Let me help you," Rob said, and stood with his hand extended.

Waylon swatted it away. "Nah, quit that." He slowly got to his feet. "I need whiskey," he declared, and shuffled toward the kitchen.

Rob followed and asked, "Are you talking about the Chow dog food company?"

"Yep, that's the one," Waylon replied as he took two glass tumblers and a fifth of Jim Beam down from a cabinet. He poured two fingers worth in each. He slid one over to Rob then took his and headed back into the living room. He sat back on the couch with a grunt, careful not to slosh his drink.

"Geez, they must be the biggest dog food company in the world," Rob said, amazed.

"Back then they were up-and-coming and dabbled in more than just dog food. The big news during that time was they had just created a formula of chicken feed that was fortified in calcium and enhanced the omega-3 content in eggs. Big deal back then. Laying hens were big business in North Texas, and it seemed I was covering story after story on the topic.

"I had just helped Joe and Erma move to a little farm in Anna, Texas. He was eager to use it as a live set for creating product advertisements. He made an elaborate photo set in the back of his small barn to take photographs of the packaging and even had pens with chicken coops, too, so his new chickens could lay eggs. He had accumulated a substantial amount of the feed, because he used pallets of it as the backdrop. He was a natural at creating scenes that held true to life. His ads of those chickens eating the feed and then eggs in a frying pan were in all the periodicals of the day. They were just about to start a commercial campaign for television, and suddenly Chow pulled the plug on their contract with him." Waylon paused and took a sip and a hit.

Rob sipped his drink too. He wasn't a whiskey drinker, but he really enjoyed the warmth in his belly as he listened to Waylon piece together the events from back then. He was enthralled. He never knew much about his grandparents, and Waylon was a wonderful storyteller.

"Why did they do that?" asked Rob.

"Same question I asked him, but he said they didn't elaborate too much. Just decided to go a different direction and sold the rights to all their products to some company based out of Maryland, of all places. The new company assumed the Chow brand and moved all operations to the Baltimore area. Rumor was after they moved, they branched into all kinds of exotic animal feed, like monkey and such. Even tiger and wild boar food. I never understood why they focused on jungle animals, but I guess in the Far East it might have been a thing back then. Maybe Chow had something going on over there. I can attest they eat anything over there that has fur," Waylon said, and emptied his glass. He struggled to his feet again and pointed to Rob's glass and asked, "Another?"

"No, sir, this was just right."

"Okay. I think I'll do one more," he said, and shuffled into the kitchen.

As Rob listened to the sounds of another round of bourbon being served up in the kitchen, he tried to piece all this new information with the clues he already had. He was still baffled. No clear answers yet. Waylon shuffled back into the living room with his refreshed tumbler in hand.

"Anyhoo, your grandmother had to go back to work, and that left your grandfather home with your dad and aunt." Waylon picked up his story as he sat back on the couch. This time he did slosh a smidge of his drink, but paid no mind.

"They were young. No older than ten years old or so as I recall. Your grandfather found he could sell eggs for hatching and kinda went nuts with it.

Tried to get me to get in on it. I told him I hadn't the time. I was all over covering the news of the day," Waylon recalled and took a sip.

"Do you know what really happened that night?" Rob broached the subject. This is what he had really waited to hear.

"Not the details, no. But I do recall some fun facts about that evening though. He had just tangled with a problematic rooster he named Colonel Sanders. You know, like the fried chicken guy?" Waylon chuckled.

"He and that bird used to go round and round, and I guess he got the best of old Joe that day and sent him to the emergency room for stitches. It was later that night when the shit hit the fan. I was staking out a city councilman who was rumored to be on the take of some local power co-op. I kept a police radio with me at all times. I heard some radio traffic about a guy that opened fire on his family. Then I heard the address. I took off immediately, and by the time I got there the circus was well underway. Cops, ambulances, fire trucks, so many unmarked vehicles sprinkled around." Waylon continued. His words now slurred slightly.

"You mentioned there were other fun facts?" Rob prodded gently.

"The feds were on the scene. How they got there so fast and where they came from, I still don't know. Their being there is what told me Joe was in real trouble. I do believe they are the ones who framed your grandfather and said he was crazy and murderous. I knew better, so I spent every second I could investigating, but they had everything sewn up tight. No one talked about it. All the information the media got from authorities was Joe went crazy and tried to kill his family," Waylon said as he shook his head in disbelief. "The judge threw the book at him, and before I knew it he was in prison and they weren't allowing him visitors. I continued covering the story, but all information soon dried up. Your grandmother was nearly killed in the whole mess that evening. I visited her in the hospital a couple of times. She made a full recovery except for her missing ring finger. She still had an uphill battle once out of the hospital with Tommy, your father. The child suffered so much trauma he was in and out of therapy until he was sixteen, I think. Then when Erma found out Joe had died in his prison cell, she just lost it. She already carried the stigma of being the crazy man's wife while she raised two kids in a small suburb. Tommy turned eighteen and joined the army, and the day after he shipped out to boot camp Erma asked me to take her and Annie to the Mexican border, where she met some of her family. I never heard from any of them since," Waylon said somberly.

"Wow." Rob said. It was all he could say. There had to be something else, something that explained what really happened. "Anything else you can remember about that night?" he pressed.

"No, that's it," Waylon murmured. Then, "Well, there was one more thing I recall about that night."

"Oh yeah?" Rob brightened a bit.

"It was the moon."

"The moon?" Rob asked with a wrinkled brow.

"Yeah, the moon. There was a fifty-year supermoon that night. I remember cause I had to write a community piece on it. It's the absolute closest the moon comes to the earth. And it was damn bright." Waylon smirked as he remembered. "They say the crazies come out during a full moon. Even though that night was crazy, I just don't believe it was caused by your grandfather," Waylon said as he looked at Rob. Then he raised his near-empty glass to the ceiling. "I blame the moon!" he shouted, and drank the last swallow from his glass.

Rob could tell the bourbon's alcohol had begun its job on Waylon.

"Fifty years ago?" Rob asked, and made a quick calculation in his head. "That means it should appear again this year."

Waylon grinned and said, "Yep, but more accurately it appears tomorrow night. It will mark fifty years to the night from 1970."

Waylon cackled then coughed several times. He picked up his oxygen mask to quell the fit. Rob sat there lost in thought. He didn't know why this last revelation about the moon had him so unsettled. He wasn't superstitious, but he felt his own nightmarish connection to that night had slowly begun to reveal itself.

Chapter Twenty-Four

"Time to drain the old lizard," Waylon declared as he struggled to stand. This time when Rob offered him a hand, he took it. Waylon patted Rob on the arm and shuffled down the small hall to the bathroom.

"Do you mind if I use your laptop for a sec?" Rob hollered after him.

"Go for it," Waylon hollered back. "You should just have to open the lid."

Rob sat at the computer desk and opened the laptop's lid. He typed into Google's search engine the words "escort services in Dallas, Texas." Nothing useful came up. Most of it was geared to Las Vegas, where escorts were legal. Waylon had begun to relieve himself, and Rob could hear his effort through the thin wall of the cabin.

Waylon began to whistle a tune.

Then a flush.

Then a door opened.

A light switch clicked.

Rob jumped when Waylon spoke over his shoulder.

"I guess I must be poor company," he said, looking at the search results on the laptop's screen. "But alright, I can go in halfsies with you, but I doubt we will get any of those pretty ladies out this far," Waylon joked as he patted Rob's shoulder.

Rob laughed and said, "No, I'm not looking for escorts per se. I'm looking for my sister, Mel." Rob explained how he had learned Mel was a prostitute and why he needed to find her. "I don't know where to find her, so I figure the fastest way would be if I found what agency she is with and request her to visit me at a hotel or something. I'm just scared that every minute she is out there she is in greater danger," Rob said as he looked up at Waylon.

"Well, I doubt you'll find anything useful on the clear web. The dark web is where you'll most likely find actual escort opportunities outside of Las Vegas," Waylon informed Rob.

"The dark web?" Rob asked curiously.

"Scooch over," Waylon shooed, and sat down in front of the laptop. "I wasn't a vice reporter, but I hung around a few and covered plenty of prostitution on the crime beat. My understanding is there are two main prostitution rings in the greater Dallas area. Both cartel driven. One called Late Evening Divas, and the other, I think, is something like Tonya's Page or something," Waylon said as his bony fingers flew across the keyboard.

He clicked on a VPN program which informed him that a secure IP address in the Netherlands was applied to his connection. Then he double-clicked an onion icon from the computer's desktop. It opened a special web browser that said "Welcome to Tor." One message after another appeared that confirmed various secure steps and protocols had been successfully created then applied to the online session. Finally a simple search engine appeared.

Certainly Waylon was no Luddite. Rob was impressed how he knew so much about technology at his age. Next, Waylon typed into the search line "Late Night Divas," and they viewed the page. There wasn't anything that referenced Mel or any individual girls. Just diversity in girls and their services. On each webpage a muskrat mascot that wore dark shades gave a thumbs-up that guaranteed a good time. The second search was for Tonya's Page. It was simpler and resembled classified ads in a newspaper. It had a section that showed the girls and their availability. Waylon scrolled down the list, and Rob studied each one. He hadn't seen Mel in several years, but surely she hadn't changed too much. So far none of the girls resembled her.

Except one. "Wait, scroll back."

Waylon swiped up on the laptop's touchpad, and the webpage reverse scrolled.

"That's her!" Rob exclaimed. She definitely looked more mature, but still the same cute lil sis. He was sure of it.

"She is a pretty girl, but I can see a tiredness in her eyes," Waylon said sadly.

Rob agreed. She looked tired and lonely. His heart ached. He had to find her soon, he just knew it.

"Crystal Bunny," Waylon read below her photo. "Must be her alias."

"I can't believe we found her," Rob said as he looked for the phone number to call and set up an appointment with Crystal Bunny.

In the distance began a low whump, whump, whump noise. It sounded like it was approaching their location. Waylon's hearing was not as keen as Rob's younger ears. He still worked the laptop's touchpad to find the phone number.

"What's that noise, Waylon?" Rob asked. He listened intently now. Waylon paused and looked up. He listened now too.

"It's a chopper! And it's moving in fast." Waylon said quickly. Within a minute it seemed just outside the cabin making the walls shudder. He jumped up, now back to his spry self, and hustled to the hall closet. From it he grabbed a Walmart sack and tossed it to Rob. "Put that in your backpack," he said hurriedly.

Rob caught it and did as he was told. Waylon went back to the laptop. He shut the lid and rolled up the power cord. He handed those to Rob too and told him to put them in his backpack. He then scribbled something on a small notepad. He tore it out and folded it.

"Take this. Don't look at it now. We don't have time. It's the name of someone I know can help you fill in the rest of the details about that night.

124

He has a similar connection to it as your father, but I was never able to locate him." Waylon said with urgency. He moved over to the window and peeked out. There was a loud double crack, and the glass spiderwebbed but didn't break. Someone had shot it.

"Come with me," he said as he shuffled quickly down the hall into the spare bedroom. He grabbed the foot of the bed and picked it up easily. It raised up flush against the wall and revealed a rug. There must have been a counterweight in the wall, or Waylon's adrenaline had given him superhero strength. He moved the rug, and Rob could see a square hatch flush to the floor.

"Open that lid and crawl down. It leads to a small tunnel that will take you about a hundred yards into the woods toward the road we came in on," he said quickly.

Rob opened the hatch and climbed down as a barrage of more powerful bullets than the ones that hit the window ripped through the roof and sent splinters and plaster everywhere. Waylon covered his head then headed for the hallway.

"That's an M2 fifty cal! It'll turn this cabin into swiss cheese. Now move it!" he yelled back at Rob.

"What about you? Come with me!" Rob pleaded with only his head above the floor.

"Go, Rob! I'll cover you! I have some tricks of my own up my sleeve I've been itching to try on those pinko bastards!" Waylon yelled. He smiled like a sly, slightly crazy fox. With that he was gone into the hall when another burst of machine-gun fire ripped through the roof. Rob ducked hard and fast, which caused him to lose his footing on the makeshift ladder. He fell several feet in the pitch black and hit hard. His backpack fell too and smacked him on his head.

To his left was a three- to four-foot-round tunnel. He couldn't see a thing but could feel a slight draft coming through it. He entered it and crawled as fast as he could. A huge blast shook the ground, which caused dirt to fall on him. He could have sworn he heard Waylon give a celebratory whoop. However, he feared the tunnel might collapse and he would be trapped, so he crawled even faster.

His heart raced. His fingernails gripped the earth with each reach forward. The tunnel seemed to go on forever. Waylon said it went about a hundred yards, so Rob imagined himself crawling the length of a football field. With that in mind it did seem like a long way to him, but he pushed on in the confined space.

Another boom shook the tunnel. This time the earth did fall in on him and pinned his legs. The weight of the soil was immense. He struggled to free himself. The walls seemed to close in on him, and he felt he couldn't breathe. Stars began to fill his vision as he gasped for air. Finally he freed one leg, then the other. He took several deep breaths then forced himself forward.

Ahead he thought he saw things lighten a little, but couldn't tell for sure. Then, yes, he could tell there was lighter darkness instead of the pitch black he had been in. Without warning, his head hit a dirt wall. The impact bent his neck, and he collapsed. He was stunned and thought for a second he had broken it. He found he could sit up and was able to move it painfully back and forth. He looked up and saw a pinhole of light. He felt for a ladder. He found it and climbed up. Once at the top he pushed on the lid. It wouldn't budge. He pushed harder until it finally gave an inch, but no more. Did Waylon have it chained closed and forgot? Rob craned his neck to the side to put his shoulder against it. Pain from his neck shot down his back, which caused him to cry out. He pushed with all the strength in his legs. The lid ripped through the thick thatch that had grown over it. He pushed it open the rest of the way and climbed up, completely out of breath. He fell to his side with a gasp and held his neck.

He then heard the chopper from back toward the cabin. He could see the front porch floodlights had illuminated the front area of the yard. In the middle was Waylon. He stood there and looked up. The helicopter hovered above him. A loud voice from a PA barked orders, but Waylon just stood there and looked up at it like in a trance. He held a strange device hooked to something similar to what Rob recalled the Ghostbusters wore strapped to their backs.

"Waylon! Run! Get outta there!" Rob screamed, but Waylon didn't acknowledge he heard Rob's plea. The helicopter was about forty feet up. It lowered slowly. Rob expected to hear shots at any moment and see Waylon crumpled to the ground. Suddenly, a bright orange-and-red tongue of fiery goo shot up from the device Waylon held and licked the bottom of the chopper. The wide chopper looked like a teapot that hung over a campfire. Flames flickered up the chopper's sides. Rob could barely make out a long rebel yell then something about BBQ and commie pigs.

The fiery goo stuck to the bottom of the chopper, and it became engulfed in flames. It banked hard toward Waylon. Like a Weed Eater, its large rotor sliced through Waylon then into the cabin and exploded.

"Waylon," Rob breathed. He couldn't believe what he just saw. Then he noticed dark shadows coming out of the woods that ran toward the fire. Terrified, Rob sucked in a breath of cold air then took off. He ran until he came to the smaller county road and turned toward town still at a sprint.

Chapter Twenty-Five

Ahead in the distance was the glow of the greater Dallas skyline. The cold air burned Rob's lungs as he ran to put as much distance as between Waylon's cabin and himself. Ahead he saw a pair of headlights round the corner. He slowed and ducked into the tree line. He lay down at the foot of a tree and watched the vehicle drive by. It appeared to be just another car on the road and not the purposeful black sedan. Once it passed, Rob sat up and opened his backpack. He pulled out the Walmart sack Waylon gave him and felt inside. Inside there was a shrink-wrapped package that contained a prepaid phone. The other items consisted of three prepaid data cards, two Snickers bars, a 16-ounce water bottle and a canister of pepper spray. He opened the phone's package and powered it up. The screen flickered to life with the splash screen of the manufacturer. He checked the signal and had two bars. Plenty. He browsed the app store and downloaded Uber. It took three minutes, and then he was able to log in and search available cars in the area. No fleas crawled on his screen. He opened the water bottle and took a long drink. He then shoved everything back in the backpack except the phone, which he pocketed, and one of the Snickers bars, which he tore open and took a bite as he stood. He shouldered the backpack and continued forward toward the distant city lights.

As he walked, he thought through the recent events and what Waylon had shared with him. A pang of sorrow washed over him as he thought of his brief time with Waylon. Already he missed him and knew he would never forget him. But he knew Waylon went out on his own terms, just the way he wanted to. In spectacular fashion. Fires that blazed bright and commie pigs on the barbie. He had to smile at that, but a pang of loneliness shot through his heart, warding the smile away. He missed his family.

He checked the Uber app again, and one flea crept slowly on the main highway ahead. Rob requested it on the app to take him to the Galleria Mall. It was the most central place to where he needed to be he could think of. And the most public. The app responded that driver Kristina was en route to his location and should arrive in ten minutes. Rob breathed a sigh of relief. He thought he might have had to walk all the way into Dallas. He dropped to his knees and rummaged through the backpack for the piece of paper Waylon had handed him just before he went into the tunnel under the bed. He recalled what Waylon said. It contained a name of someone who could help Rob piece together the details that remained of that night in 1970. He also said this person had a similar connection to that night as Rob's father, which puzzled him.

Rob found the paper and opened it. Waylon's handwriting was awful, and to make it worse, there was very little light on the side of that county road Rob was on. He squinted to read Waylon's scratch. When he thought he could read it, his eyes bulged out. He blinked several times to be sure the tears from earlier weren't crusted to make him misread. But as he stared at the paper he realized that name was definitely what Waylon had written: Benjamin Masters.

"How does that guy have a shared connection with my dad?" Rob said to himself as he looked up. In the distance ahead, he could see headlights. He sat there on his knees and stared, bewildered. If there was a connection, it couldn't be a good one. Benjamin Masters had tried to kill him and Dr. Sheltie, not help them. Waylon must have been mistaken.

Rob hadn't noticed the crunching gravel from the minivan that slowed in front of him until he saw the illuminated Uber sign in the corner of the windshield. Slowly he got up and went to the side as the door slid open and revealed a very comfortable-looking captain's chair. He slung his backpack in first then climbed in. The door slid closed and locked as driver Kristina put the van in gear and did a U-turn. Rob leaned back and enjoyed the silence and the plush seat. His thoughts swam as the van sped off toward the city lights. He watched out the side window and could see the reflection of a large smartphone screen extended from the dash on an adjustable arm. Uber encouraged their drivers not to engage in conversation with passengers unless the passenger engaged first. Even on the app there was a designation a passenger could choose that was the equivalent to a Do Not Disturb sign. Driver Kristina had all the info she needed, and courtesy of Dr. Sheltie, the means to get paid for her efforts, tips included, through the Uber app. All of this technology amazed Rob. And his thoughts drifted back to Waylon and how his razor-sharp mind was so in tune with it even at his elderly age.

So the driver's silence in the dark van didn't trigger any concern for Rob. But her hand that extended a burly pointer finger to tap on the phone's screen did. Rob caught his breath. Clearly Kristina wasn't a she. Rob hoped he was a he that identified as a she. The ever-evolving transgender alphabet still eluded him. At least Rob could make some sort of sense in that. But somehow he doubted this was the case here. Careful to not move too quickly, he slid his left hand down toward his backpack. His fingers fumbled the zipper, but he was able to slide it open enough to slip his hand in. The plastic Walmart bag inside crinkled as he searched inside it. He kept his eyes on the driver, who he now could tell had a masculine silhouette. He gripped the pepper spray canister in his hand with his thumb on its top, fat button.

As if the driver read his mind he reached up and pushed on the driver's-side reading light that revealed a familiar rugged smile in the rearview mirror. The man adjusted the mirror, and Rob could see a familiar weariness in the man's eyes. Rob froze in terror in recognition of them.

"Master Rob. We meet again," came the smooth voice.

Rob quickly reached up with his right hand to open the door. The door handle did nothing. The child locks had been applied.

"It can't be. I thought you . . . you," Rob stammered in fear.

"You thought I was dead?" Masters finished Rob's sentence. "Well clearly I am not. I am much too wily, you see."

"Where is the driver, Kristina?"

"Home caring for her family, I suppose. I borrowed her van for our reunion drive."

"How did you get her phone with the Uber app?" Rob asked reluctantly.

Benjamin Masters didn't speak; his eyes just narrowed, and his smile faded slightly.

"She will be just fine, I assure you," he said, irritated.

Rob doubted that. Benjamin Masters liked to hand out assurances. Like the one he gave Dr. Sheltie that the CIA had nothing to do with Dr. Klaskin's death.

"Where are you taking me?" Rob asked.

"Somewhere we can get caught up on things."

"Why is the CIA after me?"

"You are a boy full of questions."

"Well, if someone would start answering them I wouldn't have to keep asking them," Rob said defiantly.

They rode in silence for a bit. Benjamin Masters looked in the mirror and responded, "They are not after just you, master Rob."

"Who else are they after?" Rob said, frightened. He expected Masters to say his sister's name.

A beat ticked by, then Benjamin Masters said, "Me."

Chapter Twenty-Six

Rob read on the dashboard clock it was 10:08 PM when the van pulled into the Shangri-La Inn in Addison, Texas. The place had the look of a bed bug infestation. They coasted to a stop in front of room 113.

"Do not try to run," Masters said as he held up a large pistol. "I am a dead shot, I assure you."

Again with the assurances.

Masters put the van in park, and the locks released, but Rob sat still. He waited for Masters to come around and open the door slide. He gripped the pepper spray in his left hand, still inside the backpack, and watched Masters approach his door. Masters held the gun up as he stood back and punched the automatic open button on the key fob. The van door slid open mechanically. Rob let go of the pepper spray. Masters wasn't going to get close enough for it to be of any use. He was too wily for that.

"Ease out of the van, sir," Masters directed with the gun's barrel.

Rob did so and pulled his backpack out with him. Masters guided him to the door of the motel room and tossed him a key. Rob used it to open the door. Then he felt the barrel of the gun press between his shoulder blades.

"Nice and easy there, young man," Masters said as he pressed Rob into the room using the gun.

The room smelled of mildew, bleach, and a tinge of vomit. Masters sat Rob in a hard wooden dining chair that looked fourth or fifth hand. From behind, he bound Rob's wrists with a large plastic zip tie. Then he tossed the gun on the bed and sat down across from Rob. He rubbed his face wearily and exhaled.

"I must give you credit. You've been hard to catch," he told Rob.

Rob cut to the chase and asked, "Why is the CIA after you?"

"That's not your concern. What is your concern is helping me."

"Why would I do that?"

"For several reasons."

Rob thought about continuing the argument but felt it was futile. Masters was a seasoned spy and would never divulge anything until he felt he had something, whatever it was he wanted from Rob.

"What do you want from me?" Rob asked.

They stared at each other for several minutes. Rob could see the dark circles under Masters's eyes. How they were bloodshot. He recognized his old buddy the Sandmeister at work. He worked hard to make Masters surrender. Rob was all too familiar. Then it clicked.

"You're having nightmares," Rob concluded.

"Very astute of you," Masters conceded.

Another minute passed, and Masters's eyes looked heavier by the second.

"Let me guess. An abomination of a rooster crushing your skull?" Rob felt the tables shift slightly to his favor.

"Not exactly. I have my own abominations tormenting me, but the effect is just the same," Masters said. There was desperation in his gaze.

"I know a nightmare plagued you. I need to know how you rid yourself of it. I haven't slept in months. It started here and there, and now every time I blink I can see it," he said, eyes squinted hard. "I know Dr. Sheltie must have been involved, so tell me."

"How did you know I was having a nightmare?" Rob asked.

"I have my ways," Masters said evasively.

"Why not talk to Dr. Sheltie yourself. Why not just make her help you instead of all the effort to catch me?" Rob said. He feared the worst in Masters's answer. If Masters had harmed a hair on Dr. Sheltie's head, he would lose it.

"For a couple reasons. I figure she would have to help me willingly. I gather it is some hypnotic mumbo jumbo she has to do. I don't have time to delay using other methods to motivate her to help. Sometimes honey works fastest," he said as his patience shortened.

Rob relaxed a notch. So Dr. Sheltie was okay.

"Yes, if she is to help you she will have to be willing to do so. But I don't think she would be. I'm sure her face is still throbbing," Rob said with a snide look.

"I regret hitting her. I will certainly apologize when I see her again. But she did have a gun pointed at me, and she had the look of someone who intended to use it. A look I've seen many times in my career," Masters said. Rob felt the man was genuine in that statement.

"So you want me to call her and sell her on the notion to help you?"

"Please. And I don't use that word often, I assure you," he said in mock surrender.

Rob pondered things a little longer. Although Masters might have been shooting him straight here, Rob still didn't trust the man.

"I will. But first, I want to know the truth behind that night in 1970. I want to know what really happened, or no dice," Rob said as seriously as he could muster.

Masters jumped up and ran his fingers through his hair, which gave his thick salt-and-pepper mop a wild touch. "I can't! You are not cleared for that information, and you never will be." He lunged and grabbed Rob by the throat. His grip was like a vise. His fingers were placed at practiced points that cut off the oxygen to Rob's brain. Rob's vision began to swim as he failed to breathe. His windpipe was being crushed. Masters got within an inch of his face. Specks of his spit hit Rob's lips. Hot coffee-laced breath burned Rob's nose.

"You will call her"—Masters shook Rob's neck—"and you will tell her to help me, or I will be forced to persuade her myself. Trust me, my boy, you don't want that. I have my ways . . . I . . . assure . . . you," he emphatically whispered as he tightened his grip even harder.

Rob could feel his eyes bulge slightly. His tongue thickened and pushed out between his quivering lips. It took every ounce of courage and strength for Rob to shake his head no. He had to know the truth. His vision grew dark. His resolve began to weaken. This definitely was not how he wanted to go out. Just as he was about to give in, Masters released his neck with a shove that nearly toppled Rob backward. He rocked back, and then the old dining chair landed on all fours and jarred Rob's abused neck. Rob struggled to inhale, but couldn't. He started to panic, and then finally, chokes of air passed through his constricted throat into his starved lungs. He sucked huge gulps of sweet, vomit-laced oxygen.

"Fine, I will tell you!" Masters screamed with rage as he ripped the flat-screen TV off the wall and turned over the small dining table.

Masters knew if he killed Rob, his chance of getting Dr. Sheltie to help him was gone. And he needed sleep in the next few hours, or he would go mad. He pointed his finger directly into Rob's face and breathed, "But if you leak this information to anyone, I won't just kill you. No, I won't stop there. I will murder your whole family and everyone you know. I'll wipe the whole miserable lot of you off the face of this earth. Do you hear me, boy?"

Rob also felt the genuineness of that statement.

Chapter Twenty-Seven

Masters was in the bathroom. He looked in the mirror and confirmed he looked like hell, which was how he felt. He splashed cold water on his face and dried it with a towel before he sat on the bed across from Rob.

"I am going to talk, and you are going to listen. No questions. I haven't the time. I will go through this only once, and then you are going to call Sheltie, got it?" he said.

Rob nodded.

Masters sighed. "Good." Then he began to explain what he knew.

"The Central Intelligence Agency didn't get that name until 1947 under President Truman in response to the Soviets dragging us into the Cold War. But before the agency was officially christened CIA, they consisted of a small group of American and German scientists captured after World War II. They were kept under wraps by our military and charged with exploring Hitler's experiments in ways we could use against the Soviets. Hitler was into all sorts of bizarre genetic and biological studies. The Nazis were light years ahead of us in these sciences. The weaponization of anything ruled the day back then, no matter how far out and strange it seemed. Our defense department was desperate, and the stone resolve of the Soviets had them very nervous.

Of course, we had nuclear bombs and in 1945 learned of their effectiveness and also their complete devastation. They were impractical to use. Plus, the Soviets had them too. Tons of them. Genetics and space were the new frontiers in the way of weapons of war. We entered the space race against the Soviets in '55, but needed public support to fund it at the level it needed to be. But our leaders knew if the public thought it was to build weapons, they would reject it. World War II was behind us, and people were enjoying their peace. So in 1958 the government created NASA as a way to celebrate technological innovation. To the public, NASAs focus was to land a man on the moon before the Soviets, which was exciting and positive."

"But let me guess," Rob ventured, "NASA's true focus was more sinister."

"As is most anything the government is behind. It has to be. After all the federal government's job is to protect its citizens. Back then they took that seriously," Masters said defensively, then continued.

"One of the projects the CIA was working on, codenamed Organic Death, was a biological stimulant that enabled accelerated mutations in animals when ingested. It genetically altered their DNA and caused mutations beyond comprehension and nearly instantaneously. It truly was something out of a comic book. Many experiments went badly. President Kennedy pulled the plug on it after seeing a demonstration get out of control. Scientists were literally ripped apart in a gruesome fashion.

Then Vietnam happened. We were covertly involved as early as 1954, but it started turning ugly for us in the late '60s. Politics began to drive the decisions of our policymakers, and the media was going berserk in response to the growing deaths and the maimed soldiers that returned home. Atrocities were surfacing left and right. It was a hot mess and becoming a political nightmare for President Johnson. Going into his second term he pressed William Colby, the director of the CIA at that time, to come up with a weapon to end the Vietnam conflict. He was specific on two things. First, it couldn't be nuclear, and second, it had to be controllable once initiated. No fallout or blowback on his legacy. He knew the CIA had a few biological ideas up their sleeve. He needed success, not a bigger failure than what was at hand already.

The CIA lobbied Johnson to re-open project Organic Death. They said it was the program that had the potential to become the weapon he had asked them to create. Johnson did, so the CIA conspired with their kissing cousins over at NASA to develop the plan. They called it the Supermoon Protocol. Like any effective weapon, they needed a delivery system and a catalyst. The delivery system was a pet-food company outside of Dallas, Texas, called the Chow company. They were an emerging animal feed company taking over the domestic pet food industry and had already begun key pet food relationships internationally."

Rob froze at the name. Bits and pieces were coming together from the information Waylon had shared with him earlier and from what Masters told him now. His grandfather's marketing company was behind much of the Chow company's emerging success. Their print advertisement campaigns were a big part of that, and they were about to expand into television. Then Waylon said the Chow company sold out before Rob's grandfather's advertisements could hit the airwaves. As a result, his grandfather's marketing firm turned belly-up. It must have been the CIA that caused Chow to terminate his grandfather's contract.

"And the catalyst?" Rob asked.

Masters answered simply, "The moon."

Rob felt faint as things began to become both clearer and murkier at the same time. Now it sounded like Masters had ventured into science fiction. The moon? Really? He remembered Waylon as he toasted his drink to the sky and said he blamed the moon. Rob just thought the alcohol had spoken and didn't think much of it. Until now.

"How does this fit with our nightmares?" Rob asked. He grew more skeptical by the minute.

"Patience. Remember, I'm doing the talking. I'll get to that," Masters answered irritably. "The CIA created a shell company and bought out the

Chow company. They needed a public-facing brand that was already established to work behind. They eventually moved its operations to Maryland on CIA property, but not before they began experiments that fused the experimental elements into the product. That process actually started in Dallas. Then once in Maryland, they continued the day-to-day operations, but amped up their international efforts with a focus on the Far East. Specifically Southeastern Asia. Go figure, right? The plan was to drop food blocks all through the jungles in Vietnam that appealed to various jungle critters. The CIA scientists found a way for the DNA transformation to remain dormant until the animal became exposed to a very specific radiation. That specific radiation was in the form of a newly discovered spectrum of gamma ray. I'm not a scientist. Much of the details about how the modified feed interacted with the radiation and then DNA transformations are way beyond my comprehension. What I can comprehend was NASA was on the cusp of sending men to the moon. One of the astronauts picked for the mission was actually a CIA recruit. You may have heard of him. Neil Armstrong."

"What?" Rob gasped. Masters was way out there now. The man was obviously delusional from his lack of sleep.

"Stay with me," Masters warned. "Like I said, I am only saying all of this once. This new gamma ray was created from a by-product of some radioactive decay of atomic nuclei, but was not native to Earth. Sounds fancy, and don't ask me what that means 'cause I have no clue. I'm just reciting verbiage from the reports I had to memorize. Because the new spectrum did not naturally occur here on Earth, the CIA scientists had to create a device that created this specific type of gamma ray.

"The gist of the plan was for Armstrong to plant this gamma ray-making device on the moon while he moonwalked. Gamma rays are inherently short wavelengths of radiation. Knowing this, they calculated in order to ignite the DNA response in the infected animals, the moon had to get within

226,000 miles of Earth. There was no record this had ever happened before, but they believed that the supermoon slated to occur on November 14, 1970, would do precisely that, putting the moon the closest it's ever been to Earth before. Remember, Johnson required a control mechanism so things wouldn't get out of control. Putting this device on the moon was that mechanism. Once the moon orbited back to its normal distance from Earth, the effect on the animals was supposed to wear off. So theoretically, while the animals were on a killing spree against Charlie from the inside of the jungles, our military would strategically attack the Viet Cong into submission from the outside. Then the moon would release its grip on the animals, and the Vietnam conflict would be resolved. But bigger than that, if this mission succeeded, the US would effectively have a weapon that could be manipulated at specific intervals of the lunar calendar."

Rob sat there slack-jawed. Masters ignored the dubious look on Rob's face and pressed forward.

"So on July 20, 1969, while the world watched Armstrong leaping around up there, what they didn't see was he left behind this device armed and ready for the supermoon of November 14, 1970.

"Why didn't they just fly the gamma device over in an airplane. That would seem easiest and less costly," Rob wondered aloud.

"It required an enormous light source, I recall. A light source that already contained a whole other concoction of gamma radiation. Like our sun. Then there are a bunch of calculations they had to consider regarding axis tilt, the atmosphere, mirrors, timing, and a whole bunch of other smart-sounding things. That's why the moon was the best option. Frankly, I don't know, and I don't care. I'm just holding up my end of our bargain here," Masters snapped as he shook his head back and forth. Rob saw his exhaustion had mounted.

"So what happened with the mission set for 1970 in the jungle?" Rob asked. Nothing in history he could recall claimed anything about an animal uprising that turned the tide of the war.

"Nixon called it off at the last second. He took things in a more diplomatic direction and signed the Paris Peace Accords and brought our troops home. It's argued Johnson wanted a clear victory for the US and Nixon sold us out. But that is for historians to debate.

"The moon part of the weapon plan was already completed, however, and the gamma device still sits on the moon today. My theory is that the modified animal feed is out there somewhere. Your grandfather must have somehow obtained this experimental feed and fed it to his chickens. Then when the supermoon occurred in 1970, the reaction sent them into their evolutionary, murderous rampage.

"So Waylon was right! My grandfather wasn't crazy," Rob said proudly.

"No he wasn't crazy. But the CIA couldn't allow any DNA samples to be taken from the scene or any proof the animals were behind the craziness to get out. So to cover up what happened that night, they framed your grandfather as a lunatic that tried to murder his family. They performed a thorough cleansing of the scene. Then they took the cleansing a step further with your father, Tommy," Masters said, and paused to make sure Rob was still with him as he brought the story home. "They tried to cleanse his memories."

"What do you mean, cleanse his memories?" Rob asked.

"Your father struggled with his mental health after the incident. He suffered from post-traumatic stress disorder, now known as PTSD. It wasn't widely known how to diagnose and treat it back then. Your grandmother had him in and out of therapy for several years. The CIA was concerned Tommy had spilled some beans that could expose their secret during these therapy sessions. Rumors started to surface in the psychological community about what was really behind that night. The CIA convinced your grandmother to allow them to perform a series of treatments on Tommy that used an experimental serum to suppress his traumatic memories."

"Convinced? My sources tell me it was more like they forced her. She was against them," Rob cut in.

Masters continued like he hadn't heard. "These treatments and serum were also experimental discoveries that stemmed back to the Nazis, designed to eliminate the recollection of trauma-induced thoughts. The Nazis hoped to find a way to experiment on the general public eventually. They had great plans to control the minds of entire communities and eventually races of people. So they developed this serum. Unbeknownst to anyone at the time, it modified the victim's DNA.

For your dad, the serum seemed to work at first; the traumatic memories ceased. He was able to enter the army, graduate from college, marry, and have kids. He was the picture of happiness in America. Therefore the CIA deemed it a success. But the positive effects of the serum began to wear off and caused him terrible nightmares that robbed him of his sleep. And you know the rest, it ultimately sent him to the loony bin. That change in his XY DNA chromosomes was passed on to you, which later spawned your nightmare too. We haven't seen the nightmare phenomena in your sister, Mel. We suspect her being female with XX chromosomes, she didn't inherit the tainted XY DNA from your father," explained Masters.

"So you've been watching us?" Rob asked, alarmed.

"Rob, ever since that night in 1970, every member of your immediate family has been surveilled by the CIA. Everything from medical records and education records to shopping habits, vacations, and later each foster family you and Mel bounced between. Everything. Anything that might indicate the events from that night in 1970 might be resurfacing," Masters explained.

"So you saw what happened to Mel in Mesquite. You knew she ran away. You knew where she went! You know where she is now, too, don't you!" Rob accused, voice raised. His cheeks flushed red with anger.

"We were to monitor, not intervene. We allowed life to play out for you both," he pleaded.

"Bullshit!" Rob spat.

"I'm holding up my end of the bargain and telling you straight whether you like it or not. Whether it was right or wrong isn't up to me," Masters said between gritted teeth.

Robbed breathed deep. He knew being angry now would do him no good and he needed to hear the rest of this ridiculous tale.

As Rob worked to regain his composure, Masters continued, "Your father revealed with his doctor on a routine checkup that his sleep was being interrupted. That's how it got on our radar that something was up. I was assigned to his personal detail as special agent in charge. I took on an alias and posed as someone who just moved into town. I joined the same country club as your folks and befriended both him and Nancy. I hung out in the same circles to listen and watch."

When Rob heard his mom's name he flashed back to his nightmare. How his mother scrubbed blood with blood as she raved about a new man in her life. Raved about HIM. How the best thing Rob's dad ever did was to introduce her to HIM. Rob's subconscious must have remembered Masters and placed him behind the door when his mom opened it. The passing time added the vagueness of HIS face in his nightmare. But now the face was clear. Rob's suspicions were confirmed. His mother did run out on them with another man. The same man sitting in front of him now. Rage began to build in his gut as he fought against the plastic tie around his wrists.

Chapter Twenty-Eight

"Monitor and not intervene, huh?" Rob seethed.

The motel room grew warmer as the tension and anger built inside Rob. He had never in his life wanted to hurt anyone. But here and now he wanted blood from this narcissistic monster.

"Correct," Masters confirmed.

"Having the affair with my mom that wrecked our family? That sent me and Mel into foster care? That pushed her into the hands of a child molester and ultimately into prostitution! You don't think that is intervening, you asshole?" Rob was enraged. He pulled fiercely on the plastic tie and could feel it cut into his wrists. "All of that was your fault! How was that just letting our lives play out?" A moment passed, and Rob whispered, "I will never help you." A tear slid down his cheek knowing all he and Mel went through could have been avoided, except this guy had to prey on their mother.

Masters stood up quickly. Rob prepared to be assaulted, but Masters caught himself and just stared at Rob. His chest heaved in aggravation.

"Your mother was a mistake! I admit that. She was a wonderful woman and was in despair over your father. I was going through a rough patch in my life too. It just happened. I had nothing to do with her abandoning you and Mel though. That was her choice!" Masters screamed, and paced the room.

Rob just stared at the floor. The sight of Masters sickened him. He just wanted this to be over.

"So what happened between you two?" Rob asked after several minutes.

"When I found out she left you both with the neighbor and had no intentions of going back, I realized it had gone too far. Your dad was just committed and she wanted to be free. I couldn't blame her after what she went through, but dumping her kids? I couldn't be a part of that. I broke it off with her and asked to be reassigned. When the affair became known to my superiors, I was asked to retire. I had crossed a line, broken protocol and gotten personally involved," Masters said, now exhausted further. He sat back on the bed and looked at Rob.

"Last I heard she lives in San Diego. I haven't talked to her in years. I'm sorry, Rob. I truly am, but it is done, and there is no going back."

They looked at each other in silence.

"Help me now and I will be out of your life forever. I assure you," Masters said finally.

"You never explained why you are having nightmares. If this condition is genetic, why is it affecting you?" Rob wondered.

"Because I later received the same treatments and serum your father did," Masters admitted.

"Whoa, wait. Why would you get them?"

"I suffered from PTSD after an assignment in Belize tracking a drug cartel shipment. My partner and I were captured and tortured. It was New Year's Eve back in 1999. The DEA had their hands full with the failure of the war on drugs. Their resources were stretched thin. The CIA agreed to loan them our assistance since we had experience in that region. For six months we followed shipments of cocaine out of Colombia. Our mission was to see where the handoff point was between them and a Mexican cartel that would later process the drugs and move them into the US. Both were brutal regimes. It was impromptu, but my dark features and her Hispanic heritage allowed us to blend in well enough. We posed as husband-and-wife fishermen. We worked the same sea lanes we figured the runs were being made.

"Your partner was a woman?" Rob asked.

"Yes. We had worked together before on other clandestine missions in Venezuela that were more political in nature. Nothing this dangerous, but we knew the area well enough."

Rob could see guilt begin to mingle with his exhaustion and knew this story wasn't going to end well. This was the second time he had heard of cartels in as many days. The first was a remark Waylon had made about the two main prostitution rings in Dallas being run by cartels. He shivered to think Mel might be wrapped up with them.

Masters, who was lost in the recollection of the story, continued, "Finally, after months of fishing the area, we were approached by the Colombians to run a shipment up the coast to Belize. We worked with the local DEA assets to arrange an intercept in the small border city of Chetumal. We found it was there the handoffs were being made into Mexico. Once we delivered the shipment, the DEA was to take it from there. Then we could walk away. Everything worked out like we planned, and my partner and I were clear to return to the states. Our extraction was set for New Year's Eve, but we were in a fun city. It's not often we were between assignments. We needed a minute to decompress and just be human. So I pulled some strings and rescheduled the extraction until the next evening."

Regret seized guilt and twisted Masters's face as he painfully retraced his footsteps of the past. Rob sensed each emotion etched on Masters's face. Through his finely tuned ability to read people, he would usually use what he saw to make himself invisible. To blend in. Now he let the emotional rollercoaster take him. He felt the steep, slow climb up the biggest hill of this ride and knew the other side was going to be a devastating drop. But right now Masters had him teetering at the precipice. Rob braced himself for the descent.

"We were at a small coastal cantina that opened up to the beach. Loud music, lights, and laughter made a wonderful setting. We split fajitas and lined up a couple of shooters each of tequila. Stress just melted off in the humid heat with each shot. We were just enjoying the moment. Not as a couple, although she was pretty enough, but I respected her as my partner, not just an attractive woman. It was fun to see her let her hair down, so to speak," Masters said.

Masters had his eyes down on his fingers as he picked at his nails. A smile played delicately on his lips as if it had no business being there with what was to come across them next. Rob barely breathed, scared any noise may chase it away.

"We danced off the fajitas and set up another round of tequila. We toasted the moment and chased it with a warm local beer. On the beach, fireworks overtook the music, so we went over where a throng of couples began to form. Several kids ran back and forth from an ice chest full of mortars to a group of large tubes, lighting this fuse then that fuse. So we stood there and watched the colorful bursts in the dark sky.

From behind I felt a barrel of a gun in my back and a voice in my ear to stay still. Four men with guns had us walk away from the group and blindfolded us. Then, bang, it was lights out. When I awoke I was gagged and tied to a chair in a concrete room. My partner was chained to the wall naked and unconscious. She was battered but breathing. She had already been raped. The evidence of that mingled with the blood that ran down her thighs. Two men bragged about it as they dressed. One of them saw I was awake and told me the doctor would be there soon. But it wouldn't be a doctor to help her."

At this Masters worked his jaw and blinked hard. Rob felt the descent of the roller coaster underway as it gained momentum.

"The doctor turned out to be the interrogator who gained information for the leader of this group. He was a short, smug man with small round glasses. I remember thinking if I got the chance to break free I was going to embed them into his nose. But I never got the chance. He carried a large black medical bag. Out of it he began to place various tools on a table. He hooked an IV bag of fluid on a pole then expertly fed the needle into her wrist. He worked as if this was a routine procedure. He seemed detached from the situation. Because of that detachment, I knew then, this was about to go very bad. He followed a habitual process, like we were lab rats and this was just one more test on the docket for him before he got to go home to his wife and kids.

"Apparently, the DEA succeeded, and they intercepted the shipment, which exposed the Mexicans because that was the focus of the interrogation: how we did it and how many more raids were scheduled and when. They used my partner as leverage against me, but because our involvement was limited with the DEA, I didn't have much useful information. The DEA knew the bigger picture. She and I were just borrowed resources for the moment. Of course, the doctor didn't believe a word of that, so he proceeded to torture us. More so her than me."

There was a long pause.

"He took her apart limb by limb and processed her like an animal," he whispered.

Rob listened, horrified. He felt his stomach tighten to fight back a heave.

Masters lowered his head as he wiped his eyes.

"I'm sorry," was all Rob could say as the bile from his stomach pressed up his throat.

Masters's eyes were wet, and he exhaled a huge, haggard breath.

"For years after, when I closed my eyes, I still heard her pleas to them to just end the agony. To kill her. I could still see her in pieces neatly stacked on the table." Masters breathed in deep and stood. He walked over to the bureau and rested his hands on it. He looked at himself in the bureau's mirror and sucked in another deep breath then exhaled.

"Your father's early success with the Nazi serum had encouraged us. We figured we could use the same procedure for agents in the field who suffered trauma like I had. It's more common than people know, as most everything we do is buried in deep classifications. So I took the same serum treatments. It worked for a while, but like with your father, it began to wear off. And the memories are coming back now with a vengeance. It's as if they are amplified. Just like I am reliving it, but with exaggerations. Like I am in a trance and must follow a script. If Dr. Sheltie doesn't help me, I will go completely crazy."

Rob understood that despair. Not long ago he felt that same way too. Helping Masters didn't seem like such a bad thing now he felt he knew the man's motivation. But why was there a CIA search for Masters, since his trauma wasn't tied to a national security cover-up? Or was it?

"I assume the CIA covered up the incident in Belize?" asked Rob.

"Of course. It's what they do best. But the bigger cover-up wasn't what happened back then in Belize. It was who it happened to." Masters turned and looked at Rob. He ran his tongue across his front teeth and considered if he should elaborate.

"My partner was the daughter of Trey Lett. Then the Senate majority leader who was threatening to pull the plug on the war on drugs funding. Now he is the newly appointed national intelligence director."

"He doesn't know what happened to her?"

"Not entirely. He was led to believe she was kidnapped and still may be alive at the hands of the cartels. Both the DEA and the CIA hoped, as the head of the Senate, if Lett knew there was a chance his daughter was alive, he would continue to press the Senate to fund their war on these cartels in the hopes she would be rescued. So much was invested in that war they needed it to continue.

"Now that the CIA is under him as the director of national intelligence, certain bureaucrats in both agencies are trying very hard to make sure he never learns they sanctioned his daughter into such a reckless assignment and then lied about its outcome for their own gain. If there is any chance it may become exposed, these bureaucrats will eliminate the sources of the exposure to contain those secrets," Masters replied.

"In our own right, you and I have become liabilities to the CIA," Rob stated.

"It appears so, master Rob. And our survival may now be tied to us becoming allies against them," Masters acknowledged.

Rob nodded affirmatively.

"So let's make that call to Sheltie. Shall we?" Masters said as he held up his cell phone.

Chapter Twenty-Nine

The cell phone vibrated across the nightstand. It pushed a plastic aspirin bottle to the floor and rested against a half-empty glass of water. The vibrations against the glass were like a chorus of bells that jingled in short bursts. In the dark from under a plush Hilton embossed bedspread, Dr. Sheltie reached for it. She saw the late hour and the caller. She cleared her throat and answered.

"Chelsea? Is everything okay? It's just after 1:00 AM."

"Hello, Dr. Sheltie. I am so sorry to bother you. Rob Florchett keeps calling me. I don't know how he got my number. I told him I would have you call him in the morning, but he won't take no for an answer. I would turn off my phone, but my daughter is staying with a friend and in case of an emergency, you know?" Chelsea explained, highly irritated.

"Rob? Did he leave a number?" Dr. Sheltie asked. She was sitting up now, doing her best to clear the fog of sleep.

"I got the caller ID number," Chelsea replied, and recited the number.

"Thank you, Chelsea," she said, and abruptly hung up. She dialed the number Chelsea gave her.

***

Rob sat with his feet up on the bed in just his boxer shorts at the Shangri La. He hoped he wasn't being invaded by hungry crotch critters. He applied a cotton ball of peroxide from his backpack to his wrists where the plastic tie had dug in. The scabs where Dr. Sheltie dug in her nails a couple of days ago had opened back up where the tie rubbed, and that stung too. The hot shower felt amazing, and sitting there on the bed all clean made him very sleepy. Masters had left to grab them a pizza from an all-night joint on the main drag of Addison.

For the last half hour Rob had bombarded Chelsea with calls to get Dr. Sheltie to call him. Chelsea, true to her boss, made every effort to put Rob off and not disturb Dr. Sheltie this late at night. He didn't think she was going to, especially after she threatened to call the cops. He was just about to make another attempt when his burner phone rang.

"Dr. Sheltie?" he answered, hopeful.

"Rob! Oh my God, are you okay?" Dr. Sheltie asked, hopeful too.

"Yes, for the moment anyways."

"Thank God," she breathed. "I know where your father is but didn't know how to get ahold of you to tell you."

"That's great news, but we may need to put that on hold. Some things have come up. Rather a few things," Rob said. He wasn't sure how to broach this. He knew she would be adamantly against anything to do with Masters after what happened. "I need a huge favor."

"Of course. What is it?"

"You're not gonna want to do it."

"I'll do whatever I can. You know that."

"Do you trust me?"

"Rob! Just freakin' ask me already," Dr. Sheltie blurted.

Rob paused and swallowed as he tried to moisten his now-dry throat. "Rob? Are you there?"

"I need you to do to Benjamin Masters what you did for me to stop my nightmare," Rob said finally. A moment passed, and it was Rob who now thought the call had dropped. "Dr. Sheltie?"

"Okay," Dr. Sheltie answered, confused.

"Uhm, great. I figured you may not be inclined to agree, considering . . . things," Rob said, now confused as well.

"I trust if you are asking me this, then there is a good reason. I also trust you are not setting me up or putting me in danger."

"No way, I mean the being set up part. I would never do that to you. But I can't guarantee the danger part. I think because of everything that has occurred over the last few days, you may be being watched by some dangerous people who may be banking on me asking you this favor for Masters."

"The black sedan people."

"Yes, but Masters is on the wrong side of them too. Too much to explain now, but he needs your help badly."

"He is having the dream now?"

"Yes and no. We shouldn't talk too much on the phone. In an hour, go down to the front desk, and there will be a package with instructions. Follow them to the letter and remember, Masters can be trusted," Rob implored and hung up. He hoped his intuition was right. That Masters was indeed a good guy and could be trusted and Rob wasn't sending Dr. Sheltie into peril.

At that moment Masters burst into the room with his gun drawn.

Chapter Thirty

"You alone?" Masters asked as he swept the motel room with his gun. He put the pizza box on the bureau, walked quickly to the small bathroom area, and peeked behind the door. From there he opened the closet. Satisfied, he turned to Rob.

Rob could see the weariness wreaking havoc on Masters. He wondered if he was now teetering on the verge of sane.

"Yeah. You okay?" Rob asked cautiously. He wanted to trust Masters but was still wary.

"I'm fine. You speak to Sheltie?"

"Yes."

"And?" Masters prompted, impatient.

"She said yes, she will help you."

Masters exhaled in relief. "Good. Let's head over to the Hilton so I can drop off her instructions where to meet us," Masters said.

"You go ahead," Rob replied. "I think I am going to rest a bit. If Dr. Sheltie needs to get ahold of me, she has my info now."

"Gimme your number," Masters said and pulled out his cell phone. Rob did, and Masters texted Rob his own cell number.

"Okay, I'll head over to the Hilton. Call me if you need me," Masters said. And with that, he was out the door.

Rob stood and got dressed. He grabbed a slice of the pizza then took a bite. He noticed two slices were missing. He checked the time. It was 2:09 AM. He set the small dining table back on its legs. He took the laptop out of his backpack and set it on the table then opened its lid. He entered the Shangri

La's Wi-Fi code and repeated the steps Waylon had taught him to access the dark web. He brought up the page with Mel's alias and picture in the Tor browser. He found the number to order her services and dialed it.

"Tonya's," a gruff male voice answered.

"Yes, I'd like to meet a girl," Rob said, nervous. He'd never solicited a prostitute and found it intimidated him. Even felt a little dirty.

"Give me your number," the gruff voice demanded.

"My phone number?"

"Yeah, your phone number."

Rob did, and the call clicked off. Moments later Rob's phone rang. The caller ID said Restricted Call.

"You got a girl in mind or first available?" the gruff voice asked.

"Is Crystal Bunny available?"

"No. Pick another one."

"I'd really prefer her." Rob began to sweat.

"And I would really prefer you pick another one. I got two sittin' here in front of me that will have your rocks popped like you ain't never had. Cheaper and better looking too."

Silence, as Rob considered how to answer. He wasn't interested in getting his rocks popped. He was only interested in a meetup with Mel.

"Look, call me back when you decide," the gruff voice said, and clicked off the line.

Rob sat there and wondered if he had just blown his chance. What would a determined john do in this situation?

Pay more.

Rob dialed the number back.

"Tonya's."

"Yes, I was calling about Crystal Bunny and . . ."

"I told you, pal, she ain't available. Either pick another or first available or fuck off!"

"I'll pay triple her rate."

There was a moment of silence, and then the gruff voice said, "Wait a sec."

The sound of the phone receiver against a shirt was heard. Rob could hear a muffled voice but couldn't make out the words. The phone shook in his hand as he waited.

"You done business with us before?" the gruff voice asked, back on the line.

Rob wasn't sure how to answer. It was like a Choose Your Own Adventure book he read as a kid. If he chose wrong, he figured the gruff voice would dump the call and the story would end there and he would never find Mel. He could see the illustrated page exaggerate the failed choice and his character devastated.

So he said, "Yes. A couple times."

"Eight fifty. One shot at goal. Straight up play, and you pay her up front. Don't make her ask for it."

Given this was Rob's first ever solicitation attempt, he had no idea what the jargon meant nor how much a normal hourly rate might be. Again, he chose his answer carefully so he didn't tip off the gruff voice he was a newbie, but most importantly, to keep the adventure book going.

"Fine, no problem," Rob said with as much conviction as possible. Eight fifty? Yikes. He might have eighty dollars in his pocket.

The gruff voice asked for the location of the meeting, and Rob answered the Shangri La Inn and gave the room number.

"Might be three hours or so."

"Three hours or so?" Rob blurted. That would be around 5:00 AM.

"She's a popular girl, pal. You're lucky I was able to get you in her rotation at all. Just sit tight. It'll be worth it," the gruff voice explained and clicked off the line.

"Three hours or so," Rob said to himself. "Geez."

He finished his pizza and took a second slice. He went and sat on the bed. He grabbed the TV remote to flip on the tube and remembered it was busted on the floor by the door. So he sat there as he thought and munched his pizza. His mind trolled through everything Masters had told him. He recalled one comment Masters had made about how he thought there may still be some of that modified animal feed out there somewhere and the gamma ray device still active on the moon. He wondered what the odds were that tomorrow night another family might get ruined by an animal abomination. The thought sent a chill up his back, and he lost his appetite. He laid the pizza on the nightstand then set the bedside alarm for 4:30 AM. Once the alarm was set he lay on the bed, above the covers, and closed his eyes now eager for the Sandmeister to whisk him to dreamland.

Chapter Thirty-One

Dr. Sheltie rode the elevator down to the lobby of the Richardson Hilton. It was deserted and the lights were dimmed, so she couldn't wear her large dark shades, or she feared she might trip over something. She approached the front desk. A young lady saw her through a window of what looked like a small office, and she stood. She walked around a shelf toward the opposite side of the front desk and flipped on a friendly smile. She looked too fresh and pristine to be on the graveyard shift. Her dark hair was done up neat and tight. Her skin was smooth and perfect. Dr. Sheltie suddenly felt very self-conscious about her bruised and swollen face, which came fully displayed under the brighter lights above the front desk. The young lady's name tag read Cassandra.

"May I help you?" Cassandra asked.

"I think so," Dr. Sheltie replied. "Would you happen to have a package for Dr. Sheltie?"

"Hold on a sec," Cassandra said with a warm smile. She pretended not to notice Dr. Sheltie's black eye. "Let me go look," she said politely.

She walked back around the shelf into the small office. Dr. Sheltie turned and looked around the deserted lobby. The Hilton radio network lightly piped in Kenny G or some other elevator jazz all around her. Outside the glass doors that led out was eerie black darkness. Dr. Sheltie reached into her purse and squeezed her Sig Sauer. Right now she was grateful Rob had put it back in her purse before he dragged her out of her fiery home office. Feeling its thick, tacky grip helped to calm her nerves.

"Yes, here you are," Cassandra said as she came around the shelf with a padded envelope in her hand. She laid it on the counter. Handwritten with a Sharpie was the word "Sheltie." She picked it up and thanked Cassandra. Cassandra told her it was her pleasure with a concerned look on her face. Dr. Sheltie felt pity from her and interpreted Cassandra's response as it was least she could do for such a clearly abused woman.

Dr. Sheltie walked over to a group of chairs and sofa and sat down. She tore open the padded envelope and looked inside. There was a small rectangular black box and a note stuck to it that read, "Put this in your center console then turn left and just drive."

She looked up puzzled. Drive where? She assumed the device Masters asked she put in her console was for him to track her. Her skin crawled with goosebumps knowing she was being watched by the man. She didn't trust him, but she trusted Rob, so she pocketed the device, gathered the envelope, and walked over to a trash receptacle and threw it in. Then she exited into the eerie darkness beyond the glass doors.

Two minutes and a brisk walk later, she pulled out of the parking garage in her Spyder. She turned left and just drove. Fifteen minutes later she was headed North on Highway 75 into Plano, Texas. All the cities in North Dallas overlap, and the only way to really know which city a person is in is to read the water towers. They seemed to loom tall and dark like sentries sent to guard the city borders. She now passed one with a massive eagle lit up on its side that announced she had left Plano and entered the small community of Allen.

The highway wasn't crowded at this hour. But still, Dr. Sheltie watched all her mirrors. She tracked one set of headlights that seemed to pace her speed a few cars behind her. When she passed someone, it would too. Now it pulled up beside her. It was a black sedan. She could see the reflection of the street lights in its side windows. The driver's one rolled down and revealed the face of Benjamin Masters. Dr. Sheltie's stomach cringed. Her first instinct was to mash the gas pedal down and leave the slimeball in the Spyder's dust. Instead she looked over at him and motioned with her hands, "You found me, now what?"

Masters mouthed the words, "Follow me."

He motioned with his thumb to get behind him, and the black sedan accelerated. Dr. Sheltie fell in behind it as it exited the highway. She followed Masters for another few miles as they wound in and out of subdivisions. The houses here were stacked together like cordwood. The area boomed with all the corporations that fled the oppressive business climates of California and New York, but it was like these folks lived on top of each other. The houses were of the same three designs. All brick. All perfectly landscaped on postage-stamp-sized lots. There was a large two-story version, a medium two-story version, and a smaller one-story version. She began to calculate how many houses must be squeezed into each block, when the taillights of the black sedan lit up. It turned into the driveway of one of the thousand versions of the one-story model. Masters got out and punched a code into a keypad next to the garage door. It opened slowly. Inside was empty. He then pulled the black sedan into the left spot and exited. He motioned for Dr. Sheltie to pull into the right one.

Once parked she killed the engine. She slowly eased out of the Porsche and looked across the hood of the black sedan as Masters waited. She stood there not sure what to say to the man across from her.

After a long pause Masters said, "I'm sorry."

"You should be," Dr. Sheltie answered immediately. She could see now why Rob had asked her to help him. He looked like warmed-over hell. His hair was a mess and now looked more of salt than pepper. He was unshaven, and his clothes crumpled. But it was his eyes that gave away the desperation. He had deep purple circles around them, and they were a dulled haze.

"What is this place?" she asked, with hopes to move past the awkward silence.

"It's a CIA safe house."

"Is it safe to be here? I figure they would monitor a place like this for uninvited guests."

"They do. And who said we are uninvited?" he said, and turned. He pressed the button to lower the garage door. He felt on top of the house's door frame for a key. He found one and unlocked the door. Dr. Sheltie heard the security system's chime and the beeps that counted down the seconds before the alarm sounded. She was hesitant about the whole situation now. If the CIA knew she was here, was she being set up after all? Did Rob make that call to ask her to help Masters under duress? She didn't think to ask if he had a gun to head. Dammit, how could she be so gullible?

Masters punched in the disarm code into the alarm keypad in time. He saw Dr. Sheltie freeze in place and could see her apprehension. He exhaled like a teacher that held out borrowed patience for a problem student they knew had potential.

"The CIA is fractured, Dr. Sheltie," he explained. "There are those rooted in the past and those dedicated to its future."

"Which do you subscribe to?"

"Those dedicated to its future."

"Which side should I be most concerned about?"

"Those rooted in the past."

She slowly walked around the black sedan. She could feel the heat from both of the V-8 beasts as they ticked and hissed as they cooled.

The door led into the kitchen. Masters closed it behind her and locked it. Then she punched the alarm's active code into the keypad. The light switched from green to red. Armed.

"Make yourself at home, but not for too long. We have business to tend to," Masters said as he took off his coat.

The house had that eerie quietness of being empty for quite some time. It was simple and had the feel of contractor-grade everything. It was cold but kept up. She took off her own coat and draped it over the back of a breakfast table's chair. Moments later she could hear the furnace engage, and the smell of burnt dust blew from the vents. She went into the living room.

"So before we get into our business, help me understand how the CIA knows we are here and that isn't putting us in danger of that same CIA?"

"I still have friends. Friends that believe the hunt for me is bogus and help me stay invisible. I would never betray the CIA, no matter what memories resurface. But there are those hellbent on maintaining the cover-up and taking no chances."

"I don't understand what you are talking about. What cover-up?" she said, even further confused.

"You'll see soon enough. Now let's get this show on the road." Masters said and sat on the couch.

Dr. Sheltie tried not to become flustered at all his cryptic answers. "This is going to take some time and there are risks. Especially if we are interrupted."

"I hear you, Doctor. We won't be interrupted. I assure you."

Dr. Sheltie set her jaw as they locked eyes.

"Very well. Lie back and get comfortable," Dr. Sheltie instructed. She then perched on the edge of the coffee table and took Masters's hand in hers. It was calloused and heavy. His fingers were like a hand of bananas. She gripped his wrist so her thumb was on his pulse like Dr. Klaskin had trained her.

"Close your eyes. I need you to relax. You mustn't become distressed. It's important you stay calm," she softly instructed. She debated revealing the safe word and decided against it. She wasn't sure why, but maybe it was the dull throbs of pain that coursed across her cheek still.

"Take me to a place where you feel most at ease and calm. Describe it to me."

Masters began the description of his happy place as Dr. Sheltie's eyes closed dreamily.

Chapter Thirty-Two

Mel stumbled down the stairs of an apartment complex. She didn't even know where it was located. So much was blurred together. She had no idea what time it was except it was still dark. This night seemed to go on forever as she continued her rush to atone. There wasn't a single part or area of her body that didn't ache or wasn't raw. By her calculations she had another eight appointments before noon. She hadn't slept in two days. Bronco gave her a shot to boost her energy, but it wore thin already. She wasn't sure what the concoction was, but she knew she hated how disconnected from reality it made her feel. Her head swam as she walked across the parking lot to the Escalade as it idled. She was too tired to be angry with this john for lack of payment and didn't care enough to feel sorry for him about what was to come.

Bronco could see she wasn't coming around to get in, instead continuing a straight line to his driver-side window. He liked these moments because it usually meant he got to punch somebody. And he was bored. The night had been uneventful.

Bronco rolled down the window.

"Que pasa, chica?" he asked in a deep voice. He flexed his fist as he hung it out the window.

"He didn't pay," was all Mel had the energy to say.

Bronco eyed her close.

"Did you even try and get it from him?" Bronco asked in heavily accented English. He used a thick tongue to move a toothpick from one side of his mouth to the other in a slow, exaggerated fashion.

"I make the love. You make the war. I did my part," Mel said, then without thought wiped her mouth and looked away.

If Bronco came up short on the reconciliation of the payments versus the number of appointments sent to his phone, he knew even a huge tough guy like him was just flesh and bone bullets could rip through with ease. And who he reported to had lots and lots of bullets.

He turned off the Escalade and opened his door. His huge size-14 Redwing boot crunched on the pavement as his six-foot, five-inch frame slid off the plush seat.

"Get in the truck," he said and pocketed the Escalade's keys. He rolled his shoulders backward then forward. He twisted his neck to the left and then to the right. Each motion delivered a sharp crack. Then he purposely strode toward the apartment's stairs. Mel eagerly rounded the front of the Escalade and got in with the hopes of a few quiet minutes to nap while Bronco meted out his justice. But he was always so damn fast. She wished sometimes he would just savor the moment. Within seconds of settling into the soft leather, she was asleep and never heard the shatter of a picture glass window, a man's scream as he approached the earth headfirst with increased velocity. Then the crunch of head and earth as they collided. Mel awoke when the Escalade bounced into the parking lot of the Shangri La Motel.

Just two minutes prior, Rob awoke with a start as the bedside alarm clock berated him in its shrill voice. Sleepily, he slapped it until it stopped. He felt like he was made of lead. His sleep was so deep he almost drifted back into its depths then realized where he was and his reason for being there. With much effort he pushed himself onto his feet and shuffled into the small bathroom area. He splashed his face with cold water then dried it with a threadbare towel that just pushed the wetness around his face rather than absorb it.

A knock on the door jolted his system.

"Mel," he breathed.

He turned and walked to the door. He squinted his left eye and focused his right out through the peephole. A female with a bulbous head stood there on the other side. The headlights of an SUV glared behind her. He took a few breaths. He hoped to practice what he was going to say, which was why he set his alarm for 4:30 AM. So much for three or so hours. He'd have to wing it.

She knocked again—this time with a touch of aggravation.

One last breath in and out.

He opened the door, and it clanged hard against the security chain.

"Sorry!" he squeaked nervously. He fumbled with the chain. The stupid thing wouldn't let go. He fumbled it again.

"Good," Mel thought, "a newbie." She figured she could get in and take a much-needed shower to wake up and clean off. Then she could give this john her CliffsNotes version of her best skills and be back in the Escalade ready for some strong coffee and breakfast within the hour.

Rob finally unlatched the chain and pulled the door open. Mel strode in and set her clutch on the bureau and took out her phone. The muscles in her jaw worked as she smacked a stick of Juicy Fruit. She didn't bother to acknowledge Rob was there as he still held open the door. She didn't, because she didn't have to. She knew she had the power over johns, especially newbies. Plenty of her young flesh was on display to keep them speechless for the first few minutes while she texted Bronco the "good to go" message and then got settled. They always stood there with the same dumb look on their face while their two brains battled to take control of their unimpressive bodies. Johns could be so stupid. This john seemed no exception. Even worn-out tired she knew she looked to kill in her too-tight, too-short dress that made her modest chest look twice as full and her long, athletic legs look like they never ended.

Rob inhaled the scent of cotton candy, cigarettes, and female sweat as it blew past him in her wake. "That smell should be bottled," he thought as his body involuntarily reacted. He was stunned to see his little sis not so little any longer. He tried to speak, but no sound left his lips.

"I'm gonna grab a shower, honey," she said, still no acknowledgment of Rob. "But don't worry. I'll make up in my efforts what I borrow from your time." She turned and went into the shower area of the bathroom and closed the door.

Rob slowly closed the room door. He peeked out the window and was relieved to see the SUV drive away. He turned and just stood there as the shower turned on. He walked over to the bureau mirror and looked at himself. It looked like a cow had licked the entire right side of his head. A bad case of bedhead. He tried to smooth it down, but no luck. He abandoned the effort as he struggled with the thought of Mel coming back into the room. What was he going to say to her?

"Mel. It's me, your bro," he practiced. No, that sounded corny. "Hey, Mel. It's been a while. You look great!" "Uggh, no," he thought.

For the next couple minutes he tried to find the right line. Then the shower stopped. For a second he thought his heart did too.

The shower room door opened, and Mel walked out wearing a towel around her body and another covering her head as she vigorously dried her hair. Rob gulped. She leaned forward, took down the towel she used to dry her hair and slung the wet mess backward and stood up straight. In that instant, their eyes locked together. Simultaneously, they both inhaled quickly. For several seconds they just stood there in disbelief.

"I leave you alone for seven years and now I find you ordering hookers?" she said as her look held Rob in mock contempt.

He blinked and stammered. Her comment totally threw him. Then he smiled and laughed. Mel ran to him, and they hugged in an embrace beyond tight. They continued to crush each other and began to cry. They sobbed for several minutes and refused to let go of each other as headlights swept the room around them. Bronco was back.

Chapter Thirty-Three

Another dry heave racked Dr. Sheltie's body as she vomited bile. The contents of her stomach were already emptied from her initial effort to sell Buicks to the kitchen sink. Her whole body convulsed as she gripped the Formica countertop. She shuddered, afraid if she moved it would trigger another empty spasm. After a few seconds she felt it was safe to finally run the water and wash out her mouth. She took several deep breaths and tried not to focus on the horrible images now tattooed on the insides of her eyelids. The concrete room, two men in chairs. One was reading a porno magazine turned long ways, centerfold style, and the other counted a pile of money. Neither paid any attention to the short guy with round spectacles as he systematically took a woman's body apart piece by excruciatingly little piece. He skillfully did it in a way that maximized the number of breaths she took from the limited number of them she had left. He stacked each piece removed in neat piles on the table. Like when a mechanic dismantles a motor and needs to keep the parts organized for reassembly. Dr. Sheltie could still see the woman's heart rapidly beating through the bloody window in her chest where ribs had been removed. Her lungs pressed out over and over behind the few exposed ones that remained. The woman's screams, more like her pleas, to just die echoed in Dr. Sheltie's head.

Another heave, and this time she felt her swollen eye might explode as she strained. Near suffocation, she sucked in a gulp of air and picked up a dried, hardened dish rag laid over the center of the sink. She ran water over it to soften it back to life. She wiped her face gently and turned to look into the living room. On the couch Masters snored deeply. Her efforts to relieve him of his nightmare seemed to have worked. But to what end for herself? She went to the fridge and opened the door. She was relieved to see three bottled waters. She took one and held it to her swollen cheek, then opened it and drank deeply. The cold water felt good as it washed her stomach acid back into its proper place. She walked into the living room and collapsed into the oversized recliner and passed out.

***

Meanwhile back in room 113 of the Shangri La Inn, Rob brought Mel up to speed on the events from the last few days. It was a lot to discuss in the forty minutes they had left on Rob's dime, and he could tell Mel understood little of it. They heard a short beep from a horn outside. It was Bronco's two-minute warning. Mel and Rob jerked their heads to the window then looked back at each other.

"I gotta get going," she said, and went to the bureau to get her purse.

"Where are you gonna go?" Rob asked, surprised. She walked back to Rob, who sat on the bed.

"I have to go. Now I know how to find you. I will contact you later, but now I have to leave." She then held out her hand and flipped her fingers in the universal signal for "hand it over."

"I need the money," she said.

"What money?" Rob asked, confused. Beep, beep, from Bronco.

"Rob, really. I have to go. I need the $850 you promised to pay." Panic filled her voice. Rob sat there unsure what to say. He certainly didn't have $850. Not even close.

Mel shook her head slowly then faster. "No, no, no, Rob. Don't tell me you don't have it!" she began to cry and paced back and forth.

"Tell numbnuts out there I skipped out, or I can just take off running. I doubt he can catch me. This has to happen all the time, right? Deadbeats? What's the big deal?"

Mel just stared as the tears rolled. "He will kill you. They will find you and kill you. Especially for $850 dollars! Rob, what the hell were you thinking to agree to pay that?" Mel was tired and going into shock. "You don't mess with these people, and Branco is by far the last one you stiff the payment on." She held her hand to her forehead in disbelief. "And certainly not right now with what I am going through. This could get me killed too!"

Rob didn't understand why she was so freaked. But clearly she was, and that began to scare him. Mel's phone dinged that she received a new text message.

She looked at her phone and breathed, "Shit."

"What?"

"I got thirty seconds and then he's coming in."

Rob wished Masters was here. He would think of something clever to do. Or he would just shoot it out. But Rob didn't have a gun. What would Masters do in this situation without a gun? Rob knew he wouldn't just sit here, uncertain.

"I got an idea, listen. Remember in school when . . . ?" and Rob quickly explained the rest.

"You're nuts," Mel said in disbelief. "That's your plan?"

"You got a better one?"

Without an answer she rolled her eyes, turned on her high heel and walked out the door. Rob followed and stood on the sidewalk in front of the large plate glass window of room 113. Mel continued her walk directly to Bronco's driver-side window.

Bronco saw the scrawny white guy come out after Crystal Bunny. He stood there on the sidewalk and held a backpack like a kid at a school bus stop.

From the look on the poor chump's face, he was sad his time was up. Kid must've been desperate to pay so much for sex. But to each their own, Bronco thought. It just increased his cut of the pie. He must have been an energetic dynamo to take Crystal Bunny the full ride, though. Her in-and-out average was thirty-two minutes, so Casanova over there must have a shovel in his pants. Bronco smirked to himself as he thought further into that.

Then he saw Bunny's trajectory wasn't toward the passenger-side door, which would mean the meeting was complete and they could move on. He was hungry. It was to the driver's-side door, which meant his truck was to stay parked and there would be a situation that must be dealt with. His smirk faded, and instantly, his blood pressure shot up. He gripped the wheel so hard it bent. Crystal Bunny walked to his window and just stood there. His eyes were glued on the wimpy kid who also just stood there. His lizard brain felt something was amiss. He rolled down his window. He didn't take his eyes off the kid.

"He didn't pay," she said quietly.

"What?" Bronco said, teeth clenched tight. His eyes locked straight ahead.

Mel swallowed, then said, "He doesn't have the money."

"Chingada madre," Bronco spat.

He opened the door and slammed it shut. He didn't pull the keys from the ignition this time. He was too pissed, and deviated from his own standard operating procedure for these types of situations. He wasn't about to supplement this financial shortfall from his own wallet; $200 was one thing, but $850? No chance. He stomped toward Rob. His anger rose with each step. Rob saw the mountain of a man as he exited the SUV and started toward him. He now agreed with Mel how stupid his plan might actually be.

Once Bronco was zeroed in on Rob, Mel slipped out of her heels and stalked quietly behind him. She saw Rob stand there like a frightened child as its father approached to dish out some tough love for disobedience. But Mel figured what was to be dished out here wouldn't be love and far more deadlier than tough. Rob, in turn, watched Mel as she struggled to keep pace with the behemoth's long strides. He feared she might not close the distance in time. Right as Bronco stepped over the parking block with his left foot, Mel kicked his right one across it, which caused his legs to tangle. At that precise moment, Rob dropped to his hands and knees. Bronco now twisted to see who kicked him just as Mel launched forward like a tightly coiled spring. Her long, strong legs fully extended, and she gave Bronco the hardest shove she could gather. With his own legs still knotted, they hit against Rob's body, and Bronco flew face-first into the large plate glass window. Glass erupted into the motel room with a crash.

Bronco slammed his neck across the window's jagged sill. He rolled out of the shattered window onto the sidewalk. Dark red blood sprayed across the underside of the white awning like the first pass of a painter's spray on a wall. A long shard of glass stuck out of Bronco's neck. He grabbed it and yanked it out, which caused him to apply a more thorough second coat back across the awning. Rob crab walked backward to avoid the spray.

"Let's go, Rob!" Mel screamed as she ran to the Escalade. "We gotta go now!"

Rob grabbed his backpack and followed. He jumped into the passenger seat of the Escalade and slammed the door. The mariachi grito of Vicente Fernández filled the cab from the Cadillac's premium stereo. To both their surprise, Bronco had gotten to his feet and limped toward the Escalade like a zombie. He had a gun in his hand and struggled to level it at them. Blood still gushed from his opened neck. Mel screamed. She jammed the gas pedal to the floor and cut the wheel hard to the left. The huge SUV lurched forward with a squeal of its tires. The right side of the front bumper slammed into Bronco's hip and spun him around like a top with his gun pointed at the sky.

Rob looked back at Bronco as he spun around in place behind them, and thought he looked like a yard sprinkler. Mel thought he looked like a demented ballerina. They both sped out of the Shangri La's parking lot with Bronco now in a heap behind them.

Chapter Thirty-Four

"She's not picking up," Rob said to Mel as Dr. Sheltie's cell rang its seventh ring before her voicemail picked up. Mel was focused on the road ahead. She worked in her mind where the safest place for them was at the moment.

"Jefe Manuel will see this as a full-on declaration of war," Mel said, almost to herself. She thought for a second he could possibly view this as a kidnapping situation. Maybe the john killed Bronco then nabbed her and stole his vehicle. But after what he said to her in the rear of the bus with Jimmy, about her arrest being an attempt to alert law enforcement of his operations, she discarded the hopeless thought as quickly as it entered her mind. Plus, no one got the best of Bronco. That's why Jefe Manuel assigned her to him.

"I can't believe my idea actually worked," Rob said, amazed.

Mel saw the same shock in Bronco's eyes when they turned and met hers before his throat was laid open by the motel's shattered window. Statistically speaking it should be her and Rob in a bloody heap back there, not Bronco.

Rob called Dr. Sheltie's phone a couple of times more with no answer. Next he tried Masters's phone.

"Come on, pick up," he said to himself. There was no answer either.

"We need to get somewhere soon. I can start to feel eyes on us," Mel said urgently. Her own eyes now darted in all directions. To her, every person they passed was an informant of Jefe Manuel. They had cheated the odds once, and she knew they would not a second time.

"All aboard! Hahahahahahaaaa! Ay-ay-ay-ay-ay-ay," Ozzy Osbourne screamed. This led to the sound of deep thumps from a kick drum. Then a vibraslap cleared the way for a rhythmic assault of one of the best electric guitar riffs of all time. Dr. Sheltie was on the first row of Ozzie's final farewell tour. He had just launched into one of his biggest hits, "Crazy Train." Her screams of excitement blended with 79,999 others in the sell-out crowd at AT&T Arena outside of Dallas, Texas. They all sang along with their arms in the air.

> Heirs of a cold war, that's what we've become
> Inheriting troubles, I'm mentally numb
> Crazy, I just cannot bear
> I'm living with something that just isn't fair

"I'm going off the rails on a crazy train!" she sang as her body was filled with the electricity of the moment. She felt good. She felt free. On the stage was a magnificent performance of the defiant heavy metal Ozzie's band was best known for throughout the 1970s. They fought the system and pushed the boundaries of political correctness. What Dr. Sheltie loved most about the band was their name, Black Sabbath. Its roots originated from a film by her favorite cult classic horror icon, Boris Karloff.

Dr. Sheltie watched the special effects of the performance dazzle the crowd. There were fires and explosions. Ozzy was in rare form as he ran from one side of the stage to the other like he was twenty-something again. His heavy mascara ran down his sweat-covered face and created a hideous clown look. The crowd closed in on her. They pressed against both her sides. The communal odor of a locker room during the halftime of a hot, sweaty ball game filled her nose. People here and there rushed the stage, and security personnel grabbed them and flung them back into the crowd. The assailants landed on a sea of hands and surfed away out of sight.

From behind her, items were being tossed onto the stage. She was pressed and pushed around by the mob. Dr. Sheltie tried to make out what the items were. At first there were a few. Then several more hit the slick stage, bounced, and slid into drifts. They were small and black. And they moved. More accurately, she could see now, they flapped. Ozzy caught one in midair and raised it over his head. The crowd went crazy. He ran to her side of the stage.

The crowd chanted, "Bite it off, bite it off, bite it off!"

Ozzie sneered and bared his big white teeth.

"Bite it off, bite it off, bite it off!"

Now Dr. Sheltie could see what he held was a black bat. All around him bats were being thrown in droves. Now the stage was covered with them. They all flopped and flapped underfoot of Ozzy as he ran here and there and solicited more support from the crowd.

He stopped center stage. He took the bat and crunched into its neck with his teeth then yanked its body free. The crowd's noise reached a crescendo, and the compression of the crowd against Dr. Sheltie was immense. She felt she would be smashed. Bodies all around her gyrated up and down like pistons. Their belts grated against her like she was a piece of cheese. She couldn't breathe, like the air was devoid of oxygen.

Ozzy now bit head, after head, after head off the bats. Between bites he spit the wet hulls into the crowd. Fans clawed and fought to get them. The heat, noise, and pressure built further. Things were out of control, and the whole arena began to swirl around her, when something wet splattered against her face. Ozzy had blessed her with a gift, from his mouth to hers. Everyone in the arena dove for it. They created a furious dogpile, and she was at the bottom being trampled, crushed.

Dr. Sheltie awoke in a gasp then took several deep breaths. She was in the oversized recliner at the CIA safe house, soaked in sweat. She could see light outside the drawn shades. She grabbed her cell to see what time it was and saw several missed calls from Rob. Then her phone vibrated in her hand as her Ozzy Osbourne "Crazy Train" ringtone broke the silence. It caused her to shriek in surprise. It was Rob.

"Rob?" she answered.

"Dr. Sheltie! Thank God. I've been trying to reach you for over an hour."

"Sorry, I must have dozed off. Where are you? Masters said you stayed behind at the motel?"

"Yes, I met up with Mel."

"You found her? That's wonderful, Rob!"

"Yeah, but more trouble has found us. Is Masters there? I need to speak with him."

Dr. Sheltie realized Masters wasn't on the couch any longer.

"Uhm, I really don't know where he is at the moment. He was asleep, but now I don't know."

At that moment Masters came into the room from down the hall, his thick hair still wet from a shower. His face was shaved smooth, and he buttoned a clean white shirt over a fresh pair of black slacks as he walked.

"There you are," Dr. Sheltie said, and handed her phone to Masters. "It's Rob. He needs to speak with you."

Masters took her phone.

"Master Rob!" he announced pleasantly.

"Masters, listen. I found my sister, but we've gotten ourselves into some trouble." Rob explained to him what occurred after he left Rob at the Shangri La.

Masters put Dr. Sheltie's phone on speaker so they both could listen.

178

"Mmm-hmm. I see. Ahh, hmm. I understand," Masters commented as Rob explained.

"Any ideas?" Rob asked after Masters was brought up to speed.

The situation had compounded. Now, not only was the CIA after them, but the cartel was too.

"You and your sister need to get out of town. There is too much heat on you here in Dallas," Masters said.

"Where do we go?"

"Anywhere away from Dallas. I need to catch up on the situation with my sources now that I am rested and clearheaded," Masters replied.

"Maybe go see your father. No one will think to look for you where he is," Dr. Sheltie offered.

"And where is that?" Rob asked.

"Reynosa, Mexico."

Chapter Thirty-Five

Mel punched McAllen, Texas, into the Escalade's GPS system. The screen calculated and showed the quickest route was by way of Austin through San Antonio. A total of eight hours away, McAllen was the last stop in the US on the route before it crossed into Mexico. Mel was concerned about heading south with the cartel behind them. This could potentially make them the meat and cheese of a cartel sandwich. Rob was indifferent. His opinion was until they understood the impact of tonight's supermoon, the CIA would hunt them to their death. So one way or another, danger would be with them a little while longer.

"How much money do you have on you?" Mel asked. "I'm starving and need to get out of this dress."

Rob answered, "About eighty bucks."

Mel took them through a Whataburger just south of Dallas once they broke free of the morning rush. She and Rob both ordered double cheeseburgers. She took fries with hers, and he grabbed a large side of onion rings. Two extra-large sodas and some spicy ketchup rounded out their feast. They didn't speak much in the parking lot as they scarfed their tasty burgers and sides. Finally, Rob broke the silence.

"I'm glad you left with me back there."

"Your broke ass didn't leave me much choice," Mel said, then stuffed several fries into her mouth and took a long pull of her soda.

"Sorry about that. Sometimes I don't think things through enough."

"Well, this time I am glad you hadn't. The writing was on the wall. Either I was going to be killed by those I work for, or I would eventually end my own misery," she said. Her eyes looked ahead out the window as more cars entered the drive-thru line.

"I can't imagine what you've been through," Rob said. He couldn't understand the level of misery and hopelessness a person must experience to kill themselves. Of course he heard about people doing it all the time, but he had never spoken to someone who might actually be close to doing it. Even while he was sidled with that nightmare and greatly deprived of sleep, he never once thought of suicide.

She choked out a laugh. "And I hope you never do. You may have dreamed nightmares, but I've lived them," she said, eyes still locked on the line of vehicles that waited in front of them.

Rob sat there in silence, not sure if there was anything he could say to comfort her except, "Well, I am glad you are here."

She turned and smiled, "Me too, big bro."

Rob smiled back. Then his phone jingled. It was Masters.

"Hello?"

"Master Rob! I received an update from my team. Like all bits of information, there is good news and bad news. And as a gentleman, I always offer the choice of which you'd like to hear first."

"I need some good news. So start with that."

"Good news it is," said Masters. "So far we have temporarily succeeded in getting off the CIA's radar. It seems we gave them the slip out on that country road where I picked you up. They have been scouring the woods and areas around there, and my sources believe they have no idea we are working together now, nor either of our whereabouts. However, this is a brief victory, as their resources are endless. It's a matter of time before they pick up our scent again."

That was good news. Rob's primary source of anxiety was the CIA's pursuit of him rather than the cartel's pursuit of Mel. He figured it was because he had witnessed the ferociousness of their hunt for him firsthand. He hoped the cartel would let bygones be bygones. He always figured that prostitution was a door that revolved often, and Mel would simply be replaced by another girl soon enough. However, Rob didn't fully understand the depth of Mel's involvement in Jefe Manuel's operation as a waypoint lieutenant. She wasn't normally a prostitute as Rob thought. She was only paying off a debt to Jefe Manuel through prostitution as punishment. In reality, she was a key operator with extensive information that could collapse Jefe Manual's most lucrative business locations and maybe even his whole international operation. About this truth, she hadn't shared a whole lot with Rob. There hadn't been much time since they met back at the Shangri La. This underestimation by Rob would soon reveal itself. Mel was a huge loose end that couldn't be allowed to live.

"And the bad news?" Rob asked Masters.

"The bad news is two-fold. First, my fear that there may be some sort of supermoon reaction tonight from the GMO feed left over from 1970 has been drastically confirmed. The Chow company under the CIA's ownership made some mistakes back after the 1970 exposure with your grandfather."

"What do you mean by mistakes?" Rob asked, and put his phone on speaker so Mel could hear.

"Because Organic Death was cancelled by Nixon, the CIA had no purpose in further ownership of Chow, so they sold the assets to some foreign national in Argentina. They, in turn, continued aggressive expansion throughout the globe, however not with the original Chow formula. They continued their expansion and growth using the CIA's GMO formula."

"So hold on. Am I hearing you right? The GMO version is the version being sold today, fifty years later? Are you positive?" Rob said. The Chow company was the largest animal food supplier in the world, and not just by a small margin either. His mind grappled with what this meant if actually true.

"Yes, I am positive. Several weeks ago I had one of my lab guys run down to their local feed store and grab some Chow right off the shelf. Now that we know what to look for, he analyzed it and confirmed the GMO signatures were present. I fear tonight's supermoon will invoke the initial uprising planned in Vietnam back in 1970. But not on some small farm in Anna, Texas. I mean on a global scale," Masters explained. "And it gets worse."

"Of course it does," Rob retorted sarcastically. His mind still tried to comprehend the ramifications of what Masters had explained to him.

"Which brings me to the second half of the bad news. This was no accident. We think there is a mastermind at work behind this. We are working to try to figure out who that is and stop them. But I'm afraid there just isn't enough time. The moon will come within its closest distance to the earth around 10:00 PM tonight and trigger the gamma ray device, then the evolutionary reaction of the GMO feed in the animals that have consumed it."

"I can't believe this," Rob said.

"It's true, I assure you," Masters said.

Rob felt the genuineness of that assurance as he did of each one given before it.

"There is one ray of hope, but it is a long shot," Masters mentioned. "We think your grandfather did something back in 1970 that may have prematurely broken the evolutionary reaction."

"I'm not following," Rob replied.

"During the events of that evening the animals reverted back to normal before the moon had moved back into its original orbit. We think something your grandfather did caused that to happen. If we knew what that was, then maybe we would have the beginnings of a way to remedy this if it occurs. Granted, it may be after the fact, but still better than nothing."

Rob was silent as he thought about this. "Who was in the house that night that may recall what he did?" Rob asked.

"Well, your father, your aunt, and—" he paused a second before he said "—your grandmother."

"My grandmother? She died years ago."

"We see no records of her passing if she has. But of those three, we think she is the best chance we have of finding out what your grandfather may have done."

"Where in the world is she if she is still alive?" Rob wondered, afresh in more disbelief.

"We are looking. Dr. Sheltie is working with us on this. She mentioned during your hypnosis that the phrase 'La Casa Bailarinas' was revealed to you."

"Yeah, but it doesn't mean anything to me."

"We think it may be where Erma Florchett has been living since your father went into the military."

Rob recalled Waylon explained how he had taken Erma and Annie to the Texas border after his father entered the Army. He said from there they went into Mexico with her family, and he hadn't seen them since.

"So what now?" Rob asked.

"Proceed as Dr. Sheltie suggested. Visit your father in Reynosa. See what he may know. In the meantime me and Dr. Sheltie will keep researching on our end. Let's touch back once you leave there."

"Will do," Rob replied, and the phone clicked off.

He looked over at Mel. "This is news of the worst kind. Everything will change if all the animals that have consumed Chow transform into primal killing machines tonight." He shivered and thought, "A true animal apocalypse."

Chapter Thirty-Six

"Bathrooms so clean they'll make you slap your mama?" Mel read from another billboard advertisement for Slappy's as she and Rob sped down the interstate. They had been driving for an hour, and already she had seen five such billboards. Each with some catchy phrase about quality standards that condoned smacking around your mother.

"Slappy's is the ultimate gas station experience in Texas," Rob explained. "I can't believe you've never been to one."

Mel had never been out of the greater Dallas area if the truth was told.

"No. Can't say that I have. I didn't realize gas stations were something that could qualify as an experience." "Only in Texas," she thought.

"Oh, we gotta do this," Rob said with a grin. "There is one this side of Waco. Just a few miles ahead."

"As fun as it sounds, we need to conserve our cash. You sure we should?" Mel asked with apprehension. "Probably going to need every penny for gas."

The Escalade had a full tank when Mel and Rob left the motel. Already the gas needle began to sink further toward empty.

"You can change your clothes like you wanted, and we can just look around. Stretch our legs," Rob said with more excitement than Mel thought a person should have over a gas station visit.

A few minutes later Mel signaled right to take the Slappy's exit from the interstate. Ahead, off the service road, a large awning that covered dozens

186

and dozens of gas pumps started to materialize. Mel slowed and turned into the huge lot.

"That's a lot of gas pumps," she remarked as she carefully weaved the Escalade through the tangle of pumps to find a parking spot in front of the huge storefront. The Escalade blended in with the sea of family vehicles that jockeyed in and out of the pumps, which calmed her nerves slightly. Mel grabbed her bag off the backseat that contained a fresh set of clothes and various toiletries required for a call girl's success and got out of the truck. Rob decided he needed a change of clothes as well and wondered if Bronco at least had a fresh shirt in the back somewhere. If there was one, it would probably look wilted as it hung off Rob's thin frame, but at least it would be clean. He got out and headed to the back liftgate.

The gate lifted, and sure enough, there was a big black duffel bag on top of two hard-shell suitcases. The bag looked the kind that someone kept spare clothes in and if he was lucky, maybe a few bucks too.

"Let's see what we have here," Rob said, and slid the bag toward him. He grabbed the zipper and pulled it across the top.

"Oh my God." Mel gasped.

"Whoa! Jackpot," Rob said with wide eyes.

Inside the duffel were bricks of $100 bills wrapped in cellophane. Four of them, to be exact. Each about five inches thick. Plus two Glock pistols. One a model 23C .40 caliber and another model 27 subcompact, also .40 caliber. Also, two fifty-round boxes of KTW Teflon-coated brass .40-caliber slugs, also known as "cop killers" due to their ability to pierce Kevlar vests. There was also an accounting ledger, some burner phones, a pair of brass knuckles, large plastic ties, and various packets of pills, powders, and marijuana.

Next Rob opened the smallest hard case. Inside it was lined with thick foam padding with six circles cut out. In each circle was a silver canister. The top three had green pins in them. The bottom three had red ones.

"Tear gas and flashbang grenades," Mel informed him. "Check the other case. I have a feeling I know what's in it now."

Rob slid the second larger case to himself and undid the latches.

Mel whistled. "Oh yeah."

Inside the case was more molded foam padding. On the bottom was some sort of stubby gun with a short barrel that was about six inches wide. Between the trigger guard and the front grip was a large opening for a huge magazine. Stuffed into the cutouts in the lid were the magazine and six more grenades.

"Grenade launcher with frag canisters. These types of grenades can either be shot out of this baby or thrown by hand," Mel explained, then grabbed the Glock subcompact pistol and ejected its magazine.

Rob was taken aback by Mel's knowledge of the small arsenal they found.

"It's full," she announced. She slammed it back in the grip and racked the slide.

"I'm impressed, sis," Rob declared as he took a step back.

"Don't be until you see me shoot it," she replied with a smirk. "Now close that up before someone gets interested."

She dropped the Glock into her duffel. She then ripped the cellophane on one of the bricks and removed a few of the bills.

"I bet this place sells clothes," she said as she took in the size of the building's exterior.

"And then some," Rob said, still in awe of his sister's confidence around the items in the duffel bag. Like Dr. Sheltie, Mel seemed comfortable around weapons. More so than he did by a long shot. Also like with Dr.

Sheltie, he took awkward comfort in this. His male ego easily conceded to their prowess.

"Then let us go shopping, shall we?" she giggled with a girly grin and shook the wad of bills at him.

***

Jefe Manuel stood over Bronco's stiff, pale body. It lay on the stainless steel floor in the back of the huge black bus. Bronco's skin was already gray and pasty from lack of blood. Rigor mortis had staunchly set in. Opposite Jefe Manuel were the two soldiers of his personal detail, each with a serious look etched across their faces. They had learned of Bronco's dead body from the owner of the Shangri La Inn who watched the confrontation unfold between Bronco, Mel, and Rob. He was asleep on a couch in his office when he heard Bronco slam the driver's door of the Escalade. He peeked out his blinds as Bronco stalked toward Rob. He saw the girl sneak up from behind and kick his leg, which tripped him into the plate glass window. He recognized the Escalade as it squealed out of his parking lot. As a loyal informant, he had an obligation to call Jefe Manuel. He almost couldn't dial the number because his hand shook so badly.

Within minutes a lime-green 1964 Chevy Impala lowrider silently crept onto the scene. Two cholos jumped out and quickly began to clean things up. They swept up the glass in front of room 113 and wiped everything down inside it. They left an envelope of cash on the bed that had the words "For window" scrawled on it. Then they sprayed the awning off with a garden hose from around the side of the building. They tucked Bronco away in the car's huge trunk then crept away as silently as they'd come.

"She had help," one of the serious soldiers reported.

"Her accomplice asked specifically for Crystal Bunny," said the other.

"She wasn't supposed to be in the usual rotation. I had her clientele prearranged," Jefe Manuel remarked quietly.

"He offered three times her rate. Our dispatcher made a mistake and allowed it. He said he was only thinking of profits, so he worked her into Bronco's agenda," said serious soldier number one.

Jefe Manuel took a deep breath. Bronco was his best and toughest handler. He felt his neck warm as he worked to keep a calm appearance.

"From what the motel manager told us, it doesn't look like the cops. He said the two used a trick he hadn't seen since grade school to trip Bronco into the window," said serious soldier number two.

This enraged Jefe Manuel even more. That his top enforcer was bested in such a juvenile manner.

"I want them hunted down at all costs. That bitch must not be allowed to live," he said and looked up at both serious soldiers. "Do not fail me, amigos."

He held their gaze a few seconds longer. The look in his eye reinforced his seriousness. No other words needed to be said.

"Ahora vete!" he barked. The two serious soldiers scrambled out the back door.

Jefe Manuel stood there a moment longer and stared at Bronco's body. He contemplated the extent of damage Crystal Bunny could do to his business if she talked. Too much.

He closed his eyes then yelled, "Estúpido maldito idiota!" then kicked Bronco hard in the open wound on his neck. He left his Berluti leather slipper wedged between Bronco's shoulder and jaw as he turned and left the room with his other slipper still on his foot. He exited the room behind the solitary desk then slammed the heavy steel door closed.

"This is why I should not allow for second chances," he said to himself bitterly then slapped the red button on the wall. An electric hum could be heard. Then a splash. Then the sound of a high-pressure spray like a touchless car wash.

Chapter Thirty-Seven

Mel's head snapped back violently and hit the passenger window of the Escalade.

"Ouch!" she laughed painfully. She reached back and rubbed her hair.

"Watch out now. You're gonna pull your teeth out!" Rob warned.

Mel had just taken a hard yank at some of Slappy's world-famous beef jerky.

"I know, but I love this stuff. I can't believe I didn't know about that place!" she squealed while she laboriously chewed on the tough meat. She moaned as she savored the salty teriyaki flavor. "You were right! Slappy's is da bomb!" she declared with a hoot.

Rob laughed. "I know you just didn't say da bomb. I haven't heard that since . . . actually I can't remember the last time I heard that," he jibed her.

She clamped down for another attempt at the leathery yumminess. Rob winced at the thought of her head taking another bounce off the window, but was happy to see it stopped just shy of it. It was nice to see her old playful self being revealed little by little.

Both she and Rob were freshly showered and shaved. Mel's honey-colored hair was still wet and pulled back in a tight ponytail. She had washed off the thick layers of eyeliner and makeup to reveal her youthful features. She looked sixteen again, but still a bit weary around the eyes. They found new comfortable clothes, plus more labor-intensive jerky-like items, with sixty ounces of Slappy's Creek Water for each of them to wash it all down.

Rob topped off the fuel, and they sped toward McAllen, Texas. He felt good as they joked and laughed together. He couldn't remember the last time they had. It was way before they were dropped off at the neighbor's that awful day so many years ago. He knew that for sure. He missed Mel more than he realized. He had his best friend back. If it weren't for them being hunted by the CIA and a vindictive murderous cartel, it might be the best day of his life. Now that he thought about it, it still might be.

"Are you ready to see Dad?" Rob asked Mel after several minutes of silence.

"I don't know. I've tried not to think about it. I'm more scared than anything," she answered.

"Why's that?"

"I vaguely remember how he acted when Mom had him committed. It scared me seeing him that way."

"Yeah, me too. But we were young," Rob pointed out. "My fear is he doesn't remember us."

They drove along another few minutes then Mel asked, "You remember what he looks like?"

"Yeah, but I'm sure he's aged some."

"I barely remember how he looks at all," she replied in a sad voice. She adjusted her seat back and turned toward the window. Rob could see her reflection in the dark tint as her eyes closed and she drifted to sleep. He knew she must be tired, so he sat in silence and let her rest as the smooth ride of the Cadillac took them down the highway.

The trees gave way to scrub bushes the further they pushed south. The landscape got flatter and flatter. Rob wasn't sleepy, but he was exhausted all the same. This ordeal had started to wear on him. He couldn't believe the twists and turns. He looked over at Mel, who rocked gently with the road. She looked peacefully asleep. It was just after 2:00 PM. Rob wished this all were a dream. In a way it seemed like it was. CIA cover-ups of murderous animals in the moonlight and drug cartels. Until this week he had only heard of spies in fiction he read as a kid, but today he could say not only did he know one, but also his life might well depend on him. With that, Rob's thoughts drifted to what Masters and Dr. Sheltie might have learned by now. What other doses of good and bad news would be served up when they spoke next? All good, he hoped. A wise man once told him, "Hope for the best, but prepare for the worst." Which was what Rob feared was ahead.

The sixty-ounce jug of Slappy's Creek Water had run through him, and he needed to release it back into nature. Up ahead he saw San Antonio was the next twelve exits. He took the first one that displayed a gas station. Mel must have felt the Escalade begin to slow. She sat up and stretched.

"Where are we?" she asked sleepily.

"Just getting into San Antonio. I need to pee," Rob admitted.

"Okay. Want me to drive?"

"Yeah, if you don't mind. I was thinking I might try to grab a nap."

"Sure, no problem," Mel said with a yawn.

Rob pulled into a large truck stop. It wasn't large by Slappy's measure, but a good-sized one nonetheless. He coasted to a stop on the side corner of the building. He got out and made his way into the store. He saw the neon restroom sign in the far corner and headed that way.

Another Cadillac Escalade pulled in the farthest gas pump about the time Jefe Manuel's cell phone rang.

"Sí?" Jefe Manuel asked into his cell. The caller ID showed the name Squeaky. Squeaky was one of Jefe Manuel's handlers in the San Antonio area. Jefe Manuel figured Mel and Rob would flee Dallas, so he had all his associates on high alert throughout the state. The $1 million bounty had them all beyond vigilant. It looked like he hit pay dirt with Squeaky and might have to pay it out sooner than expected. Squeaky could barely keep his high-pitched voice from quivering more than usual.

"I see the girl you are after, senor Jefe," said a squeaky voice that resembled Speedy Gonzalez's.

"Where are you?"

"Just inside San Antonio at the Green Leaf truck stop," squeaked the voice.

"Are you alone?"

"Sí. But I'm pretty sure I can take her. She's just a little chica," Squeaky said with a mischievous grin.

"Is she alone?"

"No, senor. She is with some gringo who just went inside the store. But he is scrawnier than I am, senor Jefe."

"Don't engage them. I want them followed until I can arrange a proper takedown. Do you understand?" he asked.

"Sí, Jefe Manuel," replied Squeaky, disappointed.

"Good. Call me back when they are on the road."

The line clicked off. Squeaky walked to the back of his SUV and pretended to get gas. He continued to watch Mel as she opened the back hatch of Bronco's truck. All the gas stalls were full except the one in front of him. Then a black Ford Mustang GT backed in right up to the front of his Escalade and revved its throaty exhaust before it turned off.

"Hey senor Speed Racer," Squeaky barked to the driver when he got out. The guy turned around and looked at Squeaky. "Move your car, *ese*. I need that spot open," Squeaky demanded. The man was another Latino, but bigger. He saw scrawny Squeaky and laughed.

"Why you need two pumps, *pendejo*?"

"*Pendejo*?" Squeaky questioned back. He nodded his head and repeated the insult to himself in feigned contemplation then replied, "Yeah, you do look like you could use another asshole. Let me help you with that," he snarked, then reached into his jacket pocket and pulled out a pearl-handled switchblade and pressed its release button. The blade zinged out and glistened under the bright awning lights.

He started to walk to the bigger Latino when a car driven by an older white lady pulled up behind and blocked his rear. Several of the gas stalls were backed up in a similar fashion.

Squeaky couldn't believe his eyes. He turned and stomped back toward the car with the lady in it.

"Hey, esa no es una 196uena, vieja perra blanca! Move your shit, gringa!" Squeaky hollered at the lady. He waved his knife around just enough to be seen. He hoped it would convince her to move on. She didn't budge, just honked her horn. People started to take notice. He continued to her car ready to lay the intimidation on more heavily. She rolled her window down as he approached. He continued with the Spanish insults.

"No comprende, beaner. Go finish pumping your gas and stop pumping your jaw," she replied and beeped her horn again.

"Who you callin' a beaner, bitch?" Squeaky said, now genuinely insulted. He took a more aggressive step toward the woman's open window, when he felt a cold gun barrel against the back of his neck. He froze.

"Drop it, *ese*," a voice demanded.

Squeaky dropped the knife, and it clanged on the concrete.

"Apologize to the lady."

Rob finished his business and walked out of the restroom. As he made his way across the store, he took a casual glance through the large storefront windows toward the gas pumps. He saw what appeared to be someone with a gun to a guy's head. He hustled faster to get Mel so they could get out of there before something bad happened that caused the cops to show up. Then he skidded to a stop and did a double-take. He walked to the window for a better look. That someone with the gun was Mel!

"I don't apologize to bitches. It's a matter of principle," Squeaky said matter-of-factly. "And I certainly don't take no orders from them either." He turned quickly and made a blind swipe for the gun. Mel took a step back and dodged his attempt with ease. She delivered a fierce kick to Squeaky's balls, which caused him to double over and grab them in agony. He let out a higher-than-normal squeak Mel was convinced only dogs could hear. With a smooth, quick motion, she brought the butt of the Glock down hard on the back of Squeaky's head. He went down lights out on the concrete. Applause erupted from all around from patrons at other pumps.

"What the . . . ?" Rob's jaw loosened. Then he gathered his wits when he saw the crowd as it moved in for high fives and fist bumps. "Dammit, Mel," he muttered, then ran to Bronco's Escalade.

Mel hadn't realized that she attracted a small crowd. Several of the women hooted and hollered their praise for her standing up to a man. Even the guys whistled and yelled, "Right on, little lady!" Bronco's Escalade screeched to stop behind her, and Rob reached over the passenger seat and threw open the door.

"Come on, Wonder Woman! We gotta get outta here!" Rob yelled. Mel took a bow to her fans and jumped in. Rob mashed the gas just as her feet left the concrete. He didn't speak until they were back on the interstate.

"What was that back there?" he asked, both amazed and panicked.

"What was what? That greaseball was about to hurt that old lady. Someone needed to do something." Mel shrugged like it was no big deal.

"Where'd you learn those moves?" he asked, still shocked. He mimicked a couple kung fu chops at the steering wheel. She just smiled and shook her head.

"There's so much you don't know about me, big bro," she said under her breath as she turned and watched out the window as San Antonio disappeared behind them in a hurry.

Chapter Thirty-Eight

Huge plumes of dust rolled out from under the black bus as it roared to life. Jefe Manuel's private detail performed a final checkoff around the outside perimeter before their departure. Inside, the maître d' looking man moved around quickly. He stowed the last of the cargo and battened down the furniture to make room for the retraction of the four large slides. Normally, this routine easily took an hour. However, Jefe Manuel demanded they leave in less than fifteen minutes. All hands scrambled to ensure they could. Even Marcell, the borrowed French chef, pitched in and made sure the kitchen was buttoned up before he exited the bus to catch a plane back to Mexico City.

Once everything was secured, the air brakes released a hiss of air like a bull ready to charge. The two Volvo turbo diesel engines whined as they urged forward the ten huge Kevlar-lined Michelin X bus tires. Serious soldier number one was behind the steering wheel and guided the behemoth out of the industrial park on the outskirts of Dallas. He pointed the wide, flat nose of the bus south onto the interstate and accelerated in a jet-black cloud of exhaust.

***

Masters sat at the breakfast table in the kitchen of the CIA safe house. Across from him sat Dr. Sheltie. Both had their noses against the screens of laptops. A cell phone vibrated on the tabletop. Masters picked it up and pressed the speaker button.

"Scott. What do ya got for me?" Masters said into the phone. Scott was one of the CIA's techno-geeks committed to team Masters, an MIT grad who from time to time joined Masters on dangerous projects in the field. They had been through more than a few tight situations. When he got the memo that Masters was now considered a rogue agent, he gave it the middle finger and silently began to help him stay alive. When Masters reached out to him to go buy some animal food manufactured by the Chow company at his local feed store a few weeks ago, he did so with no questions and delivered the feed to Marty. Marty was a CIA chemist also on team Masters. Marty's deep-seated connection with Masters was merely that Masters was Marty's godfather. When Marty received the same rogue agent memo, he simply placed it over one of the many Bunsen burners in his lab and turned it to ash. Both Scott and Marty knew of the political rift that had formed in the CIA and that their friend was at the center of it. Other key people in Washington, DC, knew there was a farce afoot in an effort to scapegoat Masters too. So Masters was not alone. Like he said, he still had friends.

"Okay, I located Annie Florchett," Scott began. He chewed something and swallowed. "She is a doctor that specializes in progressive brain disorders. Works at a mental hospital in Reynosa, Mexico, called the St. Dymphna Institute."

"That's where my sources tell me Tommy Florchett is being treated too. That's where Rob and Mel are heading right now," Dr. Sheltie chimed in.

"It's actually a nice-looking place. I expected it would be some cold concrete building with orderlies in white coats wiping drool off the windows. It's more like a Club Med. And the cafeteria serves damn good tamales," Scott raved, and continued to chew into the phone.

"How does he know that?" Dr. Sheltie looked up and asked Masters with a furrowed brow.

Masters shifted uncomfortably in his seat. "I asked Scott to do some boots on the ground reconnaissance." Then he looked down at the cell phone and said, "Not a culinary critique."

"Sorry, boss. I'm all about some Mexican food," Scott admitted before he slurped from a drink.

Masters ignored the noise and said, "Proceed with the objective and report back."

"Ten-four," Scott acknowledged and clicked off the line.

"So you already knew about Tommy Florchett's whereabouts?" Dr. Sheltie asked.

"Yes, we've known about Tommy for some time. What's interesting is we didn't know Annie was there too," Masters thought out loud.

"If you knew Tommy was there, then your evil cohorts must know as well."

"Yes, I assume they do."

"Then we may be sending Rob and Mel into a trap!" Dr. Sheltie said. She stood up quickly, which caused her chair to skitter backward as she glared down at Masters. "What is Scott's objective? What are you not telling me?"

***

Squeaky crossed himself with his right hand when he saw the huge glossy black bus slow and turn into the Green Leaf truck stop in San Antonio. It's safe to say he wasn't a devout Catholic, but since he hung up with Jefe Manuel after he told him the girl cracked his skull and was gone when he woke up, he might as well have put on a priest's white collar. He was instructed not to move an inch. For the last four hours he sat in his Escalade at the same gas pump. Before he saw the bus pull in he prayed to every patron saint he could recall. Which wasn't many. Now that he saw the black bus had pulled into the trucker's lot of the Green Leaf, his prayers bypassed the saints and were directed to the big man himself. And more fervently than ever.

Serious soldier number one parked the bus next to one of the big rig gas pumps. He began to fill the massive fuel tanks as serious soldier number two crossed over to the passenger car side of the truck stop to retrieve a very shaken Squeaky who watched through wide eyes from the driver's seat of his Escalade.

"Hola hombre! Como estas? Come with me, por favor," said serious soldier number two with a friendly smile as he opened Squeaky's door.

"Sí, sí," Squeaky said as he slid off the driver's seat.

"Let's review the facts of what happened," serious soldier number two said as he closed the door and guided Squeaky toward the bus. "You were watching the southbound lanes of the interstate like a devoted soldier when you saw the Escalade driven by the girl. You followed it into this truck stop."

"Sí," squeaked Squeaky.

"You reported it to Jefe Manuel. Then you proceeded to watch the girl as instructed."

"Sí, sí."

"While you watched her some guy blocked you in. And you threatened him with a knife in front of a few people. Then a gringa grandma insulted you, so you decided, what the hell, and began threatening her with even more people watching."

"Senor, I was trying to . . ."

"I talked to a couple employees on the phone on our way here, and they said you were putting on quite a show. Yelling and waving around your knife. Pretty entertaining stuff," interrupted serious soldier number two. "Then the girl beat your ass, and here we are. You have no useful information on where she went 'cause you were busy licking the pavement." They had reached the rear of the bus as it idled. "Is that about right, sí or nada?"

"Sí," squeaked Squeaky.

Serious soldier number two nodded then opened the back door of the bus and motioned for Squeaky to enter. Squeaky climbed the steps, and the door closed behind him. Moments later there was a sound like a balloon had popped. Serious soldier number two walked around to the side door of the bus and entered. Jefe Manuel sat in one of the plush leather recliners and took a satisfied puff from his cigar when he heard the splash from the back of the bus. No more second chances. Serious soldier number one walked up from the rear of the bus. He slid his Beretta 9 mm into its holster on his hip and slid into the driver's seat. He shifted the huge transmission into gear, and the big bus continued its rumble south.

Chapter Thirty-Nine

The sky was blood red in the west as the sun closed in on the horizon. After they left the Green Leaf truck stop in San Antonio Mel took over the wheel and proceeded to McAllen while Rob grabbed a few winks. The Escalade had just entered the McAllen city limits. Unsure what the plan was now, she nudged Rob to wake up. He sat up and wiped the drool from his chin.

"I am so sleep deprived," he complained as he drank a few gulps of the melted ice in his Slappy's Creek Water cup.

"I think we both are." Mel agreed. She began to blink hard the last few minutes herself.

"Is this McAllen?" Rob wondered as they cruised by a Best Buy and a Hobby Lobby.

"It appears so. What's the plan from here?"

"Make our way to the border. I understand getting out of the country is easy. It's getting back in that can be challenging," Rob said. He could see the sun had set, and that set him on edge. Ten o'clock would be there before he knew it. Rob checked his phone for new messages. None. He scrolled back to the instructions Dr. Sheltie sent him about the location of his father. Visits were allowed until 8:00 PM. They still had time to clear the border and get to the facility.

Mel stopped at a stoplight and looked around. Everyone was Hispanic. This didn't bother her on the face of it. But when you are hunted by a Mexican cartel, it helps to have a few gringos around to add contrast to your

204

pursuers. Her paranoia began to elevate as it seemed everyone around them stared at her. She gripped the wheel as she flashed back to the bus's death chamber and Jimmy's brains splattered against the back wall. She could see herself as she looked down the barrel of Jefe Manuel's huge Les Baer .45 then heard a BANG!

She shrieked.

"Mel, you okay? I think that was a car backfiring," Rob said when his sister nearly jumped out of her skin.

"Yeah, yeah." She swallowed hard. "I'm fine. Just jumpy I guess."

"The light's green." Rob pointed out gently. He looked at her, worried. A car honked and some Spanish was thrown at them. She proceeded forward. It occurred to her that she and Rob stuck out like a sore thumb here. The problem was twofold. First was their skin color, but second she realized there was a heavy presence of the cartel this close to Mexico, and she knew by now Jefe Manuel had given Bronco's Escalade description out. And knowing him a sizable bounty had been put on her head too. So maybe the problem was threefold. Either way, she and Rob were at a clear disadvantage.

"I think we need to dump this truck," she said suddenly.

"I was thinking about that too."

Up ahead they saw a group of blue lights across the road.

"Shit," Mel said and made a quick right turn. Further in that direction was another group of blue lights across that road. A single pair of the blue lights broke away from the group and headed toward them. Then a second. Then a third.

"I think we've been spotted," Rob said. He gripped the handle above his head so hard his forearm began to burn.

Mel yanked the wheel hard to the right again and slung the SUV into the parking lot of a strip mall. She gunned the big motor, which caused everyone to look her way. People scattered as the Escalade zoomed past. A lady and her kid stepped out into the Cadillac's path, oblivious. Mel slammed the brakes, and the vehicle skidded forward and stopped just shy of the pedestrians.

They just stood there and stared with disdain. Mel hammered the horn and screamed for them to move out of the way. The woman just turned her head and meandered. Mel cut the wheel, and the left tires popped onto the curb, and she gunned it through several sidewalk racks and a trash can. It crumpled under the big truck and sent garbage in all directions. Rob looked back and saw the cops had turned in behind them.

"They're gaining on us!" Rob commentated.

"Hold on!" Mel screamed, and cut the wheel hard to the left, which led into an alley. It was narrow, and there was a dumpster on Rob's side. There wasn't room for the Escalade's girth to pass, and Mel wasn't going to slow down. Rob covered his face and pulled up his knees as the SUV slammed into it. Mel pressed the gas harder as the dumpster was pushed in front of them. Sparks showered onto the windshield as it scraped down the side of the building. They were just about at the end of the ally when a cop car appeared from the right. The dumpster smashed into the front of the cruiser, and it spun it away, which opened enough of a gap for the Escalade to turn left into another alleyway.

Ahead she could see cross traffic as that alley ran into a side road. She smashed the gas pedal to the floor, which made the 6.2-liter Detroit powerplant demand more torque from the hearty GM ten-speed transmission. It shifted down instantly in response. The tires barked, and the backend squatted to the ground just as another police cruiser tried to block their path. Mel gripped the steering wheel at the nine and three position. Both of her arms were locked, and she braced for impact, but her right foot didn't let off the gas. The cop heard the big V-8 before he saw it and slammed on his brakes, which probably saved his life as the Escalade sheared off the front of his car as it barreled past at seventy miles per hour. Mel locked the brakes and cut the wheel to turn on to the street. The Escalade's rear end slid sideways out of the alley and slammed into a parked car on the opposite side of the road. The Escalade's engine still ran, and no airbags deployed, so Mel jammed the gas pedal back down and accelerated down the street.

Rob was balled up in the passenger seat with his seatbelt in a death grip when Mel asked him if they were being followed. He opened one eye then the other and looked around, thankful they were still alive. He had burns on his neck from the seatbelt, but otherwise he was okay. He sat up and peeked behind him. The coast was clear. He exhaled and silently thanked the Lord then looked over at his sister like she had lost her mind.

"Yep. Gonna need a new ride," she said as she checked her mirrors and found them all missing.

***

"Master Rob! Great to hear from you, sir," Masters greeted Rob when his cell rang. "Have you visited your father?"

"No. We ran into car issues. Literally. We're still in McAllen," Rob replied flatly.

"Time is ticking. You should be in Reynosa by now."

"Yeah, well. We have McAllen's finest breathing down our necks," Rob explained. He looked around the empty new construction of the house he and Mel hid in. The Escalade began to overheat after they left the alley, and by chance the road led into a new subdivision. They saw a house in which the front door without knobs and locks was open. They entered and put the Escalade in the garage and manually pulled the garage door down. It was far from secure, but made do in the pinch they were in.

"Hmm. Let me check something," Masters said, and shouldered his phone.

207

For the last eight hours he and Dr. Sheltie had been on shaky terms. She accused him of not being straight with her on what he was up to in regard to Rob and Mel. He assured her his only motivation was to see them through this situation and get the CIA's heat off of them. He explained he owed her that much, at least, for her efforts to rid him of his nightmares. Plus, it gave him time to assess his own danger with them. She was very concerned for Rob and Mel's safety all alone down there. He assured her they were not alone and now was the time to reveal their assistance to them. Had he done it any sooner it would have tipped the CIA hunters of their whereabouts.

"I don't see the BOLO issued by the CIA extending into McAllen. So for roadblocks to be waiting for you is certainly peculiar," Masters said.

"There were at least a dozen cars in total that we saw. They banged up our ride pretty severely. We are holed up in an empty house. Kinda stuck," Rob explained.

"I have an asset in the area. His name is Scott. He is CIA, but you can trust him. He should be in McAllen by now. Give me the address of the house you are in, and I will have him pick you both up. He will assist in getting you into Mexico. If the locals are alert to you then I suspect the authorities at the border will be too."

"Okay. We'll keep a look out for him."

"And, Rob?"

"Yeah?"

"Be extra careful. I fear much hangs in the balance of you finding your grandmother. Call after you speak with your father, and I will bring you fully up to speed with what Sheltie and I have learned."

"We'll do our best."

"Godspeed," Masters wished, and clicked off the line.

Chapter Forty

Jerry Reed blasted from the Peterbilt's discount store speakers.

Keep your foot hard on the pedal

Son, never mind them brakes

Let it all hang out 'cause we got a run to make

The boys are thirsty in Atlanta

And there's beer in Texarkana

And we'll bring it back no matter what it takes!

"I'm east bound, just watch ol' 'Bandit' run!" the driver sang loudly as his rig full of Lone Star beer sped down the interstate. In his rearview, he caught sight of a large black vehicle as it weaved in and out of traffic and gained on his position. The sun was about to set, so it was difficult to see any details, but he was sure whatever it was, it was a big one. He looked down at his speedometer, and his rig's governor held it steady at 80 mph.

"Sumbitch must be rolling over a hundred easy," the driver said to himself. He lowered Jerry Reed to a whisper and grabbed his Uniden BearTracker CB mic.

"Breaker 1-9. This here's Crazy Cracker."

"Go ahead, Cracker," came the static-laced reply.

"I'm headed south from Alamo City. Any drivers see that black stagecoach driving the Monfort Lane, feeding the bears, over."

"Copy that. She blew by me reading braille the whole way," came a reply.

"Affirmative. Needs to lay off the hammer. Nearly blew my doors off," came another.

"Should we set up a turtle race? Slow dat sumbitch down before he sends somebody shiny side up?" Crazy Cracker asked.

"I hear ya, Cracker. This here's Country Bumpkin. You in that Lone Star thirsty truck?"

"Yes, sir."

"10-4. I'll be on your donkey in two."

Country Bumpkin pulled his rig up behind Crazy Cracker. He waited for a car to speed past then put on his left turn signal. Slowly he moved over into the left lane. He pulled up beside Crazy Cracker, and they began to pace each other at 70 mph and blocked both lanes as Jefe Manuel's bus approached.

"Our inside sources with the McAllen PD have confirmed the girl is in McAllen. They caught sight of her as she approached a roadblock fifteen minutes ago. There was a short pursuit and she slipped away. But they will catch her. I was guaranteed of it," serious soldier number two explained to Jefe Manuel as he sat and nursed a crystal tumbler of Macallan M single malt scotch whiskey.

"Somehow I am not convinced," he replied. "How far out are we from McAllen?"

"Less than an hour."

The bus braked hard, and both serious soldier number two and Jefe Manuel lurched forward. A splash of $5,000-per-bottle scotch spilled from the crystal tumbler and splashed Jefe Manuel's Italian herringbone chinos.

"¡La madre que te parió!" Jefe Manuel spat in anger. Once the bus's ride stabilized, he walked up to the driver's cabin to see why the sudden use of the brakes. Ahead he saw the backend of two 18-wheelers side by side, and neither advanced ahead of the other.

"What is going on?" he asked serious soldier number one.

"The idiot truck on the left can't get enough speed to pass the idiot truck on the right."

Several minutes passed as they both watched the two rigs continue at the same pace. Serious soldier number one grabbed the bus's CB mic and turned on the unit. He had never used it before, as cell phones were now commonplace for communications, even on the open road. The CB defaulted to channel 19, and there was laughter and some banter between several truck drivers related to the impedance they caused the big black bus. It became apparent from the CB chatter they blocked their way on purpose. Serious soldier number one blasted the bus's huge air horns.

"Whoa there, buffalo. Don't get your lil tailpipe twisted up," Crazy Cracker said in response to the air horn.

"This is the buffalo you speak of. Move your redneck asses or I will," said serious soldier number one into the CB's mic.

Country Bumpkin noted the Spanish accent and retorted in an exaggerated Southern drawl, "Should've known it was some illegal wetbacks in an Obama bus. Chinga whey, asshole."

Jefe Manuel narrowed his eyes then turned and walked back into the sitting area. He pulled out an iPad. He sat in his plush recliner and opened a special custom app. The iPad picked up the bus's Wi-Fi network and loaded several camera views from around the bus. He chose the front camera that displayed the two rig trailers. He tapped a series of other items on the screen. In the front of the bus, a rectangle panel that spanned almost the entire width of the bus's front slid up above the bumper. It revealed six gun barrels grouped in a circle. They belonged to a modified General Electric M134 Minigun capable of up to six thousand rounds per minute. This one was loaded with armor-piercing incendiary NATO rounds with depleted uranium penetration cores. They were made to shred the most robust tanks on the modern battlefield.

On the iPad's screen appeared a gun sight. With his finger, Jefe Manuel zoomed and moved it onto the rear axle of Country Bumpkin's trailer and tapped the screen. This locked the Minigun to the axel. The gun itself was fixed on a series of pneumatic arms which allowed it to float in spite of bumps in the road. Now locked onto its target, it tracked the axle with precision.

"Getting a case of the red ass back there, amigo?" Country Bumpkin taunted and held his middle finger out of his window.

Jefe Manuel programmed a short burst option of just twenty rounds. Next he chose the lowest rate of fire setting at 2,400 rounds per minute. Then he pressed the fire button. In less than two seconds the Minigun spun its six barrels and released the twenty NATO rounds into Country Bumpkin's trailer wheel assembly. All four sets of dual wheels severed themselves from their axles and blew off in different directions. They bounced wildly like runaway rubber balls. With its wheels obliterated, his trailer landed on the concrete interstate and fishtailed wildly back and forth. Huge gouges in the concrete trailed behind it. Country Bumpkin lost control of his rig and slammed into Crazy Cracker, which sent his rig into a fishtail of its own until both trailers slapped together. Then Country Bumpkin and Crazy Cracker bounced apart. This created a gap for the bus to blaze through. Each rig went in opposite directions. Country Bumpkin crossed the median and met another rig that transported jet fuel head-on in the northbound lane, which erupted in a huge explosion. Crazy Cracker caught a glimpse of the fireball in his side mirror as he flew across the right-hand ditch and across the service road out of control. He slammed into the huge steel leg of a two-story electronic billboard. His truck ripped into two halves and sent a misty foamy wave of beer cans bursting into the air. The huge billboard shuddered then slammed to the ground on top of the frothy heap in a wild display of sparks and lightning. The twin diesel engines of the bus shrieked loudly as the Volvo accelerated beyond 130 mph within seconds and left the redneck carnage in its dust.

Chapter Forty-One

Forty-five minutes passed since Rob's call with Masters. Mel watched through the empty doorknob hole of the front door. It was dark out, but there was a street light at the corner of the lot that ten minutes earlier had flickered to life. Mel caught sight of an electric-blue Toyota Yaris pull into the house's driveway. She saw a wiry blond guy with a flattop haircut get out. He wore a light jacket and denim jeans. He looked in all directions before he walked to the front door. Mel slowly cracked the door open and stuck her head out. Behind her back she held the Glock pistol, locked and loaded.

"Scott?" she asked.

"At your service," Scott replied. "You must be Mel?"

"Yes, sir."

"A mutual friend asked me to assist you and your brother to the border. Where is he?"

Mel swung the door open, and Rob appeared. He held the two cases that contained the grenades from the Escalade.

"A pinball car?" Rob said when he saw the Yaris.

"We need to blend in, and these compact cars are the most widely driven across the border," Scott explained. "Let's get a move on. I understand you guys are on a tight schedule."

He took the cases and stacked them on the backseat of the passenger side. Mel followed with the black duffel bag on her shoulder.

"This is all our stuff," she said, and handed the duffel to Scott to find the best place to stow it in the tiny car.

"Alright. Load up," Scott said. He put the duffel in the small cargo area. Rob grabbed the shotgun seat, and Mel got in the back behind Scott.

They pulled away from the house. The Yaris sat low with all the bodies and cargo in it. Once they exited the subdivision onto the main drag, Mel said to Scott, "You don't look like a CIA guy."

He laughed an easy, pleasant laugh. "What do ya mean?"

"I thought you all wore black suits," Rob interjected.

He laughed again. Scott seemed very laid-back and easygoing. A stark contrast to the intensity of Masters.

"You mean I don't look like James Bond?" He laughed some more. "That's because I'm not a field agent. I'm just a techno-weenie that gets to play around in the field from time to time," he explained. He noticed the worried looks on Rob's and Mel's faces.

"Don't worry. I still carry a gun and know all the secret handshakes," he remarked, and nodded with confidence. They slowed to a stop at an intersection behind several cars. The light was red. Ahead to their left a massive black bus negotiated a tight right-hand turn toward them. Mel caught her breath as it eased into the oncoming lane. Horns began to honk around them. Several cell phones appeared out of windows and snapped photos to be shared on social media.

"That's Jefe Manuel," she said as panic raised her voice.

"In that rock star bus?" Rob said in awe. Dr. Sheltie's Porsche Spyder was the coolest car he had ever seen, but this massive black bus that lumbered ahead amazed him even more. It struggled to make the turn in the traffic. After another minute it fully entered the oncoming lane and crept slowly toward them.

"That's a badass bus," Scott marveled as it approached.

Mel wanted to slink down, but her knees were already jammed in the back of Scott's seat. She couldn't lean over into the seat next to her because of the stacked cases. She was forced to sit straight up next to her window. The bus came along beside them. She couldn't make out where the windows started and the sleek sides ended. It looked completely smooth. She stared at the Yaris's reflection in its glossiness. An interior light flicked on that illuminated the inside of the bus behind a window above Mel. It caught Mel's attention and she looked up. Standing in the window was Jefe Manuel, and he stared down at her. He gave a small wave, and then the light went out and the window disappeared into the side of the bus again. She gasped.

"Go, Scott, go! He saw me!" she yelled, and slapped the driver's seat.

The bus exhaled a long hiss from the air brakes as its transmission was slammed into park. Scott saw a man come from around the back of the bus to his left. It was serious soldier number two. Rob could see he had an Uzi and stalked slowly toward them. The Yaris was boxed in. Scott slammed the pinball car into reverse and backed into the truck behind them. He hoped to push it back a foot or two. However, true to its nickname it pinballed off the big truck's front bumper with little result except a Spanish insult from its driver. Scott put it back in drive and tried to cut into the lane on their right. But cars whizzed by one after another. There wasn't time. Serious soldier number two was just three cars in front of them.

"Here, take this," Scott said as he handed Rob a large envelope from under his seat. "It's the IDs you need to use at the border going and coming back. Go through the lane marked SENTRI Express." He got out of the car. A gun materialized in his hand. He took a shot at serious soldier number two to gain another second more. He shouted back into the car for Rob to drive and slammed the door. Rob jumped over into the driver's seat. Scott was a little shorter than he was, plus the seat was up to accommodate Mel's long legs in the back. He couldn't get his right foot into the driver's footwell. It caught the gear shifter and the radio knobs.

Scott had moved around to the back of the car to avoid a line of fire from serious soldier number two, who now was another car closer. From behind him serious soldier number one crept around from the front of the bus. He, too, had an Uzi. The driver of the truck Scott backed into saw Scott get out of the Yaris and thought he wanted a confrontation, so he opened his door and exited his big truck, which blocked serious soldier number one's path. Scott cut between the Yaris and the big truck. He jumped into the lane of traffic to their right and waved his arms for the cars to stop. The traffic screeched to a halt. Horns blared. A momentary gap the Yaris could fit into opened next to Rob. He saw his chance, but his foot was hung.

"Go, Rob!" Mel screamed when she saw what Scott had done.

Rob pulled his leg hard. His shoe raked across the front of the radio. The knobs broke, and Kenny Loggins blared from the speakers about a highway to the danger zone. Rob cut the steering wheel to the right and clipped the bumper of the car in front, but was able to squeeze the Yaris out. It jumped forward into the gap Scott held for them.

Serious soldier number two saw the Yaris move into the far lane and ran between two cars to cut them off. Rob gassed it and nearly took him out. They sped by as he jumped back between the cars. He sprayed the Uzi wildly, but nothing hit the Yaris as it sped away. In the passenger mirror, Rob could see Scott run into the congestion of cars that came out of a Taco Bell across the street. He felt relieved to see Scott get away. But that relief didn't last long. He noticed a red Tesla Model X literally come out of the side of the bus and turn toward them into oncoming traffic. Cars swerved and crashed into themselves until the Tesla squeezed into Rob's lane behind him. It was several cars back but weaved in and out erratically as it passed cars one at a time as it caught up to them.

Serious soldier number one's path became blocked when the driver of the big truck swung open his door and got out. Through the windows of the truck he saw the Yaris speed off. He doubled back around the front of the bus to the opposite side. He used his fingerprint to open the bay door of the cargo hold in which the two Tesla Xs were stowed. The one closest to him eased out automatically just enough for the driver door to open. Serious soldier number one got in and took off into the direction the Yaris had fled. The congestion around the bus was thick and chaotic, but the small Tesla finally broke free and accelerated. With its Ludicrous Speed enabled it launched from zero to sixty in 2.6 seconds and passed cars with ease. He tossed the Uzi in the passenger seat and took out his Smith & Wesson 5906 Mexican Special Forces-issued sidearm. He wasn't left-handed, but he trained in the COIFE, the Special Forces Corps of the Mexican Army, to be a deadly shot with either.

He was two cars behind the Yaris. He swung the Tesla into the left lane and leaned out the window with his gun to shoot across its hood. He pulled the trigger twice in rapid succession then swerved back into his own lane. One bullet sailed high, and the other harmlessly pinged the pinball's rear fender. The Yaris swerved back and forth then sped up. One of the cars between them moved over to the shoulder out of the way. Now just one car between them. He laid on the horn and motioned for the car that remained between them to move over. The driver saw the man scream behind her and wave his gun. She didn't want any part of a gunfight, so she braked and put on her blinker then moved right. Now no cars between them.

Serious soldier number one aimed again out the window and shot, but the Yaris swerved onto the shoulder, and his shot missed. Enough of these over-the-hood shots. The Tesla had superior speed, so he could easily approach from the side before the Yaris knew it. Then it would be a right-handed shot across the passenger seat. Easier to aim with a more guaranteed result. He rolled down both passenger windows and stood on the gas. The powerful electric motor revved up and catapulted the small car forward beside the Yaris. He fired into its backseat window. The glass blew out, and he now saw the girl scream and cover her face. Ahead a truck closed in on him, so he braked and swerved back in behind the Yaris.

He could see that behind the oncoming truck the road was clear. Once it passed he would again pull up beside the Yaris and unload his pistol into the door of the backseat. His orders were to kill, not capture, and his .45 cop killers would shred the thin door like it wasn't even there. With luck he might be able to take a shot or two at the driver, but the girl was the priority. The truck screamed by, and serious soldier number one gassed the Tesla and swerved out. Instantly, he was beside the Yaris and about to unload his magazine when something flew into his own backseat window and clanged around the back glass. Between the distraction of the object and the Yaris now with its brakes locked up, he missed his chance. He felt around in the backseat and grabbed what he thought was a soda can. He was in disbelief he was thrown off by such a tactic. His patience was thin, and in a sudden rage he looked at the can and realized it wasn't soda.

* * *

Mel screamed when her window exploded on her. She felt the slipstream of the bullet just miss her face as it passed out the other window. Rob didn't know what to do. The little 4-banger under the pinball's hood gave Rob all it had, which wasn't even close to what the Tesla could deliver. If he stopped he and Mel would be no match for the cartel thug. He slowed to try and make a turn he saw in the distance.

218

"Don't turn! Keep going! Make him come around again," Mel hollered from the backseat. He could hear the clasps on one of the hard cases unlock.

"What are you doing?" Rob yelled into the rearview mirror. He saw Mel remove one of the frag grenades from the bigger case.

"Just let him come back around. It's our only chance," she said. She broke off the plastic seal that allowed the grenade to be thrown versus shot from the launcher. Out the rear window, she could see the thug as he waited for the oncoming truck to pass. The truck zoomed by, and with stupid speed the Tesla was right next to her, its front passenger window even with hers. She threw the grenade and immediately saw the hard wind push it back. She didn't think about their speed and its effect on something thrown out the window before she tossed the grenade. She thought she missed and felt her blood run cold as she looked down the barrel of the thug's gun pointed straight at her.

She screamed at Rob, "Hit the brakes! Hit the brakes!" as she braced for a shower of bullets to shred her door. But what she didn't know was that she hadn't missed. The grenade just barely made it into the open rear window of the Tesla. It bounced off the door frame into the back of the car. It clanged off the rear window then landed on the backseat. When Rob locked up the brakes of the Yaris the Tesla sped ahead of them. It swerved one way then another before its roof exploded and its doors shredded. It rolled end over end then side over side before it came to rest in the ditch. It looked like a tin can turned inside out from a shotgun blast. Rob and Mel sped past it and exited the highway for the McAllen Hidalgo International Bridge to cross over into Mexico.

Chapter Forty-Two

Mel had joined Rob in the front seat of the Yaris. They both exhaled nervously and looked at each other in relief as they slowly drove under the Welcome to Mexico sign and away from the border crossing checkpoint.

"That was intense," Rob breathed. He checked his side mirror to make sure they were free and clear of the inspection. Rob's phone jingled, which caused both of them to jump. He saw Masters on the caller ID.

"Hey," Rob answered on speakerphone.

"Master Rob! Scott is on the line as well."

"Hello! So glad to hear your voice, Rob. How is Mel?" Scott chimed in and asked.

"I'm here!" Mel answered.

"Great! Sorry for bailing out like that. I couldn't think of a faster solution to get you both on your way and out of the danger zone. Those were some bad hombres packing some major firepower."

Rob and Mel traded a humorous glance at Scott's mention of the danger zone. The knobs were still busted off the radio. Thank goodness for the second set of radio controls on the steering wheel. He proceeded to fill Scott and Masters in on what happened after Scott exited the Yaris.

"Impressive work. That was some fast thinking. I now take it you made it through the border checkpoint and are cruising into Mexico?" Masters asked.

"Yeah. We totally forgot we had those grenades until the Mexican border patrol approached us for our turn to be inspected to cross over. By then it was too late to ditch them," Rob replied.

"The SENTRI paperwork I gave you to use at the crossing are aliases we use to move critical things into Mexico in situations like this. Going into Mexico is easy. It's coming back that is more rigorous. Sorry I didn't explain that, but I was kinda rushed," Scott said with an easy laugh.

"In other words, Master Rob, don't forget to lose that cargo on your return trip," Masters pointed out.

"Gotcha."

"So what's the plan from here?" Mel asked.

"Continue to the rendezvous with your father. You should still have about thirty minutes to see him when you get there. Unfortunately, Scott wasn't able to make contact with your aunt before I pulled him away to assist you both in McAllen," Masters explained.

"Our aunt?" asked Rob, surprised. He looked at Mel, and she shrugged.

Scott fielded the question. "Yes. Annie Florchett is a doctor at the same facility where your father resides. We believe she is the link we need to find your grandmother. However, I figure she is more of an eight-to-five employee. By the time you get there she may be gone for the evening. As a contingency for this, in that same envelope with your IDs I gave you, there is a small USB thumb drive. Plug that into any computer you can once inside the hospital and be sure the computer is powered on. The Trojan horse program on the thumb drive will install then ping my laptop's IP address. Once I am inside the computer I can move around their network to find their personnel records, hopefully finding her address."

"I have it here," Mel said as she dug the small device out of the envelope and inspected it.

"Excellent. Lastly, under the passenger seat is a set of Mexican car tags I took off a car in Mexico before I picked you guys up at that empty house. At some point you'll want to swap them with the Arkansas tags that are on the rental. Otherwise it will be no challenge for the cartel to spot you. You must be very careful. You are on their turf now," Scott advised.

"Call us back after you've visited with your father. Hopefully we will then have more information on your grandmother's whereabouts," Masters instructed.

"Will do," Rob replied, and clicked off the call. He pulled into the parking lot of a grocery store, and they swapped out the vehicle's Arkansas tags with the Mexican ones. He put the Arkansas tags in the backseat then pointed the Yaris toward the St. Dymphna Institute and sped away.

***

Serious soldier number two slowly steered the black bus through the Mexican border checkpoint. He was being guided through a special lane designated for political figures and their "friends." The security was light, and they weren't required to stop. The top of the lane gate and chain-link fence were mere inches away from the bus's roof and sides as it crept through. Serious soldier number two's brow and hands sweat. Serious soldier number one was the primary driver, and this was only the second time serious soldier number two had ever been behind the wheel. He could tell Jefe Manuel watched this tight passage with scrutiny. His mood was very dark ever since they rolled up on the blown apart Tesla in the ditch. Serious soldier number two knew now was not the time to put a scratch on Jefe Manuel's most treasured home on wheels.

Prior to their approach to the border checkpoint, Jefe Manuel had been on the phone with both the local federales and his own lieutenants to be on the lookout for the electric-blue Yaris. He adamantly instructed them not to approach, but only report back to him personally on its whereabouts once they confirmed the girl's identity. This bitch was his to deal with. His anger seethed through his veins. All he involved were highly motivated by the generous bounty and eager to begin the hunt. It didn't take long for the first sighting of the Yaris to be had. Reynosa wasn't a huge city, but it wasn't small either. With a population just over six hundred thousand, it ranked thirtieth in size amongst all other Mexican cities. However, due to the lax immigration policies of the US at the time, it was among the fifth-fastest cities in growth. With this large increase in transient people, the cartel, too, had swelled in numbers. This meant thousands of sets of eyeballs were instantly on the lookout for an electric-blue Toyota Yaris driven by a gringo and gringa. A nondescript tan sedan exited the interstate behind an electric-blue Yaris. Then it pulled in behind it at the St. Dymphna Institute ten minutes later.

***

"The GPS says this is our exit coming up," Mel navigated to Rob.

He tried to read the road sign to confirm, but the bullet holes had knocked much of the paint off of it. This made the language barrier already in place even larger.

"Should be another ten minutes then on your right," Mel continued her navigation as they exited the interstate.

Rob pulled into the St. Dymphna Institute's parking lot. He checked his phone, and it was 7:30 p.m. As usual, Masters was spot on. They had thirty minutes to get inside and find their father before visiting hours ended. As they walked up the front walk, they didn't notice the tan sedan park a few spaces back from them. Behind its wheel was a small Mexican man who could already feel the independence and security of the million-dollar bounty in his bank account. Once Mel and Rob entered the building's front doors, he got out to check the vehicle for something to verify its passengers. He knew without a positive ID his call to Jefe Manuel would end badly for him. Word about Squeaky's demise traveled fast in the digital age.

He stood behind the car. It had Mexican tags, which caused him concern. Maybe this wasn't the right car. Jefe Manuel had said the girl and her partner had just come across the border from the US. So he figured the car would have US tags. He would have to identify them another way. He thought about an ambush when they came out. He could hold them at gunpoint and check them for IDs, but Jefe Manuel was clear no one was to approach them. Frustrated, he walked alongside the car. Then something reflected off the overhead lights and caught his eye. He realized the backseat windows were rolled down. More accurately, they were shot out. Now he could see the shattered glass sparkle from the lights. He ducked his head in and saw the Arkansas tags that lay in the backseat. He smiled big. His first thought was to call Jefe Manuel. He pulled out his cell and hit the speed dial. His next thought was what he was gonna do with all that money.

Chapter Forty-Three

The inside of the St. Dymphna Institute was quite nice. The large lobby had a similar feel to a Hilton hotel. Comfortable furniture clustered here and there around coffee tables, a huge stone fireplace to one side. It had the look of little use, probably because it was always so warm there. Lots of art, vases, and artifacts perfectly decorated on stands and shelves all around. It conveyed an indigenous South American feel throughout the place. There was a long walnut check-in counter. Rob and Mel approached it. They were greeted by a pregnant Mexican woman who seemed both polite and bothered at the same time.

"Hola. ¿Como puedo ayudarte?" she asked.

"Speak English?" Rob asked, hopeful.

"Sí. Yes. How may I help you?" she answered, then asked her question again, less polite and more bothered this time.

"Is Dr. Annie Florchett available?"

"Dr. Florchett has left for the evening."

"May we visit with Thomas Florchett?"

The lady didn't answer right away. Rob could tell she wasn't sure about this request.

"Who are you?" she inquired.

"I'm Rob, and this is Mel Florchett. We are his kids," Rob introduced.

The lady was clearly taken by surprise with this bit of information. She said, "Hold on. Let me see if he is taking visitors."

She went into the side office.

"I don't like this. I am having déjà vu," Rob said warily.

"Yeah. Me either," Mel replied. She noticed the top of a thin computer tower over the Walnut countertop. She reached into her pocket and removed the USB thumb drive Scott had left them. She tilted the tower forward and saw four USB ports. She pugged the small drive into the first one and let the tower back down.

"I am sorry. I don't see Mr. Florchett having children in our records. Only verified family and visitors are allowed to visit patients," she said with clear skepticism as she walked back over to them.

Rob and Mel looked at each other then back at the lady. Neither knew what to say to persuade her.

After another moment of silence Rob asked, "How do we get verified?"

"Mr. Florchett is Dr. Florchett's patient, and she must perform the verification. Maybe return tomorrow after 9:00 AM when she is in?"

Mel saw the woman flick her eyes over their shoulders. She didn't want to give away that she saw the woman look behind her and Rob, so she didn't turn around. Instead, she looked behind the woman for any shiny surfaces that may give her a reflection to see what the woman looked at. Nothing shiny, reflective.

"Thank you for your help," Rob said kindly. He and Mel walked back through the lobby and outside.

"I feel like we were lied to," Rob said as they descended the outside steps.

"We were. Dr. Florchett was there, and she was watching us," Mel said. She looked around and noticed there were still several cars in the parking lot.

"You got that feeling too?"

"Yep. Can you ring Scott? I have an idea."

Rob pulled out his phone and dialed Masters.

On the second ring, "Master Rob!"

"Is Scott on the call?" Rob asked.

"Give me a sec," Masters requested. The line went quiet.

"Scott here," Scott answered.

"Are you seeing the ping from the hospital computer?" Mel asked hurriedly.

"Yes. Loud and clear," Scott replied. Several taps on keys could be heard.

"Is there any way to use the info there to hack the DMV or whatever they call it here to see what kind of car Annie Florchett drives?"

"Ah, mistress Mel. Thinking like a spy, are we? Not feeling like you were told the truth in there?" Masters cooed playfully.

"I can do better than that," Scott answered. "I see they require parking permits and am looking up the good doctor now." More taps on a keyboard. "Dr. Florchett drives a white 2020 Volkswagen ID.4. Plate number FNN-86-23," Scott reported triumphantly.

They thanked Scott. He said he would text Dr. Florchett's home address once he found it. It seemed the hospital's personnel records were more secure than the spreadsheet that contained the parking permit information. They clicked off the call then scanned the lot for a White Volkswagen. In the third space from the front was such a car. They walked over to it and compared its license tag to what Scott had told them. A match.

"Well?" Rob asked.

"We wait for her to come out, and confront her. We need to see why she wouldn't talk to us."

They made their way back to the Yaris and got in to wait.

***

"Sí," Jefe Manuel answered.

"Senor, I have located the girl for which you are searching," said the small Mexican man from inside the tan sedan. He explained the events that led to that point as well as the shattered windows and the Arkansas tags in the backseat. He then conveyed the location of the hospital. He was told to stay on the line and watch.

"Do not hang up. I am on my way."

Jefe Manuel wasn't going to let the girl slip through his fingers again. He told serious soldier number two the hospital's address, and the black bus rumbled in that direction.

***

Fifteen minutes later a tall woman in a white lab coat came out of the building and walked toward the white ID.4. She held a briefcase and looked down at a paper in her hand. She didn't notice the two figures that stealthily moved toward her. Rob and Mel had planned to converge on her simultaneously from the front and rear of her car so she would be pinned in. As Rob moved into his position, he noticed the large white moon set low in the sky. Ten o'clock was just two hours away.

The ID.4 chirped and its parking lights flashed as the doctor approached the driver door. Before she could open it, Mel stepped forward and leaned against it with her hip. The doctor froze. Then she turned to flee, and Rob stepped between the cars behind her. Rob could see the terror in her eyes.

"Aunt Annie. I'm your nephew Rob."

The doctor stood there silent as if she tried to verify this claim by the way he looked. His accent was all American. He had the same tall, lean frame and thick honey-colored hair. She turned and compared that to the girl behind her. Same tall, lean features. Same honey-colored hair. Both resembled her brother Tommy. Resembled herself.

"What do you want?" she finally asked.

"Some things are happening. Some dangerous things. We need to talk to grandmother. She may be in danger."

Annie didn't speak. She and her mother worked hard to conceal her whereabouts and even that she was still alive. She knew nefarious forces were behind that night in 1970 and responsible for her father's false imprisonment. She always knew in her heart those people would come for them eventually. She never saw her father again once he was arrested. She was only seven years old at the time. Her mother and Tommy were the only family she had ever had. Once her mother was safely hidden away she worked to have Tommy transferred here to the St. Dymphna Institute when she heard he had been committed to a mental health facility in Dallas, Texas. A nurse at the time, she went back to medical school and became a doctor. She focused all her efforts on mental illness, determined to help her brother. But he had only gotten worse. While they stood there, he sat in a room unable to care for himself at all. A complete vegetable. Whatever had happened to him had ruined his mind. Taken his soul. It ripped her heart to pieces when she saw him like that day after day.

"I spoke with Waylon Gentry. He was a friend of your parents. He said he took you and grandmother to the Mexican border," Rob explained. He could see her trepidation to talk with him, so he began to tell her a barrage of facts he had learned in hopes something would convince her to talk.

Annie remembered Mr. Gentry. He was a very kind man. He looked after Annie and her mom after that horrible night. Rob's mention of him put a lump in her throat.

"I know what happened with your brother. Our father." Rob nodded toward Mel. "He was given a series of treatments to erase those horrible memories of that night in 1970. I know exactly what those treatments were and maybe a way to help him now. I suffered from the nightmares, too, and found help." Rob hoped this would convince her.

Annie was determined to help Tommy no matter if it killed her. She stood there and wondered whether this was her day to die or maybe her only chance to help her brother.

"Mom is safe. No one can find her," Annie finally said quietly.

"We need to speak with her about that night fifty years ago. We have strong evidence that what happened back then will happen again tonight, but only much, much worse." All three of them glanced at the brilliance the moon had become as it continued higher into the sky. "We think she may remember a critical detail that may save a lot of lives tonight."

Annie was still conflicted and stayed silent.

"Time is nearly gone. We think we have just two more hours. Please," Mel spoke up for the first time.

There was a loud hiss of air brakes that caused them to look toward the road. A huge black bus slowed to turn into the parking lot.

"Oh shit," Mel mumbled.

Annie saw the bus with recognition. Panicked, she swung her door open and jumped into the ID.4. It was an electric car, so it didn't need to start up. It immediately shot ahead and bounced over the parking block and sped away around the building. The bus door opened, and the sound of an Uzi erupted. A barrage of bullets began to ping around them.

"Run!" Rob screamed as he took off opposite the bus across the parking lot toward a patch of woods. Mel hesitated. She looked to the Yaris and thought maybe she could make it and grab the grenade launcher. Then from a tan sedan, a few cars away from the Yaris, another guy emerged and aimed a pistol at her. She took off after Rob.

Chapter Forty-Four

"Do you still have eyes on them?" Jefe Manuel asked into his phone.

"Sí, Jefe Manuel. They are talking to a woman in the parking lot. Should I try to get closer to hear what they are saying?

"Do not move. If they move, follow them. We just exited the interstate. We'll be there in ten minutes."

"Okay. I am not moving," the Mexican man said, keen to obey.

The bus slowed and turned into the St. Dymphna Institute parking lot. The one thing it did not have was stealth capabilities. Jefe Manuel saw the three individuals look his way as they heard the bus slow down. He slapped the button to open the bus's door and leaned out with an Uzi. He saw the Volkswagen speed away. His quarry, however, still stood there. He pulled the trigger of the Uzi. He saw her run toward a patch of trees as his bullets hit all around her. The trees were fifty yards still.

"Cut them off!" he yelled.

Serious soldier number two mashed the gas pedal of the huge bus to the floor. The massive Volvo diesels instantly responded and laid down eight trails of rubber as its rear end swung to the left. It clipped several cars and accelerated unnaturally for something of its size. It barreled over a cluster of yellow protective concrete parking posts around a fire hydrant. The bus wasn't fazed as it picked up more speed as a huge gush of water shot up in its wake.

"Run her over!" Jefe Manuel laughed a wicked laugh.

Mel heard the high whistle of the diesel's turbos engage and the squeal of huge tires as they peeled across the pavement. She looked to her right and was shocked how fast the huge bus zoomed toward her. In the passenger compartment she could see Jefe Manuel as he stood and held on to handles over his head. On his face was an evil grin. Ahead, the trees grew closer. She wasn't sure if she could make it though. Her long strides ate up a yard each. She sprinted harder now. Rob had just ducked into the trees. Her legs burned. She wasn't going to make it. The bus's lights blinded her. Its air horns blasted to declare it victorious. Rob turned just as the bus overtook his sister and sped past.

"Mel!" he screamed in disbelief and ran back to her twisted body lying in the parking lot.

***

"Yes! Crush her like the *pequeña rata* bitch that she is!" Jefe Manuel laughed when he saw she wasn't going to make it to the tree line. Unexpectedly, she stopped. Her feet slid on the loose gravel on the parking lot's surface. She held her arms out. He hoped she slid in front of the fast bus, but couldn't tell. Serious soldier number two stood on the brakes, and the bus slid uncontrollably to a stop. Jefe Manuel wasn't prepared for the sudden brake and was flung forward into the huge windshield. He hit it hard, which made it crack into a huge spider web, but it held and didn't break out. He bounced back into the floor as the bus continued its skid and finally came to a stop in a cloud of tire smoke between two buildings.

***

Mel knew she wasn't going to make it. Her instincts kicked in, and she just stopped with both feet. Still, her momentum carried her. The bus was right there, and she threw her hands out. She bounced off its slick side as it whizzed past. The world spun around several times until she slid across the ground to a stop. She was dazed but alive. She gasped for air as she stared into the night sky bathed in the light of the large white moon nearly overhead.

***

"Mel! Mel!" Rob yelled as he approached his sister. He knelt down, out of breath. He looked her over and couldn't see where the bus had crushed her. Then he noticed her chest heave as she gulped air. She was alive.

"Help me up?" she wheezed.

He lifted her to him and hugged her. The sound of air brakes hissed, and bright white reverse lights flicked on the back of the bus. A reverse buzzer filled the air with BEEP, BEEP, BEEP. It had slid crookedly into an alleyway between two buildings that connected the back road to the front parking lot. It scraped loudly as it moved back and forth to free itself, but its length made reverse tricky.

"Can you stand? We need to get going," Rob asked.

There was a gunshot, then another as a bullet wanged off the surface of the concrete. Behind them the small Mexican man took aim for another shot. Rob dragged Mel to her feet, and they hobbled into the trees for cover. Her collision with the bus had knocked the wind out of her, but she began to recover and could run on her own. They made their way through the stand of scrubby trees. Through the trees, Rob could see another parking lot for the building next door. They emerged from the protection of trees when a car screeched to a stop. It was the white Volkswagen.

"Get in!" Annie shouted out her window as another bullet struck the ground just behind the car's rear bumper. Mel jumped in the back, and Rob ran around to the front passenger seat and climbed in. They silently sped off.

No one spoke for several minutes. Reynosa roads were built in a grid pattern. Lots of stops and ninety-degree turns in all directions. Annie zig-zagged through the streets with a constant eye on her mirrors.

"You didn't mention you were being chased by Jefe Manuel. What kind of trouble have you found for the likes of him after you?" Annie said as she broke the silence.

"You know him?" Rob asked.

She snorted. "Who around here doesn't. That black bus is a harbinger of pure evil. It's the poison in these streets that terrorizes these hard-working, wonderful people."

She put on her left blinker and merged onto Interstate 40 headed southwest.

"They saw my car. They are looking for us," Annie said nervously.

"Where are we going?" Rob asked.

"The only safe place we can until he forgets about us."

"I doubt he will. He wants me dead pretty bad," Mel said from the backseat.

"Why does he want you so bad? What have you done?" Annie asked as she looked at Mel in her rearview mirror.

"I was one of his waypoint lieutenants for a few years in Dallas. He is convinced I am colluding with law enforcement to bring him down."

Annie looked shocked. "Then he will not rest."

***

The bus could not go backward any further. It was at an odd angle and risked being wedged if serious soldier number two continued to try.

"Stop!" Jefe Manuel said, frustrated. He grabbed the Uzi and stomped to the rear of the bus. He exited the back door from the death

234

chamber. The night was quiet. He hoped to see the girl's guts splattered across the parking lot. There was nothing. The bus hadn't struck her.

"*Maldita punta!*" he screamed.

From his left he heard someone in the stand of scrub trees. He started to run toward the sound with the Uzi at the ready. The small Mexican man came into view. He saw Jefe Manuel and stopped with his hands on his knees. He huffed and puffed so hard he struggled to speak.

"They . . . they went—" he swallowed and gasped another deep breath "—through there and got in the car with—" another deep gasp "—that woman they were speaking to."

Jefe Manuel recalled the white Volkswagen when it sped away. He quickly ran into the front doors of the St. Dymphna Institute. Moments later a short burst from the Uzi was heard. He ran out and opened the rear door of the bus.

"What can I do to help?" asked the short Mexican man. He now stood more steadily, concerned his bounty had started to slip away.

Jefe Manuel stopped and turned. With a quick upward flick of his wrist, he released a short burst of .45 hollow points from the Uzi into the man's body. Before the short Mexican body hit the pavement, he had already turned into the bus and slammed the door shut.

He marched to the front of the bus and grabbed serious soldier number two by his collar and pulled him out of the driver's seat.

"Move it. I am taking over the wheel. Ready all forward-facing assault weapons. I know who that woman they were talking to is and where they are now headed," Jefe Manuel explained as he slid into the driver's seat.

Serious soldier number two went to grab the iPad and check on some other weaponry.

Jefe Manuel pressed his foot on the gas pedal, and the bus moved forward out of the alley and onto the back street. It had been a few years since he had been to La Casa Bailarinas. There definitely was unfinished business there, and now was a fine time for a reunion to finish it.

Chapter Forty-Five

"Your grandmother's family has deep roots in law enforcement here in Mexico." Annie explained as they left the interstate and now cruised West into the countryside. "Your great, great grandfather, Ernesto Gomez, was the first chief of the Rurales back in 1886. They are the federal corps of rural police founded by the then Mexican president Benito Juárez. Then his son, Neto Gomez, then my grandfather, David Gomez, were also chiefs. Now your grandmother's youngest cousin Raul Gomez is the chief."

"Wow. I had no idea." Rob said.

"The Gomez family has been influential in Reynosa for nearly a century, whether in government or in the community. This is why when President Juarez established the Rurales, he made the headquarters here outside of Reynosa. That original headquarters is now the Gomez citrus plantation. That's where we are heading now. We are already on the property. With the moon so bright tonight, you can see the rows of lemon, lime, and orange trees."

Mel and Rob watched out the window in the bright moonlight as groves and groves of citrus trees raced by. They listened intently as Annie filled them in on a century's worth of their family history.

"The homestead is called La Casa Bailarinas," Annie continued.

When Rob heard the name again, he nearly choked.

"La Casa Bailarinas. The Dancing House," Annie replied with a smile. "Your great, great grandmother loved to dance and would have lots of festive parties celebrating anything and everything. She was so full of joy, as were her daughters and daughters-in-law. The most influential Mexican politicians and celebrities throughout the late 1800s until the 1970s could be found there enjoying the festivities through the generations. It was a regional tradition. They even had a full-time mariachi band that gained fame all over Mexico. Mom has photo albums full of pictures. It was such a happy time."

"What happened? Do they still celebrate like that there?" Mel asked.

"No. In the late 1970s the drug cartels started to organize," Annie replied. Her smile faded to disgust. "They began to move into Reynosa. The Rurales fought them hard, but they still seeped into the city and slowly spread their rot throughout. Corruption took hold. The elections were bought and rigged. Our family began to be less and less elected into the community until we were no longer the positive political influence. The local police fell to the corruption. The Rurales were pushed out of the city altogether. A war was waged by the cartel against us, and in 1988 our plantation was nearly destroyed. A few years later the Rurales retaliated and crippled the cartel now run by Jefe Manuel. Back then it was run by Jefe Dominguez. The war raged back and forth like that until just a couple of years ago. But when it first started Manuel was just a baby. He was kidnapped by Jefe Dominguez during that 1988 raid on our homestead."

"Whoa, whoa. So Jefe Manuel is . . ." began Rob.

"A Gomez. Yes," finished Annie.

Mel was dumbstruck. That monster was her own family?

"He was raised by Jefe Dominguez in the brutal ways of the cartel business and eventually inherited it when Dominguez died. When Manuel heard your grandmother and I had returned to La Casa Bailarinas, he became angry, thinking we would attract the US government's scrutiny because of the situation with my dad. It panicked him. He tried to destroy the homestead again. It was a brutal fight, and this time he was the one that took severe casualties. Our family had grown in support by many influential people in and around Reynosa that had grown tired of the corruption—tired of the poisoning of their children. We were ready for the fight. We were ready to make a stand against the cartel's oppression and evil. A truce resulted between our family and his cartel. However, I fear today may mark an end to it."

"This is all my fault," Mel said. A pang of nausea swept over her. "No wonder he allowed me privilege above so many when I worked for him. He knew who I was."

"Now you see why he is so adamant about killing you. You have the interworking knowledge the Rurales need to end his brutal cartel once and for all."

***

The black bus roared southwest down Interstate 40. Now that Jefe Manuel knew where the white Volkswagen was headed, he sped quickly to intercept it. There was a road that spanned across federal property that would put him in front of the Volkswagen, but he had just a few precious minutes to make the turn if he was to reach the point in time. The traffic on the interstate wasn't heavy, but there was enough. He blasted the bus's powerful air horns. If that didn't clear his way, then he forced the obstructions off the road. He left a trail of spun-out cars and trucks and jack-knifed rigs in his wake.

He had to intercept the car before it reached the Gomez family homestead. In reality it was more like a compound surrounded by high, thick concrete walls. After the cartel war of 1988, the Gomez family rebuilt with potential future wars in mind. So it was like a fortress. If the bitch made it there, then it would be game over for his cartel. The Gomez family was still, practically speaking, the Rurales, which may not have the same influence in Mexico as they once had, but did have considerable influence with the United States Drug Enforcement Agency. The Rurales were their de facto most trusted partner on Mexican soil, as all other law enforcement in the country was tainted with bribes and other corruption. The Rurales had never conceded their integrity.

Although by blood he himself was a Gomez, he was disowned long ago when he was old enough to choose the cartel life. If it really was a choice at all. He grew up ultra-wealthy. He understood absolute power, and he longed for the day it all was his. Jefe Dominguez wasn't his biological father, but Manuel knew no other. He took the Dominguez name, and when Jefe Dominguez died, Manuel took over the family business. He was not about to let it be destroyed by the do-gooder Gomez family.

The turn he looked for was coming up on the right. He hit the brakes and took the turn too fast. Sometimes he forgot how bulky the bus was. Because of all the horsepower it felt light and nimble. This is why he preferred serious soldier number one in this seat. He had the extensive experience needed to maneuver this beast around easily. The back end began to float around, so Jefe Manuel pressed the gas to control the bus's drift. Once he had it straightened out he gunned the engines hard and rammed through the unmanned entrance gate of the private road. From here it was a straight shot to where he hoped the white Volkswagen hadn't yet crossed.

The moon was very bright, and he could see even without his headlights, so he flipped them off to help his concealment. The heft and width of the bus allowed him to achieve much higher speeds on gravel roads than most vehicles. It was stopping that was its disadvantage. Within minutes the fast bus crossed the span of federal land. The bus sounded like a stampede of steers as it raced across the gravel. The gate ahead marked its end and the beginning of the Gomez plantation. The bus easily plowed through the gate. It never slowed as the road to intercept the Volkswagen came into view ahead. Sure enough, he saw the headlights of a small car in the distance to his right. The moonlight glistened off its white roof, and he could see the cone of dust behind it. He mashed the gas further and felt the bus drift slightly as the huge rear tires struggled for traction on the gravel.

"Do you have the weapons ready? I see them ahead!" he hollered over his shoulder to serious soldier number two.

"Sí, Jefe Manuel. But there is one issue."

"I do not want to hear about issues! If we miss this chance I will gut you like a pig!"

Serious soldier number two focused on the iPad. The Minigun didn't respond when he tried to move it side to side. It appeared on the screen to point to the left in a useless fashion. It must have become damaged when he drove the bus over the fire hydrant back in the parking lot. He closed that app and opened another one. The bus was outfitted with several weapons that no car could outmatch. He tapped the screen for another option. On the roof of the bus, two four-inch circular tubes extended up. They were the muzzles of M224 mortar cannons. Loaded in each were M1061 MAPAM mortars. These SAAB-designed munitions had a range up to nearly four thousand yards. Serious soldier number two had four burst options to choose from: proximity, near-surface, impact, or delay. He chose impact burst. Next he used the mobile app's target system to track the Volkswagen. Normally the cannons would make quick destruction of a target at that range. However, at their current rate of speed and with the bumps in the road, he didn't know for sure, and he didn't have the time it would take to get those assurances.

Serious soldier number two fired the first cannon. The mortar shot into the sky with a huge THUMP as it exited the barrel above. Jefe Manuel smiled to himself. He loved the sound of all the bus's weapons when they were in use. They meant power. They meant destruction would soon follow. Ahead he saw the explosion. It was a beautiful sight. But then he caught a glimpse of something cutting through the smoke. Less than one hundred yards ahead, the Volkswagen sped past and left the mortar's fiery crater behind it.

"Fire the second one!" he screamed in a rage as the bus slowed just enough to make the left-hand turn to follow the Volkswagen.

**

Mel saw it first.

"Look over there! I saw a flash," she said as she tapped rapidly on her window. Both Rob and Annie saw the moonlight's gleam off the shiny black bus about a hundred yards to their left. It sped to meet them ahead. Then the world exploded around them. The mortar had just missed the Volkswagen, but the percussion pushed it sideways and nearly toppled it. Annie pressed the gas, and the electric motor spun up and righted the car. Annie pressed a button on her steering wheel. Moments later they could hear a phone ring through the car's speakers.

"Hola," answered a man.

Annie screamed rapid-fire Spanish back to the voice on the phone.

The second explosion sent the car into a spin across the gravel and into the orchard. Rob's door slammed into a tree. Everything was silent.

"Everyone okay?" Annie asked.

Mel looked behind them. She couldn't see anything from the smoke and dust. But she could hear the whine of the turbos on the diesel engines and the roar of the huge tires on the gravel road.

"Drive! Drive! Go!" she screamed as she slapped the back of the driver seat.

Annie prayed while she tried the gas pedal, and the car's tires spun in the sandy soil and they began to move. She hit the Call button on the steering wheel again, but nothing happened. Her phone had fallen somewhere between the seats from the commotion. The trees were planted in perfect rows, so she lined up between two rows and gunned the electric motor.

The bus pulled alongside them on the road. Rapid gunfire sounded, and Mel could see the flashes from the barrel. Annie timed her turns between trees. The Volkswagen moved row by row to put more distance and tree trunks between it and the bus. A crossroad was ahead. It was raised a few feet. The Volkswagen went airborne then crashed down and sent dirt across the hood. It bounced a few times and kept going. To the left the bus tracked them with ease. The gunfire had ceased. Mel feared something bigger was about to happen.

***

Ahead, Jefe Manuel saw the Volkswagen spin off the road. He knew the second mortar wasn't a direct hit, and he slammed his fists on the bus's steering wheel in anger. He saw the car recover from the blast then take off to his right in the trees. He pulled even with it and opened the bus's door so serious soldier number two could fire the Uzi at it. It was no use; the Uzi was ineffective. He needed to do something quick. The homestead fast approached. He thought he saw the concrete wall glow in the bright moonlight ahead.

To his surprise he saw the car, row by row, move back toward the gravel road. He let off the gas a little to encourage its effort. Once the Volkswagen was back on the gravel road he would bulldoze right over them. A vicious grin slowly spread across his face. He gripped the steering wheel hard in anticipation. The small Volkswagen popped back onto the gravel road in front of him. Its rear end fishtailed slightly, and it began to pull away. Jefe Manuel laughed loudly and mashed the accelerator to the floor. The loud diesel engines inhaled hard and screamed for traction.

"I have you now, bitch!" he laughed and screamed as the front of the bus came mere inches from the rear bumper of the Volkswagen. He was ready. This was it. The bus rammed the small car. Then strange things happened. His seat swept to his left, right out from under him. He slammed hard against the bus's door to his right. Then the floor launched up and hit him with such force, he felt the discs in his lower back compress and explode. What had happened? He couldn't figure out what was up or down or left or right as his body was slammed against the ceiling. Or was it the floor again?

For a split second things moved in slow motion. His body twisted in midair, and he could see down the length of the bus's interior. Things seemed weightless as they crashed into this and that. Serious soldier number two tumbled into view. His skull was gruesomely crushed and his arms flailed around. Clearly loose in their sockets. The huge front bumper of a truck ripped a chunk of the roof off then was gone. He caught the whiff of formaldehyde. Priceless dinnerware shattered everywhere. His extravagant home and all of its contents tumbled as if in a dryer. Then he slammed into the steel rim of one of the four huge slides, and all went quiet.

Jefe Manuel lay there, twisted. His legs wouldn't work. Nor his arms. He couldn't take a breath. He knew he had lost to the Gomezes somehow and would never recover this time to take revenge. And he was right. He stared straight ahead when the intense heat of the diesel fuel ignited around him. It looked like a scene from the movie *Backdraft* as the flames rushed toward him. He was always a Baldwin brothers fan but would never admit it. It's funny what the brain recalls in its last moments before . . . nothing.

***

"I found your phone!" Rob said. He pulled it from under his seat and checked the signal. One bar, it might be enough.

Annie pressed the button on the steering wheel again, and two rings filled the car from its speakers. Another barrage of rapid Spanish was traded back and forth between Annie and the male voice on the line.

"What's he saying?" Rob asked. His heart raced. Mel had her head between the front seats intent on hearing their instructions.

"He wants me to get back on the road so we are lined up with the homestead entrance ahead," Annie explained, and started to weave through the trees back toward the gravel road. Neither Rob nor Mel thought this was wise, but had to trust the man on the other end of the phone call. He barked more things in Spanish, and Annie would reply a word here and there. Mel could tell their conversation was about timing something to come.

The Volkswagen popped up the slight embankment of the gravel road. Annie fought for control as the car slid sideways a bit.

"¡Darse prisa! ¡Más rápido!" the male voice yelled through the speakers. Rob thought he could hear a large engine rev louder behind the voice. Annie complained to Rob that she had the pedal to the floor. Behind them the huge front of the bus loomed closer. Mel looked back. She could see the wicked grin on Jefe Manuel's face. He had a crazy look in his eyes, unhinged.

Rob looked to his right and saw a set of headlights as they bounced on uneven ground. They appeared to be on an intercept course with them and moved very, very fast. He gripped the door handle and instinctively pulled a knee up to brace for the impact to come. Mel saw the lights, too, and screamed, afraid they were going to collide. The voice from the speakers continued to urge Annie to go faster. She cried and screamed she was going as fast as she could. The bus behind them now was just feet and then inches before it hit their rear bumper. The impact jerked their heads back into their headrests. Annie screamed as she twisted the steering wheel in every direction. Then the bus was gone.

***

The man on the phone with Annie could see the white car's fast approach from his left. The huge black bus right on its heels made it look like a toy. He pressed the gas pedal of the Roshel Senator Armored Personnel Carrier, or APC for short, to the floor. Its 6.2-liter turbo diesel responded without balk thanks to the four Nokian MPT Agile tires that easily gripped the gravel surface. This APC was one of five gifted to the Rurales by the United States DEA. Its thick armor and pointy steel nose made the perfect weapon to destroy a huge armored bus.

He feathered the gas pedal as he timed when the bus would cross in front of him. He didn't have any weapons locked and ready. He knew the huge black bus. He knew they would be useless against it. The APC he drove was the weapon. It was a guided missile on a collision course. Thirty seconds he figured, then twenty. He mashed the gas to the floor and screamed into the APC's Bluetooth microphone for Annie to go faster. In return he could hear her cries that the electric Volkswagen was going as fast as it could. His speedometer was at 80 mph then 90. Ten seconds to impact.

"Hurry Annie," he said to himself as he tracked the bus's trajectory with his eyes.

The APC's speedometer now topped 100 mph.

Time slowed down.

Five seconds.

He braced for the impact and stood on the gas. The engine's RPMs redlined. The thick muscles in his forearms flexed hard from the grip he had on the steering wheel.

Four seconds.

He could make out the passengers in the Volkswagen.

Three seconds.

He could see the driver of the bus now as well.

Two seconds.

He could see the confused and terrified look on Annie's face in the Volkswagen. Behind them he could see the wicked smile of his cousin's face as he glared down at the small car in front of him.

One second.

"Viva los Rurales!" he yelled as the APC slammed perfectly broadside into the bus. The sound was thunderous.

Chapter Forty-Six

The Volkswagen spun around like a top. Gravel sprayed in all directions until the car settled to a stop in the center of the road. All three passengers abruptly quit their screams and just sat there still braced for impact. Each chest heaved heavy breaths in the sudden quiet. Then a huge explosion rocked the small car. Tree limbs, sandy soil, and lemons assaulted the vehicle. In front of them blossomed a massive fireball. Even from the inside of the car they felt the intense heat. All three passengers were in shock. Each wondered how they were still alive. They barely registered the several pairs of headlights that surrounded them. Then each of the three was assisted out of the Volkswagen and led into the back of an ambulance. Two paramedics checked their vitals and inspected them for injuries during the short ride. None were found, just a lot of disbelief they were alive and appeared safe.

The ambulance slowed to a stop. The back doors opened, and they were helped out. Rob looked around like he was again in a dream. They were inside high concrete walls. There were lush gardens and foliage everywhere. Large fountains and statues could be seen all around. The brightness of the moonlight made everything surreal. He heard Mel express how beautiful this place was. He turned behind him and saw the front of a huge mansion, all lit up brightly. There was ordered chaos as people rushed here and there. Spanish chatter was nonstop as a small fire truck pulled out of a garage then rolled out the gate they had just come through.

A man in a neatly pressed suit approached them driving a golf cart.

"Buenas noches. Your presence is requested in the southern garden," he said in heavily accented English.

Mel and Rob sat down in the bench seat behind him, and they sped off away from all the commotion. The ride took nearly ten minutes. The air around them turned moist and cool. All they could hear were the sounds of the cart's small electric engine and lawn sprinklers in the distance. The grounds were beautiful. They rounded another large house. Ahead in the distance was an immaculately kept garden with a small courtyard in the middle of it. In the middle of the courtyard was a circle of citrus trees. In the trees' center sat a small woman in a wheelchair. Behind her was another dark-haired lady with her right hand resting on the woman's shoulder. The cart stopped at a small path that led to the courtyard. Rob and Mel climbed off the cart and began to walk toward its center. They approached the two women in the silence of the evening.

Not sure what to say, they nodded slightly and smiled. The woman was very old, but her eyes were kind and alert. Her hair was done up neatly. Her makeup was perfect. She was missing the ring finger on her left hand. They felt she deserved the utmost respect, so they waited for her to speak first. The old woman in the wheelchair just smiled back. Across her lap was a faded blanket that Rob knew was once brightly colored. Memories of him in the woman's lap as he counted numbers in Spanish flooded his head. Even though the lady was much older, he still knew exactly who she was: his abuela. Tears flowed down her cheeks as she further took in the sight of her grandchildren. She never imagined she would ever see them again, now grown up so handsome and beautiful.

Finally she spoke in a soft voice and said, "My dear Robert and Melanie. I must be dreaming. How I have prayed for this day. Welcome to La Casa Bailarinas. Mi casa es tu casa. Now come hug your grandma."

The three hugged long and hard. Tears of joy flowed from each.

"I am sorry to interrupt, senora Erma. But it is now that hour," the other woman said. "We must implement the Lockdown Protocol."

Her face conveyed sudden concern as she wheeled their grandmother quickly away. Rob and Mel were puzzled by her urgency. Lockdown? Was there still concern about cartel retaliation? They gave each other a confused glance. Then they heard it. The moon overhead was huge and the brightest they had ever seen it. Animals all around the outside of the high walls begin to howl . . . some that actually did howl and some Mel and Rob didn't think should have been.

It was 10:00 PM.

The End

Coming Soon by J.T. Fluhart

Lockdown Protocol

The world is plunged into an all out animal apocalypse, but a single hope is sought to return the order of man and beast back to normal. Mel Florchett joins the CIA team headed by Benjamin Masters as they combat this lunar induced disaster to put man back at the top of the food chain. Meanwhile, Rob Florchett and Dr. Maria Sheltie uncover the sinister plot behind the Chow company's continued intentional use of the GMO weaponized pet food. More thrilling, heart pumping action and suspense propels this story further into deeper global conspiracies of the deep state. Will man survive this animal uprising or will we take our place as the next species on Earth's extinction list?

CPSIA information can be obtained
at www.ICGtesting.com
Printed in the USA
LVHW092020160221
679324LV00003B/124